The Blackest Time

A novel of Florence
during the Black Plague

Ken Tentarelli

Black Rose Writing | Texas

First printing

ISBN: 978-1-68513-653-6
LIBRARY OF CONGRESS CONTROL NUMBER: 2025934578
PUBLISHED BY BLACK ROSE WRITING
www.blackrosewriting.com

Printed in the United States of America
Suggested Retail Price (SRP) $21.95

The Blackest Time is printed in Adobe Garamond Pro

*As a planet-friendly publisher, Black Rose Writing does its best to eliminate unnecessary waste to reduce paper usage and energy costs, while never compromising the reading experience. As a result, the final word count vs. page count may not meet common expectations.

Praise for
The Blackest Time

"*The Blackest Time* is a fascinating close perspective on what we all know as the Black Plague, great for fans of historical fiction and plucky main characters."
–The Independent Book Review

"A rewarding journey through a richly drawn past. Tentarelli's ability to immerse readers in medieval Florence's sights, sounds, and struggles makes this a novel worth diving into."
–The Literary Titan

"The historically rigorous description of the apothecary profession, including the guild that regulates it, is impressively presented by the author, whose research is impeccable. The account of the cultural life of Northern Italy, including its economic realities, is equally impressive."
–Kirkus Reviews

The Blackest Time

1

Year 1345. Poppi Village, Tuscany.

Gino cracked the skull into pieces, dropped the fragments into a mortar, and began the arduous task of grinding them into a fine white powder. "I'll make a paste from this," Gino explained, "for people with rotting teeth, and a broth for people with painful joints."

"I just snare the animals and bring the bones to you," the hunter said as he watched Gino work. "You're the *speziale* who turns them into medicines." Gino balked at the praise because, as a mere apprentice, he had much to learn before he deserved the title speziale.

The apothecary sat with a few other shops at the center of Poppi Village, the largest village in the Casentino Valley that supplied the city of Florence with much of its farm produce. The shop had two rooms. Gino worked in the room at the rear, the one that he and Signor Morelli, the owner, referred to as the preparation room. Here Gino and Signor Morelli made ointments, liquids, and powders to treat ailments from the colic of infants to the pains of the elderly. The shop's front room had a counter where Signor Morelli served his customers and chairs where patrons would sit and share their woes while their medications were being made.

In his first year at the apothecary, Gino had learned how to use dozens of plants that grew in the valley and nearby woodland hills to make medicinal formulations. A jar in front of him contained a potion to promote sleep, which Gino had made earlier from chamomile flowers he'd gathered the previous day. Signor Morelli had taught him to use even the most dangerous plants, such as belladonna and hemlock, both poisons favored by assassins, to make ointments for treating aching joints.

In Florence, members of the Apothecaries Guild who prepared medications were known as speziale. Although there was no guild in Poppi Village, locals honored Signor Morelli with the title speziale in appreciation for his many years of easing their pains and suffering. The Casentino Valley had only one doctor who circulated among its towns and villages. He could be summoned in an emergency to treat serious illnesses and injuries, but for everyday medications, people relied on speziale Morelli and on Gino, his assistant.

Before his apprenticeship, Gino Liani had worked on his family's farm. As the oldest of six children, he had always been given the most strenuous jobs. He could spend entire days plowing the fields, struggling with the plow to keep it moving straight through rocky soil. He loved the warm sun, the cooling breezes, even the chilling rain. But when out in a field gripping the plow and following behind the ox, intriguing stories he had heard from merchants of colorful events in fascinating places often played through his thoughts.

The goddess Fortuna had brought Gino and Morelli together when labels on the jars of plants and herbs had started to blur in Signor Morelli's failing eyes. Word of Signor Morelli's difficulty spread quickly through the village. He had no children to continue his legacy, and the boys in the village were farmers, none of whom had the skills needed to apprentice at the apothecary.

It was Gino's mother who saw Morelli's predicament as an opportunity. She had realized her eldest son had talents and curiosity that could not be satisfied on the farm. He needed to move beyond the family and test his abilities. At first, he had resisted her suggestion. "I know nothing of medicines," he protested. "And there's much to do on the farm. I'm needed here."

"No one begins a new job knowing the skills," she countered. "You're a smart young man. You'll learn."

Gino's father supported her argument, saying, "Your brothers and sisters are old enough and strong enough to tend the farm. You've seen your brother Fanto behind the plow. He doesn't have your strength yet, but he's capable and determined. It's time for you to make your own life."

As was the custom, young men in the valley, some even younger than Gino, had left their farms to apprentice with relatives in Florence and Arezzo. By working at the apothecary shop, Gino would have the best of two worlds. He could continue to live at home with his loving family and every morning walk the few miles from the farm to work and learn at the shop in the village. Morelli welcomed his new eager and talented helper. He took Gino foraging in the countryside for medicinal plants and taught him how to prepare the formulations known to all speziali.

Years ago, Gino had gained an appreciation for the value of native plants from his father. As the oldest child, it was always Gino who accompanied his father to gather clover, dandelion, and other grasses to make wine and ale. With that experience, he adapted quickly to the methods practiced in the apothecary shop.

When he first started, Gino's greatest obstacle had been his inability to read and write. He couldn't read the labels Signor Morelli had applied to each container. He identified the vessels containing flowering plants by looking at the flowers themselves, but he wasn't able to distinguish between similar looking dried herbs and grasses. Morelli's formulations, written on pages and filed in folios, were meaningless to the illiterate apprentice.

Initially, Signor Morelli tried to teach Gino to read letters and words, but his efforts met with little success, since Morelli had no experience as a tutor. Their frustration drove Gino to seek the tutelage of a monk from the Abbey of San Fedele. Nearly all the writings available to the monks were written in Latin. The monk who agreed to help Gino had access to only one book in Italian, Dante Alighieri's *Commedia*. Gino made steady progress using Dante's narrative, but even better progress when he brought pages containing Morelli's formulas to their study sessions.

Before long, Gino learned to read the labels and decipher the medicinal formulas and Morelli came to trust Gino to create even the most complex compounds. On pleasant afternoons, the aging man took to enjoying long strolls through the town while leaving Gino to serve the shop's patrons.

Older women didn't hesitate to describe their conditions to Gino. Some even brought their daughters to the apothecary to meet Morelli's well-muscled assistant with the lock of hair that fell playfully over one eye. But younger women were reluctant to discuss female problems with a man of only seventeen years. On Gino's second day by himself, an attractive woman, hardly older than his sister, entered the shop. Gino had never met the woman, but he recognized her immediately as Count Guidi's new bride. The Guidi family had ruled the villages in the valley for generations. Her elaborate wedding, one week ago, had drawn nobility from as far as Siena to the Guidi castle, an imposing stone structure that towered over Poppi Village. Gino thought it possible that the marriage had accorded the woman a noble title, but unsure how to address her, Gino said simply, "May I help you?"

"May I speak with Signor Morelli?" she asked.

Gino replied, "Signor Morelli isn't here. I'm his assistant, Gino Liani. May I help you?"

The woman blushed slightly, cast her eyes downward, and said nothing. She turned slightly, as though preparing to leave. Looking at her, Gino could not detect any physical ailments. Her skin was clear, her breathing strong and regular, her eyes, what he had seen of them, were bright. He took a risk by presuming her problem. "You are a new bride. Sometimes, if husbands are rough …."

She gave a barely perceptible nod, and her cheeks flushed to scarlet. "I'll be but a moment," Gino said as he walked to the preparation room where he mixed lavender, salvia, artemisia, and oil to create a salve.

He returned to the counter and handed the woman a paper cone containing the compound. "This should help."

Without meeting his eyes, she opened her coin purse, withdrew a silver soldo, and held it out. Gino declined the payment, saying, "May you have a long and happy marriage." She turned quickly and scurried from the shop, leaving behind only the scent of her perfume.

Although they never discussed it openly, Signor Morelli believed one day he would take his leave and Gino would become the village's speziale. They didn't expect the time would come so soon and so suddenly.

***

One morning, Morelli was late to open the shop because he was not feeling well. At midday, he went home to take his noon meal and failed to return. Later that afternoon, a monk from the San Fedele Abbey came to the shop. He moved slowly and purposefully to the counter alongside Gino and crossed himself. "I've come here to deliver sad news. The Lord has taken Signor Morelli."

Gino's knees weakened. He reached for a nearby chair and slumped down onto it. "How can this be? Signor Morelli said he wasn't feeling well, but he served customers this morning. He just went home to rest."

"He collapsed outside his house. Neighbors tried to help him, but they could do nothing. It's a shock to us all." The monk continued, "Sometimes the Lord moves quickly. We all loved Signor Morelli." The monk looked down at Gino with sympathetic eyes. "His death may render a burden onto you and others, but do not grieve for him. He is with God in a better place."

The monk stayed until Gino sat up straight, glanced around the shop, and said, "The village will miss him."

As he turned to leave, the monk said, "The village will find a way and you will find a way."

Gino was still sitting in the chair with his hands folded in his lap when the baker's wife came into the shop. She often came for a sweet-smelling unguent made from lavender and sage to treat her frequently recurring headaches. Gino pushed aside his despair, went to the preparation room, and took a selection of ingredients from their containers on the shelves. As he and Signor Morelli had done many times before, he took precise amounts of each item and combined them to make the headache remedy.

In little more than a week, the villagers began calling Gino a speziale. Their acceptance made him feel both proud and unworthy. Signor Morelli had been trained in Florence by a member of the Apothecaries' Guild. He had shared his knowledge freely, but Gino knew he had much more to learn before he deserved the title speziale. He dreaded the day when a villager would come to him with a problem, and he wouldn't know the remedy. With Morelli gone, there was no one to teach him.

At noon, on a cool rainy day, Gino unpacked the lunch his mother had prepared for him—bread, cheese, and pork sausage. He had just broken off a piece of bread when a stranger entered the shop. He had shoulder length dark hair, wet from the rain, and narrow-set eyes. His cloak was pulled tight as protection against the weather.

Gino set his lunch aside and asked, "How may I help you?"

The man shook water droplets from his cloak and let it fall open, revealing a stylish blue silk tunic with silver buttons. "I am the owner of this building," he announced, speaking with an accent Gino didn't recognize. Gino knew several shops in the village were owned by Count Guidi's many cousins. "My son recently graduated from the law school at the University of Padua," the man stated. "This valley needs a lawyer, and my son will fill that need. He'll be coming to Poppi, and this will be his office."

Stunned, Gino said, "But what will become of the apothecary? The village needs an apothecary. Everyone in the valley comes here for medicinals."

The man grunted. "There's an apothecary in Arezzo. It's less than a day's ride. People can get what they need in Arezzo." He scanned the room, stepped around the counter, and peered into the preparation room. He gave a dismissive wave. "Workers will come here in two days to remove this stuff and make these rooms into a respectable office for my son."

Gino shared his distress with his family at their evening meal. His mother, on the verge of outrage, snapped, "The people in this valley need an apothecary, not a lawyer. When people are sick, they need to be cared for quickly. They can't ride a half day on horseback to Arezzo. I never heard anyone say we need a lawyer in Poppi."

His youngest brother asked, “What will you do?”

Gino met the boy’s gaze and said, haltingly, “I don’t know. I’ve been able to help people, but I don’t know enough to open my own apothecary. I guess I’ll come back to the farm.”

His father pounded the table. “No, you won’t. You’ve labored to learn the skills of a speziale, and you mustn’t let those efforts be lost in the wind. You owe it to Signor Morelli to carry on his legacy… if not in Poppi, then somewhere else. Every man must take his own path in life, and you’ve already begun following yours. You must look forward. It will not serve you to look backward.”

They discussed many possibilities, and by the end of the evening, his mother had persuaded Gino that he should look for work in Florence. She said, “Every district of that city must have an apothecary shop. Surely one of them has the need of an apprentice.”

His father agreed and said, “You can expand your skills in Florence; then, after you’re accepted by the guild as a speziale, you can return to Poppi.” Gino had fidgeted in his chair as he absorbed the arguments put forth by his parents. They were right, of course, but he was already anticipating the pain of leaving his home and family.

Gino spent the next day, his last in the apothecary, making formulations. He knew which people in the village regularly had headaches, who suffered from sore joints, and who had intestinal disorders. He prepared quantities of those medications and, with the help of his brother, distributed them throughout the village. Rather than let Guidi’s workmen trash the remaining ingredients, he delivered those to the Abbey of San Fedele to monks who had experience making basic restoratives. He wrapped Signor Morelli’s recipe folio in a cloth and tied it securely. He would take that with him to Florence. One last time, he locked the apothecary door and wondered why he did so. There was nothing of value left inside, only a few simple paintings that Morelli had hung on the walls to bring a modicum of joy to his customers, and tomorrow those would be destroyed by Guidi’s workmen.

***

In late afternoon, Taddeo, a merchant, made his round of farms in the valley to collect vegetables he would take to the *mercato* in Florence. Since the Casentino Valley was many hours distant from Florence, Taddeo always loaded his wagon in the evenings, kept it at his home overnight midway between Poppi and Florence, and departed for the city early the following morning. "My son is going to Florence to look for work," Gino's father said as he helped load artichokes into Taddeo's wagon. "Might he be able to travel with you?"

"I thought he was working at the apothecary here in Poppi," Taddeo began, then in a flash of recognition he said, "Ah … it closed. Someone told me the apothecary had closed. Certainly, Gino can travel with me. I'll welcome his company. Does he have work in Florence?"

"He's hoping to find work in an apothecary, where he can add to what he learned from Signor Morelli."

Gino packed his small satchel and tossed it into the back of Taddeo's wagon. He hugged every member of his family, not knowing when he might see them again. His mother tried, without success, to hold back tears. His father embraced him tightly and placed a coin purse in Gino's hand. "You will need this until you can find work."

Gino accompanied the merchant and spent the night on a mat near the fire in the kitchen of Taddeo's house. He got little sleep worrying over what his future held.

2

Monday April 25, 1345

It was well before dawn when Taddeo came into the kitchen and thumped his boot against Gino's foot. "It's time for us to go. I have to be at the mercato early to find a prime place to set up my cart."

Gino groaned and rubbed his eyes. In the dim firelight, he could barely make out the silhouetted figure standing over him. "Were you able to sleep?" Taddeo asked. "I know the floor is hard, but the only choices were to sleep on the floor or in the barn, and my horse doesn't tolerate company. His snorting surely would have kept you from sleeping."

Gino pushed himself up and stretched. "It's not the first time I've slept on a hard floor, and at least the fire kept me warm."

Taddeo pointed to a pot at one end of the hearth. "There are rolls keeping warm in that pot. My wife made them last night. And there's an apricot spread on the table. Slather the rolls with the spread while I get the horse and wagon ready."

Gino coated two rolls with apricot preserves, grabbed his satchel, and stepped out into the night, lit only by stars. Barely able to see his surroundings, he found Taddeo at the barn by following the sound of the horse being harnessed to the wagon. He stepped carefully from the house to the barn, fearful he might trip over objects in the yard. Casting his eyes skyward, Gino exclaimed, "Wow, I've never seen a star that bright."

"Look more carefully," Taddeo said. "It's three stars, not one. They're wandering stars." Taddeo pointed up at the trio. "They're close to each other now. Last week they were farther apart and each night they've been moving toward each other."

"Will they collide?" Gino asked in a wobbly voice.

"I don't know, but if they keep moving toward each other, we'll find out before long." Taddeo hopped up onto the wagon. "Climb up. We have a long ride ahead, and we need to be in Florence before the sun gets high." He glanced at Gino. "Don't you have something warmer to wear than that thin cloak?"

Gino shrugged. Taddeo tossed him a blanket. "Cover yourself with this. The air will get warmer as we descend to the river valley near Florence, but up here in the hills, nights are cool."

Gino wrapped the blanket around his shoulders. After several miles, the rhythmic swaying of the wagon had him closing his eyes. He was nearly asleep when the wagon stopped abruptly, pitching him forward and nearly catapulting him out of his seat. Taddeo had pulled hard on the reins, swerving the wagon to the side to keep it from hitting another wagon that had come into view suddenly as they rounded a sharp curve. The wagon in front was tilted at a perilous angle and partially blocking the road. Gino righted himself and regained his senses. In the dim glow of the dawn light, he could see a man bent down next to one of the wagon's wheels.

Taddeo turned to Gino and said, "I know him. His name is Wiener. He's a merchant like me, but he doesn't sell vegetables. He brings grains to the flour mills in Florence." Taddeo climbed down and walked to where the man was struggling with a wheel. "Wiener, what happened?"

The man looked up and grumbled, "Ah, this damned wheel has come loose. It's been wobbling for the past few miles and coming down this slope made it worse. It's practically coming off the axle. Something happened to the pin. I need to replace it, but first I have to get the wheel tight on the hub."

"We can help with that," Taddeo said. "Gino, help me lift the wagon." He and Gino grabbed hold of the wagon. They groaned as they raised it to unweight the wheel, then held the wagon while Wiener reseated the wheel and replaced the pin.

Wiener wiped the sweat from his forehead, stood up, and tipped his head to his two helpers. "*Danke*. I couldn't have done that by myself. You must join me for a beer when we get to the city."

By the time they finished the repair and resumed their course toward Florence, brightness in the eastern sky heralded the coming sunrise.

"Wiener is an unusual name," Gino observed.

"He calls himself Wiener as an homage to his homeland. He's from the capital city of Austria. I only know him as Wiener. I don't know his given name."

"He's never come to our farm," Gino said.

"No, he doesn't go as far as the Casentino Valley. He goes to farms closer to Florence that grow grains like wheat and barley."

In a few miles, the road widened as it dropped from the hills to the Florentine plain. Wagons and donkeys loaded with farm produce joined from side roads and dirt paths, creating a procession headed to the city. Gino squinted as he peered at the horizon ahead. "Is that a river?"

"Yes, it's the Arno," Taddeo replied. "But we won't need to cross it. This road follows alongside the river all the way to Florence."

"The Arno," Gino said with a furrowed brow. "That's the name of the river that passes through my village, although in Poppi, it's much smaller. In summer, it's hardly more than a stream."

"It's the same river," Taddeo explained. "But as you'll soon see, it's grown in size since leaving Poppi. It flows right through the center of Florence and then on to the sea at Pisa."

When they reached the river, Gino watched the water to determine its direction of flow, then he looked upriver. "Some of this water came all the way from Poppi," he said to himself wistfully, and wondered how long it would be until he saw his village and his family again.

The river and the road curved slightly toward the north for nearly a mile and then southerly for an equal distance before straightening to a westerly course. In time, they reached the city wall. Gino looked up at it and marveled, "It's over three times my height. Much higher than the wall around Poppi."

"The city keeps growing, so they keep building new walls. This is the sixth wall that's been built around the city. This one encircles over five times as much land as the last wall," Taddeo explained.

The road turned away from the river and paralleled the wall. As they passed into the city through the Porta alla Croce gate, Taddeo patted Gino on the shoulder and announced, "Welcome to Florence, your new home."

Wiener turned his wagon to the left. Gino's gaze drifted along the road ahead until a row of poorly constructed one room wooden houses drew his attention. With surprise and disappointment in his voice, he said, "Those houses… they're just hovels. Is this how people live in Florence?"

"The poorest of the poor and the richest of the rich live in Florence. Some have shacks like these, while others have magnificent fortresses. There are even beggars who have no houses at all."

Gino scrunched up his nose. "What's that smell?"

Taddeo grinned. "What you are smelling is mostly just the people. In time, you'll learn to ignore the odor. I was aware of it when I first came to the city, but I don't notice it anymore. Florentines don't smell bad, not any worse than you or me, but it's a crowded city. Like having a thousand or more Poppi villages packed inside the city walls."

"Does it smell like this everywhere?"

Laughing, Taddeo said, "In some neighborhoods, people throw their garbage and shit into the streets. Those neighborhoods smell worse."

Gino shot his companion a look of disbelief as Taddeo said, "You'll want to avoid those neighborhoods. And be careful when you're near the district by the river where the tanneries are located. It has its own unique odor."

Taddeo paused a moment to enjoy Gino's shocked expression before adding, "But you should find the center of the city to be pleasant enough. The upper-class people who live there even wear perfumes to mask their stink. You'll find the air more pleasant when there are strong breezes blowing from the hills."

As they neared the city center, they rode in silence, with Gino awed by the tall stone tower houses that overshadowed the small wooden homes as they neared the city center. Fascinated by throngs of busy people and apprentices standing outside shops hawking goods to passersby, Gino no longer noticed the offensive smell.

Taddeo turned onto a side street and into a livery. "Welcome to your new city," he said as he and Gino climbed down from the wagon. The stableboy unhitched Taddeo's horse while he and Gino transferred the wagonload of vegetables to a cart that had been kept for him at the livery.

Poppi Village had just one main street. Gino felt lost in a maze as he gazed around at his new city, with people rushing in all directions.

3

Monday April 25, 1345

Florence had established the mercato many years ago in a narrow space under a portico as a place for sellers to display their wares. Over time, it had expanded with vendors setting out tables in the adjacent piazza until, in recent years, carts loaded with food, clothing, and household items filled the entire piazza every morning. Women selected vegetables grown on nearby farms for their evening meals, restaurateurs chose fruits from Sicily and North Africa to impress their patrons, and local artisans displayed furniture, knives, bowls, and other wares.

Taddeo weaved through the swarm of early buyers to set up his cart in a prime spot. Gino followed close behind, fearful he might become lost in the crowd. He held his arms close to his sides to shield himself from the throng of people and the barrage of sounds. So many people, all talking at once in different dialects. How could they possibly understand each other?

Other vendors were still arriving, and Taddeo had barely moved his cart into position when customers crowded close to purchase vegetables, including the artichokes that had come from Gino's family farm. A plump woman poked Gino with her elbow, pushing him aside so she could move closer to the cart. Scanning the piazza, he saw similar clashes at the carts of other vendors. Taddeo said, "These women want their pick of the finest merchandise, so they get here early. Many of them are the servants of wealthy families. Poor women do their shopping later when the prices are lowered."

"Is it this active every day?" Gino asked.

"Yes, every day, but only until midday. I usually sell everything by midday and then return to the farms to get more goods to sell the next day. Ah, that's the boring life of a merchant. Each day is like the last and the next," Taddeo added pensively, then with a quick smile he said, "But today, before I leave, we will meet with Wiener. Remember, he promised to treat us to beer."

When the initial throng of customers thinned, Taddeo introduced Gino to a nearby vendor whose pushcart was stacked with wool cloth. "This is Ercole. He lives here in Florence and knows the city better than most. Maybe he can tell you where there are rooms for rent."

Ercole clasped Taddeo on the shoulder. "You credit me more than I deserve, old friend, but I do know of one building that has rooms to rent." He moved Gino away from the crowd and pointed to a street leading away from the piazza. "Follow that street to its end, where several streets angle off. The middle one is Via del Sole. It has no nameplate, but it's the one that leads to the Santa Maria Novella church. You'll see the church ahead of you in the middle of a large piazza. When you reach the piazza, there will be a building on your left with a candlemaker's shop. See the candlemaker. He can show you the rooms."

Gino set off, following Ercole's directions. When he approached the piazza, his gait slowed as the church ahead captured his attention. "It must be three times the size of San Fedele," he said aloud as he compared Santa Maria Novella to the church in his home village.

A woman passing by smiled at the young man, whose gawking expression showed him to be fresh from the countryside.

The candlemaker's shop was visible to his left, as Ercole had said. The aromatic fragrance of hot wax reached Gino's nose even before he pulled open the shop's door. Stepping inside, he spotted a short round-shouldered man at the rear of the shop lifting a pot from the fire. The man moved to a nearby counter where he drizzled liquid wax into molds. He worked carefully to avoid displacing the wicks centered in each mold.

Without looking up, he called out, "I'll be with you in a moment." When he finished pouring, he removed his heavy apron and gloves and approached Gino. "Greetings, young man. How may I help you?"

"I am told there is a room for rent and you can show it to me."

The man scrutinized Gino, whose clothes were simple, but not those of a peasant. A quick look showed that Gino's hands had done work, but lacked the extensive bruises sustained by laborers. They had all ten fingers with no ends missing. He must be a transient, most likely from the countryside, the shopkeeper decided. The satchel that Gino carried supported that conclusion. "The building owner doesn't want itinerants, so the settlement term must be for a month or more."

"A month would be acceptable," Gino said. "I intend to remain in Florence."

"It's on the second level. Come with me." The candlemaker led Gino out of his shop to a doorway at the far end of the building, where a stairway led to the second level.

Gino followed the man into a large room, larger even than the room Gino had shared with his two brothers on the farm. A single window painted the walls with light. Gino found the musty air reaching his nose only mildly unpleasant. Adjoining the one large room was a small kitchen area. The space was far more than he needed, but it lacked any furnishings. To make it livable, he would need to buy a bed, table, a chair, and cooking utensils, at the very least. "How much is the rent?" Gino asked.

"Two hundred soldi for the month."

Gino winced. In his short time at the mercato, he had come to realize food was more expensive in Florence than in Poppi village. Now he found, to his dismay, rooms were also expensive. Two hundred soldi was nearly all the money his father had given him. If he spent that much for the room, he wouldn't have enough left to buy any furnishings … or food. In a somber voice, Gino said, "It's a fine room, but more than I can afford until I find work."

The man raised his hands in resignation. "There's nothing I can do. It's not my building. I don't set the price."

After they left the room and descended to the street, Gino asked, "Might you know where I could find a less expensive room?"

"I don't know of any other rooms for rent, but I can send you to a neighborhood where the costs will be low if you can find a room there."

Gino's expression brightened. The man pointed along the street in front of his shop. "At the end of this street, close to the river, the street on the right, Borgo Ognissanti, is filled with houses. Ask someone about rooms when you get there."

Small houses lined both sides of Borgo Ognissanti. They were narrow, not as tall as those near the mercato, and crowded close together. Trash littering the small spaces between buildings once again made Gino aware of the city's foul smell.

Unlike the streets in the center of the city, the borgo was nearly devoid of people. A distance ahead, a lone man turned from the street to enter a house. Gino ran toward the man and when he drew near, called out, "I'm looking for a room."

The man turned to face the voice calling him, gestured toward the house beside him, and responded brusquely, "Up on the second level. Three soldi."

Gino registered surprise that the previous building insisted on monthly rentals, whereas that building seemed to accept daily rentals. "May I see the room?"

In a gravelly voice, the man barked, "Up on the second level." He pointed to a stairway, but stepped aside and didn't accompany Gino.

At the top of the stairs, Gino pushed the door open and set one foot into the room before noticing a woman standing by the window brushing her hair. She smiled sweetly at her visitor, set the brush aside, and said, "Come ahead."

Flustered, Gino barely managed to push out the words, "I'm sorry," as he pulled the door closed, and hurried down the stairs.

"Someone's in the room. A woman," Gino muttered to the man who had remained in the anteroom with his arms folded across his chest.

"You don't like her? You expected a boy?"

"A room. I'm just looking for a room," Gino said defensively.

"*Bah, un cretino*," the man grumbled and made a gesture with his hand that Gino did not recognize.

Gino walked back into the street. Only when his wits returned did he realize the building was a bordello. He raked his eyes over the other buildings, wondering whether any of them really rented rooms or whether the phrase "I'm looking for a room" had a different meaning in Florence. Disappointed again at his failure to find a room, he plodded back toward the mercato.

As he walked, the image of the woman in the bordello returned. She had a pretty face with dark eyes and long chestnut-brown hair. Any man would find her attractive, but Gino had more important concerns … at the moment. Taddeo had claimed that Florence was the size of a thousand Poppi villages. Surely, somewhere in a city so big, there must be a room for rent at a price he could afford, Gino told himself.

Bells sounding midday at nearby Santa Maria Novella reminded him that Wiener had promised to treat him and Taddeo to beer, so Gino quickened his pace. The crowd of shoppers had thinned to just a few stragglers, and some vendors were removing their carts when he arrived at the mercato. Taddeo's cart was nearly empty. All the artichokes from Gino's family farm had been sold. When he spotted Gino, Taddeo held up a few undersized carrots. "I did well today. Only these remain, and my horse will enjoy them."

Wiener led Gino and Taddeo to a tavern on a side street, where he ordered a pitcher of beer and a plate of dried fruit. They were fortunate to find an empty table in the popular beerhouse. Friendly banter filling the room further raised the spirits of the two vendors who raised their mugs to congratulate each other for selling their wares quickly and at favorable prices. After downing nearly half a mugful in a single swallow, Taddeo noted Gino's somber behavior. "From your glum expression, I assume you didn't find a room."

Gino responded in an unsteady voice, "The place Ercole sent me had a fine, spacious room, but the rent is more than I can afford. I must guard my soldi keenly until I find work." He ran a finger over the rim of his mug. "The man in charge of that building pointed me to another neighborhood, but all I found there was a bordello."

Wiener nearly spat out a mouthful of beer and chortled, "Florence has a good measure of bordellos, despite being prohibited by statutes. Being fresh from the countryside, I assume you forewent the pleasure."

Gino managed a weak nod.

Wiener snickered, "Florence is a bewitching city. She may seem strange to you now, but I'll wager you'll be gripped in her vices by the next moon."

Taddeo rubbed his chin. "The city ordinances are thick with statutes condemning evils, but those rulings are ignored and forgotten as soon as they're issued. The *berrovarii* try to keep the city safe by catching criminals, but they don't shut the bordellos because berrovarii are among the most faithful patrons of those establishments. Even the magistrates who write the statutes have their favorite nests."

Wiener downed another swig of beer to calm himself. In a serious tone, he said, "The mill where I delivered grain this morning sells flour to the bakers throughout the city. Everyone in the city eats bread, so news passes readily through the bake shops. There's a good chance that one of those bakers will know of an available room. I'll take you to meet the miller when we leave here."

After the men enjoyed a second round of beer and a plate of antipasti, Taddeo pushed himself away from the table, saying, "Two farms in the Casentino Valley are expecting me to collect their vegetables this afternoon, so I must be on my way." Gino and Wiener followed him from the tavern and then headed across the city to the grain mill.

4

Monday April 25, 1345

Gino continued to be struck by the differences between Poppi and Florence. People walking through the streets in Florence kept their eyes directly ahead and took no notice of those passing by them. In Poppi, people greeted their neighbors as they passed. We all knew everyone, Gino reflected. But here in Florence, they are all strangers to each other. He sidestepped awkwardly to dodge people brushing past him. After flattening himself against a storefront to avoid colliding with a man whose vision had been blocked by the cask hoisted on his shoulder, Gino said, “People in this city don’t seem to be friendly.”

“They are wary of strangers,” Wiener agreed, “but they’ll warm once they get to know you.”

The miller’s wife was sweeping up spilled grain when Wiener and Gino reached the mill. Wiener flashed a smile. “Buon giorno, Signora. This young man is Gino. He’s just arrived in Florence and he’s looking for a room. Your husband’s customers stay informed about their neighborhoods, so I thought they might know of rooms for rent. Maybe Gino could go with your husband when he makes his deliveries.”

She set her broom aside, appraised the young man, and said, “It’s too bad you didn’t come earlier. You could have gone with him, but you’re too late. He’s out making deliveries now,” the miller’s wife explained. “If you come back tomorrow, you can ride with him.”

Gino swallowed hard and said softly, “But I need a room for tonight.”

Noting his simple clothing, the woman asked, "Where are you from?"

"Poppi." He hesitated a moment before adding, "It's a village in the Casentino Valley."

The woman returned a blank expression. Neither the village name nor the valley name held any meaning for her. She studied Gino's arms, not muscular but the sturdy limbs of one who had done strenuous work, and his face, sincere and honest. With a bemused smile, she offered, "If you can help move sacks of grain to the mill from the storehouse, I'll see that there's a place for you to spend the night."

It wasn't the long-term arrangement that Gino sought, but it would keep him from sleeping in an alley. He bid farewell to Wiener and followed the woman to the storehouse. She showed him to a stack of sacks. He hefted a sack onto his shoulder, followed her from the shed to the mill, and deposited it on a platform next to the hopper that fed grain into the giant mill stone.

Gino's thoughts drifted from the chore at hand to his blissful time at the apothecary assisting Signor Morelli, and the few precious days when he had held the position of speziale, before the apothecary shop closed. "I've taken a step backward," he thought. "I came to the city hoping to find work in an apothecary, and here I am laboring as I did on the farm."

Just as Gino had set the last sack onto the platform, the woman returned with an armful of blankets. "Ah, my husband will be pleased when he returns that one less chore awaits him," she said and led Gino through a doorway to a small room that served as an office and handed him the blankets. "These will keep you warm. My husband has a brother who sleeps in this room when he visits."

Gino steeled himself to spend his first night in Florence, and his second in as many nights, on a hard floor. But his eyes brightened when he stepped into the room and saw a cot against the far wall and next to it a stand holding a water pitcher for washing. And unlike the mill room, the office did not have a thin coating of flour on every surface.

"What brings you to Florence?" the woman asked.

"I'm hoping to find work as an assistant in an apothecary."

"An apothecary? Why an apothecary? If you're looking for work, you'll have more success finding a job as a stonemason. They're building the new cathedral, so there's always a need for stone workers."

"I have experience working at an apothecary. I worked at the one in my village until the shop was closed."

"Young men like you must find farming disagreeable because they're constantly coming to Florence looking for work. Most end up as laborers. Can that be better than farming?" she asked rhetorically. "Ah, but you have experience working in an apothecary shop, so maybe fortune will find you."

As the woman turned to leave, Gino said, "There's ample daylight remaining. I'd like to use it to explore my new city. I saw a church when I was outside."

"Santa Croce," the woman said.

"Even from this distance, it looks huge. Earlier today I passed Santa Maria Novella and this one … Santa Croce looks to be even bigger."

"And it continues to grow. The first stone was placed before my birth, and I may be summoned to the Lord's kingdom before the last stone is set. Enjoy your stroll, but don't become lost," she quipped. "If you get twisted, always look for the river. Walk along the river and eventually you'll find your way back here to the mill."

The most direct route from the mill to Piazza Santa Croce led to the rear of the church. Scaffolding clinging to the church's transept confirmed the woman's assertion that the building was still under construction.

As Gino got closer, he was mesmerized by the building's unusual texture. Unlike other buildings that were constructed of smooth cut stone blocks, all sides of Santa Croce were encased in thin slabs of rough brownstone. The stacks of stone upon stone reminded him of the many-layered cakes that his mother made at Easter.

Years ago, Gino's father had taken him to a quarry to get stones to enlarge their smokehouse. While his father had been negotiating prices, Gino had watched masons cutting rectangular blocks from a rock outcropping. The skilled artisans positioned their chisels along nearly invisible fault lines, then struck the chisels with hammers to cleave smooth sided blocks. To sever large blocks, two masons teamed together with both men striking their precisely placed chisels at the same instant. Occasionally, small slabs of stone broke away and were set aside in a pile. It was those small fragments that Gino's father used for his smokehouse, and similar small stones had also been used to build Santa Croce. Perhaps this was another sign that the building was not yet finished. Maybe, in time, the rough stones would be covered with an attractive façade.

Gino followed two elderly women into the cavernous church. Pausing at the doorway, he stared in awe into the nave. High above, a frightened bird darted between wooden trusses, trying desperately to escape to the sky. How could Gino possibly describe the gigantic structure to his family? Would they believe it true if he told them that Santa Croce could hold within it four San Fedele churches?

Although the church's exterior was unfinished, its interior was beautifully decorated with paintings on the walls. A monk approached as Gino marveled at one painting. "Saint John the Baptist. He has a special place in the hearts of many Florentines," the monk informed the admirer.

"It's painted on the wall," Gino said dubiously. "The church in my village has paintings on wooden panels, but this is painted directly on the wall."

The monk smiled. "They're called frescoes. The artist applies paint while the plaster is still wet. I'm told that the technique lets the plaster absorb pigment so the paintings will stay vivid for many years."

"Frescoes," Gino repeated and added, "The colors certainly are bright." He wondered, "How many wondrous new things await me in this city?"

After browsing through the church, Gino stepped out into the piazza, where a sign identifying an apothecary drew him onto a narrow street. Perhaps it is a sign of good fortune, he thought, that on his first venture into Florence, he came upon an apothecary.

The shop was closed at the late hour, but Gino pressed an eye close to the linen cloth covering the shop's window to peek through a small hole in the fabric. The darkened interior kept him from seeing anything inside, but his discovery of a potential place to seek work gladdened his spirit. He planned to return the following day.

The apothecary sat on a corner, where an intersecting street veered off at an angle. Its skewed direction and lack of a nameplate brought to mind the miller's wife's warning against getting twisted. From his current position, Gino could see neither the river nor Santa Croce church. Wandering further could easily get him lost. A glimpse of the dark clouds filling the sky and the dwindling daylight convinced him to retrace his steps and return to the mill, where he spent another restless night staring into the darkness. Alone.

5

Tuesday April 26, 1345

A rhythmic sound roused Gino from his slumber. He swung his feet off the cot onto the floor, stretched, then made his way to the mill room, where the spinning mill stone's rough surface and steady spin mesmerized him. On the platform above the wheel hub, the miller was pouring grain into a hopper from the sacks that Gino had carried the previous evening. The man poured carefully with a steady flow to prevent clumping. At the stone's rim, an apprentice collected flour into sacks. Without taking his eyes off the hopper, the miller called to Gino. "Buon giorno, young man. You've eased my day's work by lugging these sacks from the shed."

"A small task for a night's lodging," Gino said cheerfully.

Gesturing toward a small table, the miller said, "My wife left a muffin and a pitcher of water for you."

Gino devoured the muffin and, still feeling hungry, went outside in search of something more to eat. He spied a stream of locals entering a nearby pastry shop and joined the queue. Once inside, he stepped aside to observe what the locals were ordering. The pastries with a red jelly-like filling and those with peach nectar were most popular with the locals. People getting the peach nectar confections ordered them using a name Gino didn't recognize. He tried repeating the word, but either he heard the name incorrectly or he mispronounced the local jargon, so he resorted to pointing.

He found the pastry dough to be chewy. "Not flaky like my mother's torte," he told himself. The filling was made from berries he didn't recognize and had been sweetened excessively for his taste. The peach nectar, although refreshing, had the consistency of a thick syrup. Even the food in Florence is different, he mused, wondering whether he'd ever gain a taste for it.

Gino intended to accompany the miller when he delivered flour to the bakeries, but while the miller was still grinding grain, Gino had time to re-visit the apothecary shop he had seen in the Santa Croce neighborhood the previous evening. He retraced his route along Borgo dei Greci and turned onto the short side street. The apothecary shop windows were still covered with linen cloth, making it appear that the shop was not yet open, although nearby shops were already serving customers.

As Gino reached out to grasp the door handle, the door swung open and a thin man with a bony face rushed from the shop, coughing and snorting as he hurried past Gino. A pungent odor of cabbage flowed out of the shop in the man's wake. Gino couldn't recall any medicinals with ingredients that smelled like cabbage. Perhaps speziali in Florence used formulations unknown to him. If so, he might not be as skilled as he had believed. Upon entering the shop, a young man with dark eyes, bushy brows, and wavy black hair greeted him. In Gino's mind, speziali were old men like Signor Morelli, but this man was young. "Are you the speziale?" Gino asked.

"No. My uncle is the speziale. He's away now, but he'll return soon. I'm his apprentice."

"I arrived in the city yesterday and I need a job. In my home village, I worked in an apothecary shop and I'm hoping to find work as an assistant to a speziale here in Florence."

"My uncle doesn't need to hire anyone because I started apprenticing with him last month." Seeing Gino's shoulders slump, the young man added, "But there are apothecaries in every district of the city, so you should be able to find work in one of them. Try the San Lorenzo district. It has two apothecaries."

Gino nodded, gave a half-smile, left the shop, and headed upriver toward the grain mill. He passed woolen mills and leather processing mills along the riverbank. Large mills sat on the bank while smaller ones floated on platforms in the river. All used wheels to draw power from the flowing water. The miller's apprentice had already begun piling sacks of flour on a wagon bed when Gino reached the mill yard. He grabbed a sack and helped with the loading.

After Gino set the last sack on the wagon bed, he climbed aboard the seat next to the miller. "I deliver to two neighborhoods," the miller said. "First, to bakeries in San Giovanni and San Lorenzo. Later, to the Santa Maria Novella quarter."

He eased his horse forward out of the mill yard. "My wife said you are looking for a room and hope the bakers might help you find one. She's probably right. Bakers have a good sense of what's happening in their neighborhoods."

They set out on the same road that Gino had walked the previous evening. Near the city center, a pile of timbers blocked the road, forcing the wagon to divert onto a narrow street skirting a large piazza. "That's where they're enlarging the new cathedral," the miller explained. "Consuls of the major guilds decided that for Florence to be seen as an important city, it must have an archbishop. And to have an archbishop, it must have a majestic cathedral. Santa Reparata isn't big enough, so they're making it larger." His tone suggested he didn't favor the project.

"Couldn't one of the existing churches become the cathedral?" Gino asked. "I visited Santa Croce yesterday. It's a massive building and lovely inside with beautiful,"—he searched for the word—"frescoes."

With obvious sarcasm, the miller said, "Ah, but Santa Croce isn't as big as the cathedrals in Pisa or Siena. The consuls won't settle for Florence being second or third. We must have the largest cathedral." In a less disparaging voice, he added, "Architects have been flocking to the city, each with a proposal grander than the last. For half a century they've been squabbling over the design and mostly what we have are piles of timber and stone blocking the roads."

They passed the old bridge reconstruction site and, a short distance later, turned onto a street angling away from the river toward Santa Maria Novella church. The bakery was one of only a few shops on that street. Most of the narrow two-level buildings lining the sides of the road had living space on both levels. Gino queried the baker about available rooms while they carried sacks into his shop.

"I don't know if there are rooms available, but Stefano would know. He manages all the houses on this street. He doesn't own them, he just manages them." Pointing toward a gray stone building at the far end of the street, the baker said, "He lives there on the ground level." The baker hefted another flour sack onto his shoulder. "Don't mind Stefano. He can be cranky."

Gino hurried to the building the baker had indicated. A slender man with a dour expression answered his knock. "What?"

"I'm looking for Stefano."

The man grunted, which Gino took to mean the man was Stefano. "Are there rooms available?"

"Always there are rooms. Just you or a family?"

"Just me."

Stefano eyed Gino's simple clothes, then pointed to a building on the opposite side of the street. "There," he said and began walking toward the building, leaving Gino to follow. He led Gino through a passageway alongside the building to an entrance at the rear, unlocked the door, and stepped inside. "One room. Twenty soldi for the month."

Gino scanned the room. A table, two chairs, a bed against one wall and a fireplace for cooking along another wall. Gino would need a few other things to make the room comfortable, but it had the basics. The price, twenty soldi, was a mere fraction of the two hundred soldi quoted to him for a room not far away in the same district. He pulled out a coin purse hidden under his tunic and counted out twenty silver coins. Stefano pocketed the coins, handed Gino a key, and turned to leave.

Gino asked, "Is someone living in the other room, the one in front?"

"No one lives there. The person who lives above uses it as an office."

"An office? Is he a doctor or a lawyer?"

Stefano growled, "I collect the rents. I don't ask people about their business."

Gino chuckled as he surveyed his new home, thinking his mother might have considered it an omen that his hunt for a room began in the Santa Maria Novella district; then, after a fruitless search elsewhere in the city, he had success in the Santa Maria Novella district. "The district accepts you," she might have said, and then advised him to look for work at an apothecary in that district. Gino put little faith in omens; still, who could fault him if he were to visit the church and light a candle?

Gino retrieved his satchel from the miller's wagon, thanked the miller, and headed to his new home.

6

Wednesday April 26, 1345

Gino awoke the following morning eager to look for work, but first he would meet with Taddeo to learn whether the merchant had any news from Gino's family. As he approached the mercato, he paused near the edge of the piazza and challenged himself to distinguish one conversation from the chatter surrounding him. Nearby, a well-dressed man was speaking. Gino watched the man's mouth move and strained to capture the words: "… wool is coming …." He caught that short phrase before being distracted by the chatter of two women passing nearby. Is this city ever quiet?

Gino moved a few steps closer to the man and focused on his deep, resonant voice, striving to ignore all the other speakers. "The ship is overdue. It should"—someone's shouts covered a few words — "England on Thursday." Gino slapped his thigh, pleased he had extracted even those few phrases from the din. Repeating the words to himself let him realize a conversation about a ship and England would never take place in Poppi. England was a distant land somewhere to the north and of no concern to the villagers in Poppi. This was another example clear of the differences between Poppi and Florence.

"Your mother is worried," Taddeo said after Gino had wended his way to the merchant's cart through the crowd of shoppers. "She hasn't heard from you and fears you might have been swallowed by the Florentine underworld."

"She doesn't really think I've met an ill fate, does she?"

"No," Taddeo laughed, "but she worries. Your father does too, although he tries to mask his concern."

Gino protested, "I've only been away for two days. Surely they can't expect to receive word from me every day."

"Mothers and fathers always worry," Taddeo said as he drifted away to attend a customer.

Across the market, Ercole, the vendor who had told Gino about the expensive room near the church, was removing a covering from the items stacked on his cart. Gino threaded a path through eager shoppers to where Ercole was readying his cart. Noticing the cart was filled with cloth and items of clothing, Gino asked, "Will you sell all of this merchandise in one day?"

Ercole replied, "Vegetable and fruit vendors expect to empty their carts every day, but the clothing business is different. I sell a few pieces each day, but I come here mostly to tell people about my shop where I sell used clothing. That's where I do most of my business. My wife minds the shop in the mornings while I'm here. I tend the shop in the afternoon."

"Your shop sells used clothing? Gino reflected.

"Yes, mine and many others like it." Gesturing toward Gino's smock, and knowing the answer he would receive, Ercole asked, "Did you buy your shirt new from a tailor?"

"No, there are no tailors in my village. On the farm, my mother makes all our clothes from spun wool she gets from a neighbor who raises sheep."

"As I would expect," Ercole said. "New tailor-made clothes are expensive. In Florence, aristocrats, government officials, and prosperous guild members are the only ones who can afford new clothes. When they tire of a style, and some women tire of their fashions with every moon, they donate any torn or badly soiled garments to the church. The bulk of their castoffs they sell to second-handers like me." Ercole chuckled as he added, "The practice lets the rich boast that they're supporting the church while mostly they're refilling their coin purses. The church passes the dregs to the indigent and, believe me, Florence has its share of paupers. I provide good used clothing to working families whose pride prevents them from accepting charity from the church." He gave Gino a friendly slap on the back, saying, "Come visit my shop when you're ready to dress like a Florentine."

Ercole changed the subject, asking, "Yesterday, you were looking for a room. Did you find one?"

"Yes, I found one, but not the one above the candle shop. It was a fine room, but more than I could afford. I found a room in the same district at a lower cost."

Ercole winked. "Closer to the river?"

"Yes," Gino replied, puzzled by the question. "How did you know?"

"The river floods periodically, so rooms on ground level close to the river are less expensive." Ercole noticed Gino tense, and said, "But don't be overly concerned, Gino. People choose to live in those houses because the rents are low. They regard the floods as mere inconveniences, and nowhere in the city is totally safe. Water from the Arno covered half the city in the great flood a decade past. Just be sure to mount your valuable paintings high on the wall," Ercole jested.

Gino bit his lip, wondering how often the Arno flooded. He pondered the question for a moment, then pushed it aside and focused on his next problem. He said, "Today I'm looking for work. I have experience working in an apothecary. Are there apothecaries in the Santa Maria Novella quarter?"

"There are two. One is near my shop."

Ercole gave Gino directions to a long two-level building fronted by a colonnade. "That's San Paolo hospital. It's the oldest hospital in the city, founded by Saint Francis when he first visited Florence. A short distance beyond the hospital is a narrow street angling to the left. You'll find one of the apothecary shops on that street."

Gino thanked Ercole for his help and headed to the shop. He almost walked past without noticing the shop's tiny sign. "This shop is smaller even than the apothecary in Poppi," he said to himself. Stepping inside, the shop's dull gray walls made Gino feel he had entered a dreary rain cloud. Signor Morelli always had paintings hanging on the walls of his shop. No one ever commented on the paintings, but Morelli believed the artwork brightened the spirits of his customers, who were otherwise weighed upon by their illnesses. Gino glanced down at the floor where his footsteps had streaked a thin dust layer. "Could I be happy working in such a gloomy place?" he wondered.

The shop seemed empty when Gino entered. He called out and a short man with bushy eyebrows came out from a room in the rear.

Gino introduced himself and stated his purpose. "I'm new to the city and looking for work. Before coming to Florence, I worked in an apothecary in my home village. Might you have need of an assistant? I can mix preparations and I can hunt for plants in the fields."

The man held up a hand to end Gino's petition. "I have no need of an assistant. As you can see, mine is a small shop."

"I understand," Gino replied, not entirely displeased by the rejection. "I was told there is also another apothecary in this district. Can you direct me to it?"

"I could direct you, but going there would be a wasted effort. You'll not find work at that shop either. It, too, is a small shop like mine. We serve the poor people of this district. Many who live in these neighborhoods can't even afford to consult a doctor when they are sick. They bring their ailments to me, hoping I can give them a cure." Gino looked confused, so the speziale added, "I help them whenever I can. I've seen many common symptoms more times than I can count, so I know what a doctor would prescribe.

"There are a few wealthy people of this district, the ones who live near the church. They frequent the large apothecaries in the city center because those shops offer more than just medicines." Gino opened his mouth, but before he could speak, the shop owner said, "There are many apothecaries in Florence. You could visit each shop looking for work, but there is a better way. Our guild maintains close contact with its members, so clerks at the guild office will know whether any shops are seeking help."

Heartened by the suggestion, Gino asked for directions to the guild office. "The Doctors' and Apothecaries' Guild office is clustered with several other guild offices, so it will be easy to find the building, but its entrance is nearly hidden. It's on a small street without a nameplate. Go past the mercato and when you reach Via Calimala, — Via Calimala is the wide street — turn to your left. Go a short distance, maybe two or three blocks, and ask someone to show you to the guilds. You can identify the Doctors and Apothecaries Guild office by its emblem, the Holy Mother with the Baby Jesus on her lap and a rose in one hand. The emblem is next to the building entrance."

It seemed incongruous, but Gino did not ask why the guild had chosen the Holy Mother and Baby Jesus as figures for its symbol. He left the shop and followed the directions without difficulty. At Via Calimala, he turned left and walked two blocks. Ahead, a young apprentice paced back and forth in front of a bakery shop, announcing to everyone within earshot the newest confection pulled from the oven. The apprentice responded to Gino's query about the guilds by pointing to a building directly across the street. "Some guilds are in that building. Others are in the building behind it."

The building identified by the apprentice had an insignia above its door, but not one of the Holy Mother. Gino walked around the side of the building and, behind it, he came to a short, unnamed street. That street ended at a three-level stone building with a sloped roof, and above its entrance was the symbol of the Doctors and Apothecaries Guild.

Gino stepped into an unoccupied anteroom and paused, listening for signs of activity. He heard nothing from the corridors branching off to his sides, but a murmur of voices on the second level floated down the wide staircase facing him. He climbed to the second level landing and stepped forward into a grand audience hall where his footfalls on the marble tiles echoed down from the high ceiling above. Full length statues anchoring the corners of the room sat atop pedestals, making the imposing figures appear larger than life. Four long tables arranged in a square filled the center of the room with enough padded high-backed chairs surrounding them to seat two dozen men.

Intimidated by the elegance, and feeling like an intruder, Gino returned to the landing by slinking backward with tiny steps. He followed the undertone of voices to a large well-lit room where four clerks sat at desks silently reviewing documents. A man standing beside the fifth desk was reprimanding a seated clerk, who fidgeted and struggled to maintain eye contact with his critic. The standing man noticed Gino, but he did not let the visitor's presence interrupt his reproval of the underling. At length, he finished his rebuke and approached Gino. "What?" he demanded brusquely.

After Gino explained he was seeking work at an apothecary, the man folded his arms across his chest and pronounced, "You're too old to be an apprentice."

"I have experience working at an apothecary. I'm looking for work as an assistant, not as an apprentice."

"What experience?" the man asked sharply.

"I worked alongside the owner of the apothecary in Poppi, a village in the Casentino Valley. He taught me how to prepare a large range of herbal remedies. Before he opened his apothecary in Poppi, he lived in Florence and had been a member of this guild."

The man gave a dismissive wave. "Do you have a family in Florence?"

"No."

The man stepped back and leveled an icy stare. "Speziali are highly respected in this city. Many Florentines would beg for the opportunity to work in an apothecary. I am certain there are no positions for outsiders." He turned and walked away.

Crestfallen, Gino left the room. If the guild knows all the apothecaries and they reject outsiders, what can I do? I can't go back to the farm as a failure. Gino shuffled down the stairs, his hand clinging to the brass railing for support. When he reached ground level, he heard footsteps approaching from behind. One of the clerks who had been working in the office came alongside him. "Don't be deflated by Peto's words. He can be a cow's ass. His appointment as senior clerk came only because his uncle is a guild consul. Elections will be held within a month, new consuls will be elected, and then Peto will be cast into the street where he belongs. Every day closer to the election, he becomes more insufferable.

"I heard you say you're looking for work at an apothecary. I know of no apothecaries in need of speziali, but a reputable shop in the San Marco district is seeking a perfumer."

"A perfumer?" Gino echoed.

"Apothecaries in Florence sell more than curatives. A perfumer is like a speziale, except instead of preparing curatives, perfumers prepare fragrances and elixirs." Noting Gino's skepticism, the clerk added, "A perfumer is a respected profession."

Gino recalled Taddeo saying rich people used perfumes to mask their smell. Although the concept of perfumer seemed strange to him, Gino got directions to the apothecary and set out for the San Marco district.

He reflected on his situation as he walked. In Poppi, I helped relieve the suffering of all the sick in the village, both rich and poor. I always felt pleasure when my potions cured their ailments. Will I be satisfied making ointments for rich people to hide their stink? How will my father react when I tell him I'm a perfumer? But if there truly is no prospect of a speziale job anywhere in the entire city, I may have no alternative other than to become a perfumer…or return to the farm.

Gino found the shop easily on one of the major roads heading out from the city center. Its sign read *apothecary di fiducia*, trustworthy apothecary. At first, he thought the apothecary was one of two shops on the building's ground level, but upon closer inspection, he realized the sign straddled both shops.

The first shop, the one most directly under the sign, was larger than Signor Morelli's shop in Poppi and much larger than the apothecary in the Santa Maria Novella district. "This must be a prosperous shop," he concluded. While Gino studied the building, a well-dressed man and woman came out of the shop. They crossed the street, strolling with the woman clutching the man's arm for support. A few minutes later, a man wearing a red robe and carrying a black leather case also left the shop. He walked in Gino's direction, and as he passed, he gave a quick nod. He was the first passerby to have paid any notice to Gino since he had arrived in Florence. Gino learned later that red robes trimmed with squirrel fur were the distinctive dress favored by doctors who treated the Florentine upper class.

Inside the shop, shelves on one wall held a display of brightly painted urns, each containing a colored powder. Lettering on the shelf gave the names of the powders in the urns. Gino recognized some names as ingredients he had used in preparations. Others were unfamiliar to him.

A tall man with an angular nose, a well-groomed mix of brown and gray hair, and a healthy color in his cheeks, came forward to greet Gino. Unlike Signor Morelli, who wore simple smocks when working in his shop, this man wore a stylish tunic embroidered at the cuffs. In a melodic voice, he said, "Buona sera, Signore. Welcome. How may I help you?"

Gino introduced himself, explained he was looking for work, and summarized his experience at the apothecary in Poppi. The man, who gave his name as Carlo Roselli, scrutinized Gino's clothing. "Poppi must be a small village," he said, noting the road grime marring Gino's smock.

Following Roselli's eyeline, Gino said, "I just arrived in Florence and haven't yet bought … city clothes."

Looking beyond the clothes, Roselli saw intelligent eyes and sensed the determination of the young man standing before him. "Help me understand how much you've learned in your small village apothecary. Florence is a large city with people having a variety of ailments. Moments ago, a woman came here suffering from constipation. The doctor prescribed Sportavecchia. Do you know it?"

Gino nodded. "Yes. For constipation, we used the leaves and had people boil them to make a soup." Realizing he was being tested, Gino added, "For more serious conditions, we combined Sportavecchia and Raponzolo."

Signor Roselli raised an eyebrow. "Did you use the same treatment for children?"

Gino shook his head. "Oh, no. Sportavecchia is much too strong for young children. For them, we used Malvia leaves and had their mothers make a thin broth."

Believing Gino possessed at least a rudimentary knowledge of curatives, Roselli rubbed his chin and explained, "Until recently, the shop next to mine sold ceramics. The shopkeeper found his trade falling to where he could no longer continue his business. He was a good man, and I was sorry to see him fail, but my trade in perfumes and pigments has been growing, so I seized the opportunity to expand by combining the two shops together. I can attend to the curatives, but I could use help to prepare the perfumes and elixirs."

Gino lowered his gaze and admitted, "I have no experience with those," then with growing enthusiasm, he added, "But I know how to create formulations, and I can read. If the processes for creating them are written, I'm certain I can follow them."

Surprised a farm boy from the countryside could read, Roselli asked, "Who taught you to read?"

"A monk at San Fedele Abbey taught me so I could read the formulations written by Signor Morelli, who owned the apothecary. As his eyesight failed, he trusted me to do more and more of the preparation."

Feeling Gino showed promise, Roselli declared, "Very well, you may have a trial for one week. Be here in the morning when the church bells sound Terce." Gino thanked Roselli for the opportunity. As he turned to leave, Roselli called to him, and using Gino's phrase, said, "Buy some 'city clothes.' Our customers expect us to be presentable."

On the way back to his room, Gino bought two stylish tunics at Ercole's used clothing shop, then he stopped at a tavern for a glass of wine to celebrate his success at having found a job.

7

Thursday April 28, 1345

On the first morning of his new job, the apothecary was locked when Gino arrived. He waited outside for several minutes, watching men hurrying to their work and women heading to the mercato, before Signor Roselli came down from the building's second level to unlock the door. "I live above the shop with my wife and daughter," Roselli explained. He handed Gino a pastry wrapped in paper. "They made sweet rolls this morning, and my wife wanted you to have one as a warm welcome to your new city."

Gino followed Roselli into the apothecary and then through an opening to the adjoining perfume shop. Roselli set three folios on a counter, pointed to one, and said, "This sheath holds the pigment recipes."

Gino opened the folio and glanced at the first page.

Blue Azurite

Dissolve copper in aquafortis.

Precipitate using calce viva.

Wash the precipitate and spread on linen cloth to dry.

Grind with calce viva powder to produce the blue color.

While Gino read the recipe, Roselli said, "Blue Azurite is the shade of blue Maestro Gaddi favors for his frescoes in the chapel at Santa Croce. The maestro rarely comes here himself. He sends his apprentices whenever he needs more pigments."

Roselli pointed to the second folio. "These are the elixir recipes." He withdrew a sheet and said, "Some recipes are labeled to show their purpose, such as this one, the Elixir of Health." He sifted through the pages until he found a specific sheet. "Others, like this one, *Elisir per il Professore Vianello*, we make especially for Professor Vianello. He discovered this recipe when he was teaching at the University of Padua and claims the Greek philosopher Aristotle created it to expand his mind. The professor says the elixir helps him to think clearly. Among its ingredients are Greek olives. According to the professor, minerals in Grecian soil give their olives a trait not found in olives grown elsewhere. To make this elixir, we have Greek olives sent to us by an importer in Venice."

Gino looked at Roselli skeptically. "Does the elixir truly improve his mind?"

Roselli held up a hand. "Elixirs are … mysterious. Their values may be shaped by a user's beliefs. Regardless, I never ask users about the efficacy of their elixirs, and I suggest you not ask either. Study this recipe because I expect the professor to come here today. This elixir cannot be made in advance, so you will need to prepare it when he arrives."

Roselli pointed to a large jug on a shelf behind them. "We always have this elixir ready because men come for it every day after work before they return to their wives … or mistresses. The recipe is called *Virile*. Men claim it stimulates their passion." Roselli paused a beat, then quipped, "This one you can try yourself and decide whether it helps you perform."

Roselli tapped the thickest folio. "These are the perfume recipes." He gestured toward the rows of colorful urns on the shelves behind the counter. "All the perfumes are made in advance and stored in these urns."

Roselli showed Gino the ways to dispense the perfumes: as a powder in a small box, as a liquid in a vial, or as a scented sachet or handkerchief. After the orientation, he left Gino to study the material in the folios.

Gino opened to the first page in the perfumes folio and had barely begun reading when two women entered the shop. Standing behind the counter with customers in the shop made him feel proud once again, as he had when he was a speziale in Poppi. He beamed. "*Buongiorno, donne.*"

One woman's eyes narrowed. "You must be new. I've never seen you before."

"I am new to this city," Gino agreed. "And on this, my first working day, I thank fortune for the privilege of serving two graceful women. How may I help you?"

The women muttered to each other briefly, then one said, "I would like Jasmine rose." Seeing Gino's hesitance, she pointed to one of the colorful urns, and said, "It's in the urn painted with pink flowers."

While she spoke, Gino leafed through the perfumes folio to find the sheet for Jasmine rose and read Roselli's note. "Women dab Jasmine rose on their bodies to stimulate sensual experiences. Dispense in a vial."

A drop of liquid splashed onto Gino's finger as he decanted a measure into a vial. He sniffed it, shut his eyes momentarily, and freed his imagination. Yes, he could believe the scent might add to a woman's allure. With his face flush, Gino handed the vial to the woman and turned to her companion. She held out a container and requested that he fill it with Sweet Water. Gino regained his composure as he read the notation in the recipe: "For perfuming clothes. Dispense in a flask."

As the two women departed with their perfumes, one commented to her friend. "He seems well-mannered."

With a flirtatious smile, the other replied, "Well-mannered and well-formed. I should find a reason to return soon and bring my daughter. She's old enough to catch his attention."

By serving customers throughout the morning, Gino found women escorted by their husbands behaved with decorum, while those who came with other women were less discrete. Unlike the custom in Poppi, Florentine women didn't come into the shop alone.

In late morning, a fashionably dressed, dignified looking man entered the shop. Surprised at seeing Gino, he asked, "Has something happened to Signor Roselli?"

After Gino explained he was Signor Roselli's new assistant, the man announced, "I am Professor Federigo Vianello."

Gino recognized the name immediately. "Signor Roselli told me about your elixir. It will only take a minute to prepare it."

"It must be made with Greek olives," Vianello cautioned. "The olives must be from Greece."

"Yes, professor. The olives were shipped here from Greece." While he prepared the elixir, Gino said, "Signor Roselli told me you taught at the University of Padua."

"Yes, that is so. I taught at the university until earlier this year when I received a commission to tutor the children of Signor Peruzzi, the banker. I much prefer teaching at the university, but I could not dismiss Signor Peruzzi's lucrative offer."

"What was your specialty at the university?"

"I taught mathematics and astronomy. Padua has the finest tradition in astronomy. Superior even to the offering at the University of Bologna."

Gino's grasp of mathematics was limited to simple arithmetic, and he had scant knowledge of astronomy. He could only comment on his recent observation and asked, "Have you been watching the bright, wandering stars in the night sky?"

"They are planets, not wandering stars," Vianello corrected. "And yes, I've been studying them. A conjunction like this, with the three planets coming together, happens only once in a century. It's a rare and ominous sign."

"Ominous?" Gino echoed.

"Yes, events in the heavens are predictors of future events here on Earth. Jupiter and Saturn are water planets. Their alignments alone would foretell of a great flood."

The mention of flooding made Gino uneasy as he recalled Ercole's description of houses close to the river being flooded easily. "When will the flood occur?" Gino asked.

Vianello tapped his fingers on the counter. "No one can say. Heavenly signs can often presage Earthly events by two or three years. But flooding isn't the most menacing possibility, because Mars has also joined the alignment. The red god of war is a sinister forecaster. I believe Mars joining with Jupiter and Saturn means we will be vexed by something far worse than a flood."

The professor's prophecy left Gino in a quandary because he had always considered predictions to be the conjurings of witches and magicians; yet Vianello was a learned scholar.

In mid-afternoon, the shop filled with patrons eager for a measure of Virile elixir. The men who gathered at the counter chatted about their work, the weather, and recent disappointing actions taken by the Signoria. The friendly banter of those standing shoulder-to-shoulder and drinking gave the shop the character of a tavern rather than an apothecary. Gino had not expected the large vessel holding the ready supply of elixir could be depleted in a single afternoon, but little remained when the shop door closed at day's end.

Gino was busily grinding herbs, the first step in creating a new quantity of elixir, when Signor Roselli came from the adjoining shop. "I see you had a busy day," Roselli said, glancing at the collection of empty mugs scattered along the counter. "I was busy as well, or I would have come round sooner."

"Is it always this hectic?"

"No. We are busiest at the end of the week, although business has thrived since the other apothecary in this neighborhood ceased operation. I'm certainly pleased to have you as an assistant. I would have struggled to accommodate everyone today without you."

Gino said, "I can't judge whether Virile elixir increases prowess, but it certainly makes men more talkative."

"It sure does," Roselli agreed. "The fruit pulp used in Virile is fermented in the same manner grasses are fermented to make beer. I believe Virile is even more potent than beer. Did you partake of it?"

Gino chuckled. "No. It would have little value for me since I have no woman waiting at home."

Gino walked along the river on his way back to his rented room and tried to judge how high the river would need to rise before his room became flooded. When he reached his house, daylight had faded enough for the three planets tantalizing each other to be visible in the western sky.

8

Wednesday May 11, 1345

After two weeks working at the apothecary, Gino found working as a perfumer to be more satisfying than he had initially thought possible. He enjoyed serving customers and chatting with them. Wiener was right when he said, "Florentines will warm to you when they get to know you." Signor Roselli, delighted with his new assistant, told Gino, "I don't know how I managed without you."

As the end of the day approached, Gino peered into the jug containing the supply of Virile elixir and found it still nearly full. Only a few men had come into the shop in the afternoon and all had already left except for one man, who was emptying his mug slowly.

"You were here earlier in the week," Gino commented offhandedly to the straggler.

The man looked up with a resigned expression. "I need this nourishment two or three times every week. My wife is ten years younger than me. She's always *appapare.*" He raised his mug. "Even when I drink this, she wears me out. My father told me to marry an older woman. I should have listened to him."

The man took another sip, then said, "I haven't seen you with a mug of your own."

"I have yet to taste it," Gino replied.

"How have you resisted the temptation? Every day you serve this elixir to a herd of men, and you've never tried it yourself?"

"I prepare many things. I couldn't possibly sample every one of them."

"But Virile is special. You must try it." He dropped a silver coin onto the counter. "Here, let your first taste come as a token from Paolo."

Reluctantly, Gino filled a mug for himself and took a swig. He recalled all the ingredients he had blended to create the drink, but none were easily identifiable in the composite. "The taste isn't what I expected."

Paolo laughed. "Taste isn't the reason men come to you for this elixir." He downed the rest of his drink, puffed out his chest, and headed toward the door, saying, "Now I'm ready for my frisky wife."

Gino finished his mug as he cleared the counter and put the shop in order. As he stepped out into the street, a recollection of the woman in the house on Borgo Ognissanti flashed into his mind. Her pretty face, her alluring dark eyes, and her soft voice. Feeling a warmth in his loins, Gino thought, Paolo spoke the truth about Virile elixir. When he reached the Santa Maria Novella district, he found his feet carrying him to Borgo Ognissanti rather than to his room. He was about to knock on the door when it swung open and a gruff voice barked, "The cretin has returned." Without a word, Gino pressed three soldi into the man's hand, turned away, and scurried up the stairs to the second level.

Gino rapped once on the door. Inside, muffled footsteps came toward him. When the door eased open, he faced the pretty face of his memory. He inhaled the scent of her perfume, delicate, yet even more sensual than Jasmine Rose.

The woman smiled, took Gino's hand, and led him across the room. "I'm pleased to see you've returned. I thought I had frightened you away," she said as she ran her fingers through his hair. Standing beside her bed, she unbuttoned his tunic and swept her soft, warm hands over his chest. "What's your name?"

In a wavering voice, he replied, "Gino."

"I'm Tessa," she whispered softly and pulled the sash from her robe, letting it fall open. It slipped from her shoulders and dropped to the floor. She lowered her hand from his chest to his leggings. "Oh, Gino," she purred, as she touched his hardness and eased him backward onto her bed.

That was Gino's second time with a woman. His first was an awkward experience with a girl in Poppi. Neither he nor the girl had found the encounter satisfying, but Tessa was well-versed in fulfilling the promises of intimacy.

Only a faint glow of daylight remained in the western sky when Gino stepped out of Tessa's building into the cool evening air. He remembered Wiener's lighthearted jest, suggesting Florence's charms would ensnare him by the next full moon. He didn't feel sinful, but if his visit with Tessa was a vice, then Wiener was too generous in his timing because the old moon still reigned. As he ambled along the nearly deserted street, Gino thought about other patrons of the apothecary who had become users of Virile, but, still in the glow of Tessa's charm, he decided he could fare well without an elixir.

Ahead, Gino spotted a woman laboring under the weight of the two bags she carried. Twice he had seen the woman coming down from the second level of his building and assumed she was the wife of the doctor whose office adjoined his room. He rushed forward, came abreast of the woman, and said, "Signora, I live in your building. I rent the room on the ground floor. Your bags look heavy. May I help you carry them?"

Too winded to speak, she huffed in response to Gino's query and held out one bag. Gino took it; then stepped around her and reached for the other bag, which she surrendered gratefully. Freed of her heavy load, she moved with the poise of an upper class woman but wore a simple tan dress befitting a shopkeeper's wife. She had a strong face with a pointy, but not long, nose. Gino guessed she was about the same age as his mother, although he never considered himself adept at judging women's ages.

He matched her gait and said, "I'm Gino."

When her panting subsided and her breathing slowed, she said, "I'm Masina. I shouldn't have gathered so much this time. It's almost more than I can carry."

Gino noticed a stalk poking out from one bag and asked, "Is this Ortica root?"

"Yes, it is," she answered, surprised he had recognized the plant. "How do you know it?"

"From my work in an apothecary. Are these plants for your husband, the doctor?"

Puzzled at first, Masina replied, "There is no doctor and I have no husband. I'm a healer. I gathered these plants in a field, and I use them as you do at the apothecary."

They reached the house and climbed to the second level. "Come inside and let me fix you a refreshing peppermint drink in appreciation for your help."

Gino watched Masina combine peppermint and two other herbs, sprinkle the mixture into mugs of water. Offering a mug to Gino, she said, "Let the herbs bathe before you drink."

"Is this one of your remedies?"

Masina smiled, "Yes, it is one I use myself to help restore my energy."

"Where did you learn to become a healer?"

"My mother and her sister began as midwives and grew their abilities. I learned from them. Women are embarrassed to discuss certain problems with a doctor, and many pregnant women do not wish to expose themselves to a strange man. I serve those women."

"Did your mother teach you to make curatives?"

"As a little girl, I would go with her to the fields to gather plants. She showed me how to identify them and how to use them to make remedies for our poor neighbors."

Gino told her how Signor Morelli had taught him about medicinal plants, then asked if he could join her when she hunted for plants near Florence. They continued sharing stories until dark.

9

Saturday May 14, 1345

Gino's first customer of the day had hair falling to his shoulders and wore a paint splattered smock. Dabs of yellow and blue paint decorated his chin. In the past two weeks, the artist painting frescoes at Santa Croce—Gino couldn't recall his name—had sent his apprentices to buy paints, but this man was too old and too unkempt to be the maestro's apprentice. Gino assumed the man was the artist himself, and asked, "Are you beginning a new fresco, maestro?"

Puzzled at first by Gino's question, the man replied, "You must have me confused with Signor Gaddi. I am Salvi di Cione and I don't paint frescoes. I just received a commission … a prized commission to produce an altarpiece for the Church of Santa Margherita in the Chianti Hills south of Florence. It will be a masterpiece, so I want to use some new colors, ones I haven't used before."

Since he didn't know the names of corresponding pigments, he and Gino were forced to work by trial and error. The artist waved a hand in the air with a flourish and said, "First, I need a bright yellow with the spirit of blooming daffodils and sunshine." Gino thumbed through the pigments folio and found a recipe called Mimosa, named after the delicate yellow flower found coloring hillside fields in early March. The artist closed his eyes and tried to picture the flower. "Perhaps," he said.

In his mortar, Gino ground a mix of flowers from two plants with a stem from another. He boiled the mixture in salted water, then filtered the precipitate with a fine cloth. "A lovely color but too intense," di Cione declared. Next, Gino found a recipe named Alpino Pasque. "I don't know of a flower with such a name the artist said, so Gino prepared a sample.

"It is pretty, but too pale," di Cione concluded. "Is there one midway between?"

The names of all the other yellow pigments, such as Sunflower, suggested they were deeper, bolder shades. With no viable candidates to choose from, Gino placed the recipes for Mimosa and Alpino Pasque side-by-side. He compared the processes for each color and prepared a sample by using steps from each formulation. Di Cione clapped his hands together and shouted "*Perfetto*!" when Gino showed him the resulting pigment. "With that pigment I can create a beautiful, rich paint color."

Gino mixed a batch of pigment for the artist and recorded his formulation in the folio. He named the color Cione Yellow and noted its color fell midway between Mimosa and Alpino Pasque.

Di Cione said, "I will need three shades of green."

Gino asked, "Are any of these familiar to you?" and read pigment names from the folio.

"I know that one," the artist announced when Gino read the name *Terra Verde*, Earth Green. "I can use it for the middle tone. Now find two others, one brighter and one slightly darker."

The artist stopped Gino again when he read, Egyptian Green. "I've used Egyptian Green before in another painting. It will be ideal for the brighter green. Now one more, a darker shade this time," di Cione said.

Gino mixed two more green pigments before finding a color acceptable to the artist. The blue, purple and red hues required no trials because di Cione knew the names of the pigments he wanted. As he left the shop, di Cione said, "*Grazie. Grazie mille,* speziale." Gino brightened at once again, hearing himself called a speziale.

Later, he confided to Signor Roselli his gratitude that perfumes were not blended to satisfy the whims of individual customers. "It would take a legion of perfumers to serve all our customers if each took as much tending as Signor di Cione."

"True," Roselli admitted. "But creative artists like di Cione bring a welcome diversion from our daily routine."

Gino's work at the apothecary kept him busy for long hours, six days each week. He valued the chance to expand his skills, and he enjoyed meeting new people, but he also relished his time away from the shop when he could explore his new city. Every day after work, he walked different streets back to his house.

Sunday May 15, 1345

Sundays, when the apothecary was closed, were the only days when Gino had time to explore outside the city. Each Sunday, he chose a new destination, a town or village in the countryside. His first foray took him to Fiesole, a town in the hills north of Florence.

Stories about Fiesole fascinated him even as a boy growing up in Poppi. He knew the Etruscans had founded the town over two centuries ago, and when the Romans came to the area, they had settled in Fiesole rather than the swampy area along the Arno River that eventually became Florence. Along the road that ascended to the hilltop town, Gino passed only a few children playing in a farm field, but deep wheel tracks were evidence that on days other than Sundays, the road carried heavily laden wagons hauling farm produce to Florence.

Gino stopped at the base of the old wall surrounding the town to eat the bread and fruit he had carried with him. From the high vantage point, he could see the entire city of Florence in the distance. Morning mist rose from the Arno River. Buildings obscured the view of his house, but he could see several churches, including Santa Maria Novella and Santa Croce. He had just finished eating when the bell at the church in the center of Fiesole summoned him and the other faithful to mass. His weekly treks let him attend mass at a different church every Sunday.

In the afternoon he sat on the steps of Fiesole's Roman amphitheater, thinking about his family. Stories of the Romans and Etruscans had also intrigued his brothers. Would they ever visit Fiesole, he wondered. Was it proper for him to be sitting idly watching a leaf spinning in the breeze while his family toiled on the farm?

He knew, with the wisdom of experience, that Sundays offered no respite from the unending chores of farming. His family always attended mass together on Sundays, but only after they had milked the cows and fed the hogs. They postponed other chores until they returned from church. By comparison, city dwellers had Sunday as their day of rest. They could spend their day, as he was, enjoying *la dolce vita*, the sweet life. A short while later, Gino tempered his view when he spotted a pauper rooting through trash in a side alley, hoping to find something to eat. Working men like me have comfortable lives, he decided, but not everyone in towns and cities is as fortunate.

The following Sunday, Gino had intended to hike to a village south of Florence, but heavy rain forced him to change his plans and attend mass at nearby Santa Maria Novella. Since he was not a member of the congregation, he took a position alongside a column toward the rear of the church. He had not expected to recognize anyone and was surprised to see Masina, the healer who lived in his building, standing farther forward across the nave.

Midway through the mass, the priest stepped behind the pulpit to deliver his sermon. Without preamble, he launched into a tirade. "Beware the evil ones among us who obey the teachings of demons. They may look like us, but their hearts are blackened by Satan's lies pouring from their mouths. Witches and sorcerers they are, who would lure you away from God with their promises and potions."

The priest's voice grew louder, and his face reddened. He gripped the pulpit tightly with both hands and swayed side-to-side as though he himself were gripped by a spell. "A woman in Milan claimed her tonic to be more powerful than prayer for curing the sick. Only when a cross was burned into her chest did she cast off her evil and beg for the Lord to help her." He pounded his fist on the pulpit. "Be watchful of all, lest witches abound in Florence."

Parishioners reacted to the diatribe with sideways glances at those around them. They moved slightly, where possible, in the crowded church, to distance themselves from others. When the service ended, people filed out of the church quietly, absent the typical friendly Sunday morning banter with neighbors.

Gino joined Masina as they both headed back to their house. The rain had stopped, and overhead the dark clouds were breaking up. "This is the first time I've attended mass at this church. Is the sermon always so fiery?" Gino asked.

Masina looked around to be sure no one else was close enough to overhear her. "Priests like him are fools. He, too, would beg for the Lord's mercy if his chest were being branded. It proves nothing."

She hesitated, then continued in a softer voice. "How can it be acceptable for nuns to care for the sick while he condemns other women as witches? The church didn't always condemn women healers. There was a time when Pope Gregory praised the contributions of women at the medical school at Salerno. Since then, the church has looked favorably on us. Only recently have some priests become embittered."

They walked silently for a few minutes, with Gino not responding to Masina's words. She looked around again, and satisfied no one was close, she said, "I believe it is the doctors in your guild who are pressuring the church. They now see us as capable rivals."

"Are you afraid of being accused?" Gino asked.

"I am careful. I treat only women and children, and I never let them take treatments away to be used at home. Whenever I give something to drink, I call it a broth, never a potion or a cure." She paused a moment, then said forcefully, "But yes, I am fearful. And my fear prevents me from talking with other healers. In the past, I could learn from others when I encountered a new condition calling for a treatment unknown to me. Now, fear confines me to using only the cures I already know."

"I'm willing to share my knowledge of curatives." Gino said.

Masina acknowledged his offer with a smile, then continued, "After childbirth, women should nurse their newborns for a year to keep the infants from contracting intestinal problems, but some poor women don't follow my advice. They wean their own children quickly so they can earn money as a wet nurse for rich women's babies. Lately, their own infants have suffered from a stomach cramp condition, and my usual remedies have failed to end their pain."

"How are you treating them?"

"With apple pulp stewed to a purée."

"Apple is good against diarrhea, but not the best for stomach cramps," Gino said. He ran through formulations in his mind, searching for a cure suitable for infants. "Are you familiar with Genziana?" he asked. Masina shook her head. "It's a flowering plant that's effective for stomach problems. Men and women can chew the roots, but for children you could make a broth from the leaves. Perhaps use honey to sweeten it. I can get Genziana leaves tomorrow when I am at the apothecary."

"The people I treat are poor. They can't afford to buy medications from an apothecary."

"There's no need to buy the leaves because I can replace whatever I take. The flower grows wild in the Apennine hills near my village. I'll have one of my brothers gather leaves and send them to me."

"Aren't you worried the church might learn you are aiding a healer?" Masina asked with concern showing on her face.

Gino laughed, "I'm certain our scheming to help sick children can be a secret held between us. You said the people you treat are poor. Are they able to pay?"

"Some feel they should offer me a token for my help, but I ask for nothing. Before the Lord took my husband, he owned a butcher shop. When he passed, I sold the shop. The money I received is more than enough to support my modest life."

Gino looked up at the blue sky pushing away the gray rain clouds. "I had intended to explore the village in the hills south of the city where the new monastery is being built, but the rain made me cancel my plan. Now, the weather has cleared, but it's too late to trek as far as the hills."

Masina said, "There is an old Benedictine monastery not far from the city. I go there often to pick flowers in the fields for my broths. I could show you."

Masina and Gino spent the afternoon in the fields around the Saint Marta monastery, letting the warm sun drive away their fears and concerns stoked by the priest's scathing sermon.

10

Wednesday June 1, 1345

Years of farm life had conditioned Gino to rise at daybreak and he saw no reason to abandon his habit when he moved to the city. He consistently arrived at the apothecary before Signor Roselli, even though Roselli lived directly above the shop. Rather than making Gino wait for him, Roselli had given Gino a key so he could open the shop and begin making the perfumes that needed to be replenished.

Roselli usually arrived a short time after Gino and well before any customers, so Gino startled when an attractive young woman followed him into the shop. She paused just inside the doorway with her eyes downcast and her hands clasped together in front of her. In a timid voice, she said, "My father is sick. He said to tell you he can't come to the shop today."

"Signor Roselli is your father?" Gino asked, his voice registering surprise.

Without raising her head, the woman nodded. Roselli had mentioned he had a daughter whom Gino had pictured as a little girl, not as a beautiful woman. Almost in a whisper, barely loud enough for Gino to hear, she said, "He asked whether you could tend both shops today."

Roselli knew Gino had the skill to prepare medicines as well as perfumes and elixirs. On occasions when the apothecary was especially busy, Roselli and Gino had worked side-by-side preparing curatives for waiting customers. Once, Gino had tended both the apothecary and perfume shops by himself when Signor Roselli had gone to his nephew's baptism, but then Roselli had been away for only a few hours. Gino thought quickly. One could never be sure, but typically, Wednesdays were not busy days. "Yes, I can manage both shops," he replied.

As the woman turned to leave, Gino said, "Tell me about your father. What are his symptoms?"

For the first time, the woman looked up, revealing the sparkle in her amber eyes. She said, "He woke during the night and he vomited … more than once."

"Could it be from something he ate?" Gino asked.

She tensed and said, "We all ate the same supper." Gino's question raised a fear she might contract the same ailment as her father. Reflexively, she placed a hand against her stomach.

"Is he hot or cold?" Gino asked.

"My mother said he felt warm."

"Is he sweating? His face wet?"

"I wasn't close enough to see, but mother wiped his forehead with a cloth."

Three times in the past week, people had come to the apothecary describing the same symptoms. Gino concluded they and Signor Roselli had fallen ill to the new malady spreading through the city. "I can make something to help him. It will take only a few minutes."

With no need to consult the list of formulations, Gino dropped three herbs into the mortar, ground them to a powder, combined them with a few drops of olive oil, and poured the liquid into a vial. When he held the vial out to her, she reached for it with a delicate hand, almost touching his. She turned and left without another word.

Gino watched her go and his eyes remained fixed on the door long after she had gone. Throughout the morning, he hustled back and forth between the apothecary and the perfume shop to serve the steady stream of customers, including two men bearing prescriptions from doctors for the same medication Gino had sent to Signor Roselli.

Near noon, when both shops were empty, Signor Roselli's daughter returned. Again, she stood just inside the doorway. She didn't look down.

This time, she made eye contact with Gino. "My father thanks you for the medication. He is more comfortable and resting now."

"I'm pleased the formulation helped him."

Gino expected the woman to retreat after delivering the message, but she did not. In an unsteady voice, she said, "My mother said I must help you, if I can." She stood with shoulders slumped as a young child might when about to be reprimanded.

"What shall I call you?" Gino asked, smiling.

"My name is Gabriela," she said, her hands fidgeting at her sides.

Gabriela, Gino repeated to himself, stretching the syllables as if they were melody in a song. A name befitting an angel, he mused. While his mind wandered, she said, "I know nothing of the apothecary. My father never taught me."

"There may be something you can do to help. Come with me." He escorted her toward the adjoining shop. She trailed behind, suspicious of where he was leading her. "This is the perfume shop," he announced.

He beckoned her to the counter, not daring to move close enough to detect whether she used perfume. He gestured to the shelves holding the colorful vessels. "Each of these urns holds a different perfume. Customers ask for them by name." Her eyes sparkled when she sniffed the fragrance Gino had dabbed on a small cloth and handed to her.

He had just finished explaining how to dispense the perfumes when two women came into the shop. "I know those women from church," Gabriela said softly.

"Ask whether you can help them," Gino suggested in a voice kind enough to acknowledge her insecurity, yet firm enough to keep her from protesting.

She approached the women, addressed them by name, and confirmed she was Gabriela Roselli, Signor Roselli's daughter. Using Gino's phrasing, she asked how she could help them. As Gino had predicted, one woman asked for a perfume by name.

Uncertain whether she should serve them, Gabriela looked at Gino, who simply nodded. She picked up an empty vial, scanned the shelves to find the perfume that the woman had requested, and filled the vial. Her lips turned up in a smile as she handed the vial to the woman. The second woman asked for two different fragrances. "One is for my daughter," she explained. "You should meet her. Cinzia is about your age."

"Even your father couldn't have done better," Gino said after the women had left. His praise elicited a beaming smile from the young woman. Hearing the apothecary shop door open, Gino said, "I must attend to a customer. You can mind the perfume shop," and he turned and walked away. Gabriela glanced around the shop as though she had just discovered a new world.

Whenever Gino wasn't busy with customers in the apothecary, he meandered to the opening between the two shops to observe Gabriela. She delighted all the women who came into the shop. As much as customers enjoyed flirting with Gino, they equally enjoyed sharing stories and expressing their feelings to another woman.

It wasn't until mid-afternoon when the first man came into the perfume shop. Gino rushed in from the apothecary, put an arm around Gabriela's waist—had he thought about it, he might not have been so bold—and guided her to the door. She looked at him quizzically. "He's not here for perfume," Gino said. Knowing his statement didn't resolve her confusion, he added, "You've done well … very well. Your father will be proud." Before she could say a word, he guided her to the door and closed it behind her.

The following morning, it was Signor Roselli who came into the shop shortly after Gino. "I'm pleased you've recovered," Gino said while observing Roselli's pale face but steady gait.

"I'm not feeling as well as I did when I was your age, but I'm much better than yesterday," Roselli said, wincing slightly.

They had little time before customers coming into the shop sent both men to work, Roselli in the apothecary and Gino in the perfume shop. Neither man had mentioned Gabriela. Roselli's mood seemed more somber than normal, perhaps because he was not fully recovered, but Gino began worrying his behavior toward Gabriela might have offended Signor Roselli. Perhaps he should not have made her interact with customers.

Gino had just finished serving one of the shop's regular customers, the wife of a wealthy banker, when Roselli came into the perfume shop. He waited until the woman left before approaching Gino. "To show my appreciation for your tending both shops yesterday, I'd like it if you could join my wife and me at our evening meal tonight." Gino said he would be pleased to join Signor and Signora Roselli, but he remained perplexed by Roselli's failure to mention Gabriela.

***

In the early evening, when Gino climbed to the second level above the apothecary, it was Signora Roselli who answered his knock. She had the same bright eyes and dimples as her daughter. "I'm Gino Liani," Gino announced.

"Yes, I know," she said and stepped aside to let Gino enter. "I'm Joanna. Welcome."

He presented her with a candle. "It is a custom in my village for guests to bring a gift to their hosts."

Signora Roselli smiled slightly, making her dimples even more pronounced. "What a lovely custom. People in Florence are not as thoughtful." She inhaled the candle's aroma. "Is it myrrh?"

"Yes," Gino replied, surprised that she had identified the scent.

They moved to the kitchen where Gabriela stood at the fireplace stirring a pot. She did not turn to greet Gino when he and her mother came into the room.

Signora Roselli said, "Unfortunately, my husband can't join us. The medication you sent helped him to improve quickly. He felt better this morning, but working for the entire day was too great a burden. He's resting now."

Gino tensed, uncomfortable at the prospect of having supper with just Signora Roselli and Gabriela. "I should go. We can share a meal when Signor Roselli recovers," he said, and turned toward the door.

"The food is ready, and I'm sure my husband would want you to stay." She ushered Gino to the table. Gino recognized her tone; it matched his mother's manner when she would accept no argument.

Gino became even more uncomfortable when Gabriela sat facing him. Even repeated sips of beer did not eliminate the dryness in his mouth. He had just put the first morsel of food into his mouth when Signora Roselli said, "Gabriela told me you had her help with the perfumes yesterday."

Gino bit down hard to keep from expelling the food. He swallowed without chewing and said unsteadily, "I'm sorry. I shouldn't have …"

Signora Roselli raised a hand. "There is no reason for regret. Gabriela enjoyed talking with the women." She drew her daughter into the conversation by asking her, "What was the name of the woman who wanted the lemony fragrance … the one who helps at the hospital?"

Gabriela's entry into the discussion dispelled the remaining tension, letting the three diners enjoy pleasant conversation for the rest of their meal. Gabriela suppressed her modesty enough to look directly at Gino and he gazed at her without feeling he had violated a social prohibition.

When it came time for Gino to leave, Signora Roselli accompanied him to the door and said, "Tomorrow evening, our church choir will sing at a service in honor of Saint Sebastian. Gabriela and I plan to attend. Would you like to join us?"

Gabriela stood to the side watching and hoping for Gino's affirmative response.

11

Wednesday June 22, 1345

Signor Roselli found Gino sweeping the floor when he entered the apothecary. Gino looked up and said, "This dry weather has everyone bringing in dust." Roselli glanced behind him at his own dusty footprints and apologized for tracking more dirt onto the floor that had just been cleaned. Gino cleared the footprints with a quick swipe. "It can't be helped. There's dust everywhere."

Roselli shifted the conversation. "The feast of Saint John is on Friday. Do you celebrate it in your village?"

"No. I know Saint John is revered in Florence, but his day has no special significance in Poppi."

"In Florence, we celebrate by going to mass in the morning. Then a city-wide horse race will take place throughout the afternoon."

Confused, Gino echoed, "A horse race? To celebrate the Feast of Saint John? I don't understand."

"I'm told the tradition of a riderless horse race originated with the Romans. The custom continues in Rome and in several other cities. Here in Florence, we hold the race on Saint John's day. The streets are blocked to make the horses run only one way across the entire city," Roselli explained. "The races are always exciting, and they'll be even more special this year because our neighborhood is sponsoring one of the horses. You should join us."

"On Friday ..." Gino said slowly, still processing the unlikely relationship between a religious holiday and horse racing.

"Gabriela enjoys the races. She'll be there with my wife and me."

Roselli noticed Gino's eyes brighten at his mention of Gabriela. "Friday is good," Gino said more quickly than he intended.

Gino finished sweeping, and as he walked into the adjoining perfume shop, a man entered the apothecary and announced himself. "I am Naldo Trinboli, the inspector from the guild. I'm here to verify all your materials and methods meet the guild standards."

"Yes, of course, Signor Trinboli," Roselli said respectfully. "I remember you from last year." He led Trinboli to the rear of the shop and gestured toward the urns containing herbs and other components used to make curatives. "These are the ingredients we use in our medicines. As you can see, they all comply with the guild regulations."

Trinboli investigated each urn, sniffed some, touched the leaves of a few plants to the tip of his tongue, and winced at the bitterness. "These seem to be proper. Now, let me see your preparations."

Roselli presented him with the folio containing the medicinal formulations. Tronboli examined a few randomly selected pages. "Good ... good." Satisfied, he closed the folio, handed it back to Roselli, and scanned the shop. "My notes say you also sell perfumes and elixirs. I don't see them."

"They're in the adjoining shop." Gino, who was preparing an elixir, stepped aside as Roselli led Trinboli into the perfume shop and to the shelves containing the colorful perfume urns. The inspector systematically removed the cover of each urn, sniffed its contents, replaced the cover and moved on to the next vessel. When he reached the end, he returned to an urn decorated with yellow flowers. He said, "I need a sample of this one." Without asking permission, he filled a vial and slipped it into his shoulder case. For his wife, or perhaps his mistress, thought Roselli, as he faked a smile.

After watching Gino for a minute, Trinboli referred to his paperwork and said, "The guild listing shows only one speziale at this apothecary. Only you, Signor Roselli. Who is this man? Is he your apprentice?"

Glaring at Roselli, he asserted, "You know guild regulations forbid apprentices from making preparations."

Flustered, Roselli said, "He's not an apprentice. He's my assistant, and he doesn't prepare medications, only perfumes and elixirs."

Trinboli waved a hand dismissively. "You should know the rules were changed last year. Anyone preparing formulations of medicines, perfumes, or elixirs must be a registered member of the Doctors' and Apothecaries' Guild. If you allow him to continue, you'll be sanctioned."

Realizing Roselli's predicament, Gino said, "I'll go," and without a backward glance, he walked out of the shop.

***

Gino sat alone in his room, his elbows on the table and his head bent forward and resting on his hands, when a sharp rap on his door startled him. "Gino, are you in there?" a familiar voice called.

He pulled open the door to face Signor Roselli. "How did you find me?" he asked.

"It was a challenge," Roselli replied. "Gabriela remembered you mentioning your neighborhood. But I had to ask several people before I found one who could point me to your building."

Gino beckoned Roselli into the room, lit two candles, and set them on the table while Roselli removed his cloak. "Do you always sit in the dark?" Roselli asked.

"Only when misfortune pushes me backward, just as I was feeling settled."

"Don't worry about Trinboli. He takes pleasure in intimidating people, but he is correct; you need to become a member of the guild. The application process isn't difficult. You can apply for membership by appearing before the guild consuls. Unfortunately, they won't be meeting for two weeks." Gino slumped in his chair.

Roselli continued, "There is something you can do until then. I spoke with my brother, who manages the funeral business."

Mystified by Roselli's statement, Gino murmured to himself, "Funeral business?"

"In Florence, apothecaries also provide funeral services. I can't do everything, so my brother manages the funeral services. He deserves a brief holiday, and if you can help with the funerals, perhaps he can have his holiday. You don't need to be a guild member to work on funerals."

"I know nothing about funeral services," Gino retorted.

"You can learn. You learned to be a speziale, and burying folks is much easier than creating medications. I'll tell my brother where you live, so he can send one of his men to fetch you."

After Roselli left, Gino blew out one candle and sat in the dimly lit room, wondering how he might explain to his family that he would be burying people instead of treating them. He could hardly understand himself why the fickle goddess Fortuna struck him once again.

12

Saturday June 25, 1345

Gino grew concerned, wondering if Signor Roselli had forgotten his promise of a temporary job in the funeral services business because no one had come for Gino on Thursday or Friday. To pass the time on Thursday, he and Masina went hunting for medicinal plants in a field outside the city wall on the road to Luca. A chilling rain and fretting about his work situation kept him from enjoying the day. Thankfully, on Friday, Saint John's Day, he had the pleasure of spending time with Gabriela.

Gino was pondering how to spend another day when he heard a knock. He opened the door to face a wiry man with a scar above his right eye and two missing teeth. Rain beat down on the man's head, sending droplets splashing from his cloak, nose, and beard. He wore a tattered smock and badly scuffed boots, like those Gino had worn when he mucked the animal pens and did other odious chores on the family farm. A grave digger sent by Signor Roselli's brother, Gino assumed.

Gino looked down at his own clothes, not his finest, but not his shabbiest, either. He was not concerned about sullying his smock or his leggings, but if they expected him to dig graves, he wished he had his old worn boots instead of new leather shoes. Unfortunately, his boots were at the farm. When he had left home, no one in his family had suggested, "Bring your old boots. You might have to dig graves."

The man said, "I take you to the signore." He said nothing further as he led Gino through the city to Ponte Nuovo, the new bridge, where they crossed the Arno River to the Oltrarno District. They walked along the riverfront toward the Porta San Niccolò gate. Opposite them, on the far riverbank, Gino spotted the grain mill where he had spent his first nights in the city. The sight made him grateful again for the kindness of Florentine strangers. After passing through the gate, they followed a dirt path away from the river, passed a stable and a carpenter's shop, and eventually came to a long, low wooden building. Gino's guide pushed open a door at one end of the building, stepped aside so Gino could enter, and said, "The signore is inside."

A man shorter and heavier than Signor Roselli sat behind a desk. When he heard the visitors arrive, he squinted and looked toward the door. "Who's there?" he asked with doubt in his voice, uncertain whether the shadow in the doorway was a person.

Gino moved closer to be in range of the man's impaired eyesight, and announced, "Buon giorno, signore. I'm Gino Liani."

"Yes, yes. Come closer. I'm Piero … Piero Roselli." He gestured toward a chair. "My brother speaks well of you."

"I'll try to justify his confidence in me. But as I told him, I know nothing about funeral services."

"If you are willing and able to learn, you'll do well." Piero leaned back and clasped his hands together on his ample stomach. "Everyone believes funerals are sad occasions, yet this is not always so. Yes, funerals are sad for poor people who only want to speed their loved one's soul to paradise. But for the rich man, finally free from a nagging wife, giving her a lavish funeral convinces those around him he was a loving husband. Then, while others continue their mourning after her interment, he races to his mistress' bed.

"Similarly, rich widows turn a husband's funeral into a spectacle to show the deceased's mistress her newfound control over the family's wealth. And it's not only the rich who use funerals as pretense. Even tradesmen and artisans use funerals to flaunt their affluence to their peers."

Gino sat quietly listening as Piero Roselli continued, "The poor only want candles in church, a simple casket, and a cemetery plot. But the wealthy demand fancy decorations in church, elaborate memorial meals, lengthy processions, elegant caskets, and carved stone grave markers." Piero's eyes brightened as he recited the items responsible for substantial profits.

Piero leaned forward and smiled. "If you expected I would send you to dig graves, then you misjudge my needs. This city is beset with paupers who constantly beg for work digging graves. The help I need is to organize an extravagant funeral for one of the city's richest men. Arnoldo Beruzzi, the patriarch of the Beruzzi banking family, is near death. Signora Beruzzi sent instructions for arranging her husband's funeral. She wants the church bedecked with fresh flowers." Scratching his head and voicing his misgiving aloud, he said,

"Even with all this rain, we can find fresh flowers, but she also wants a meal with wild boar and fresh fruit. We have berries locally, and any other fruit we'll have to get from Sicily, and I don't know where I'll get wild boar." Looking intently at Gino, he added, "She wants enough mourners to fill the entire nave of the cathedral. I went to the cathedral to determine how many mourners it will take to fill the nave. By my count, at least twenty if they stand only two abreast. Ten men work for me as mourners, so your first task is to get ten more … at least ten. Fifteen if you can find them. "

Piero noticed Gino's brow wrinkle as he puzzled where to find mourners. He said, "If you tell a group of beggars you'll pay six denari each for men to walk in a funeral procession, they'll shove each other aside for the chance to be picked. But they mustn't look like beggars in the procession. They need to wear mourners' robes." Piero shouted, "Luigi!" A thin man with a bent nose came into the office from an adjoining room. Piero said, "Bring one of the mourner's robes."

Luigi disappeared, returned moments later with a robe like those worn by monks, and handed it to Piero, who held it up for Gino to view. "We have a woman who makes these. Luigi can tell you where to find her. Your second task is to have the woman make robes for your mourners. Gray, brown, and black are fitting colors, but not white. Some monks wear white robes, but white isn't a suitable color for funerals. And tell her to work quickly because Signor Beruzzi may be called by the Lord at any time."

Piero leaned forward, his eyes locked on Gino, expecting questions. When Gino remained quiet, Piero said, "You'll have no difficulty finding beggars to serve as mourners because this city has paupers at every turn. But don't expect to find men in taverns. I've found repeatedly that men who spend their days in taverns aren't reliable. While they may promise to come to the church, they're more likely to be drunk and sleeping in an alley."

Gino rose to leave. When he reached the door, Piero called to him, "When you finish these tasks, there'll be others."

Luigi gave Gino directions to the house of the robe maker. She lived not far from Gino, down the hill closer to the river where houses had lower rents and were more susceptible to flooding. After knocking on her door, Gino heard a thumping sound inside, coming toward him. The door creaked open enough to let the smell of yesterday's cooked vegetables escape, and an elderly woman peered out. "I'm Gino Liani," he announced. "I'm here on behalf of Signor Piero Roselli. Are you Fiametta?"

The woman studied Gino, as if surprised to see a good-looking young man. "I'm Fiametta. Usually Luigi is the one who comes."

"I'm new," Gino said simply.

The door opened wider. "You're getting wet. Come in from the rain."

Gino stepped inside and hung his dripping cloak on a nearby hook. She led him into the room, holding his elbow with one hand and balancing on her cane with her other hand. She trembled as she lowered herself into a chair. Gino reached out, ready to keep her from falling. Age had made it difficult for her to walk and marked her face with lines, but her hands looked strong with fingers smooth and straight, not bent and stiff like those of other people her age. She pointed to a jug sitting in the middle of the table. "Would you like a drink? It's apple mead." She gestured toward a side table. "Get a mug."

While Gino fetched a mug, she asked, "What can I do for Signor Roselli?"

"You've made robes for his mourners," Gino replied. "He's arranging a funeral with many mourners, so he needs more robes."

"Signor Beruzzi's funeral?" she guessed.

"Yes, how did you know?"

"Florence may be a big city, but news spreads quickly when a person as important as Signor Beruzzi becomes seriously ill. How many robes does Signor Roselli need?"

"At least ten. Maybe fifteen."

"Mmm," she murmured. "Even ten could be a problem. I get cloth from a nearby used clothing vendor, but his shop is small. I doubt he has enough material to make ten robes. Maybe three or four."

Gino understood it was his responsibility to get robes for the mourners. If Fiametta's source did not have enough material, then it fell to him to find an additional source. He remembered Ercole was a used clothing vendor.

"When does Signor Roselli need the robes?" Fiametta asked.

Gino laughed. "You know about Signor Beruzzi's condition. When do you believe he will be with the angels?"

Fiametta joined his laughter. "As an old woman alone, I must be many things, but I'm not a sorceress." Turning serious, she said, "Ten robes will take time."

"Is there someone who can help you?" Gino asked.

"My sister. She sews as well as me."

***

Gino went directly from Fiametta's house to Ercole's shop and explained his need. Surprised by Gino's request, Ercole said, "You're a speziale. Why are you asking about robes for funeral mourners?"

Gino showed a sheepish grin. "I want to be a speziale and I'm grateful the owner of an apothecary let me work with him, but recently, a guild inspector came to the shop and said I can't work at the apothecary unless I'm a guild member. It will be two weeks before I can apply for guild membership; until then, I have work helping to arrange funeral services."

Ercole pounded his fist on a table. "Someone should have warned you. I should have warned you. In this city, guild membership is necessary to do anything other than common labor."

Gino returned to the matter at hand. "The woman who makes the robes believes her vendor can supply material for four robes. I need to find material for at least six and possibly eleven more robes."

Ercole said tentatively, "I have some wool in dark colors. I believe the seamstress will find it satisfactory." He paused a moment, then added more forcefully, "If I don't have enough material, I can get more from other members of my guild. I'll have it tomorrow."

***

Having made progress with procuring robes, Gino turned his attention to recruiting mourners. Piero was correct in saying Florence had an abundance of paupers. Gino pondered how to connect with them as he headed out from Ercole's shop into the rain. When he reached the mercato, the constant rain had driven vendors from the puddle-spotted piazza. The remaining vendors had their carts tucked under the protective loggia. A few women wandered from cart to cart, picking through the last of the vegetables.

Gino recalled Taddeo telling him the women who shopped in the afternoon seeking low-priced goods were the wives of laborers. The servants of wealthy families would have come to the market earlier to get the finest quality produce. Paupers never came to the mercato because they couldn't afford to buy anything, even at the lowest prices. "Masina treats poor women in his neighborhood," he said to himself. "She must know where those women get their food."

When no response came to his knocks on the door of the space Masina used as an office, Gino climbed to the second level of the house and found the door to her room partially open. "Masina!" he called.

Moments later, she came to the door wearing an apron and holding a potlifter. She smiled at seeing him. "Gino, I'm happy to see you. Come in. Leave the door open."

He followed her to the hearth. She gestured toward a pan set above the fire, and said, "I told you I get payment in many forms. Today, a woman brought this fish. I'm sure it will be delicious, but if the door weren't open, the smell of fish cooking would stay for a week. It's a big fish. Enough for both of us. Sit, tell me, have you been called yet to dig a grave?"

"I was called this morning, but not to dig a grave." He described his meeting with Piero Roselli. "He tasked me to find mourners."

Masina served each of them a generous portion of fish, sat opposite Gino, and said, "So, you came to ask for my help in finding poor people to serve as mourners."

Gino detected a stiffness in her tone, so he asked, "Do you find the request objectionable? Signor Roselli pays six denari to each mourner, and the work is easy. They have only to walk in the procession and stand in the church during the service."

Masina arched an eyebrow. "Will he pay six denari to women?"

"Women?" Gino repeated. His mouth gaped open as he considered using women as mourners. "Women mourn," he told himself. After a pause, he said, "Signor Roselli made me responsible for finding mourners and he is prepared to pay six denari each, so yes, I can pay the same to women."

Masina's lips turned up in a smile. "Poor women in this district get food from the nuns at Santa Maria Novella. After we finish our meal, I'll take you there."

***

Gino and Masina arrived at the Santa Maria Novella convent, just as a wagon pulled to a stop beside a small building behind the convent. A group of women came out of the building, removed a covering from the wagon bed, and began unloading food. Two women carried a large pot, moving slowly to avoid spilling its contents. Other women fetched armfuls of cabbage, cavolo nero, and other vegetables. One woman hefted what had once been the hind leg of a sheep. Most of the flesh had been removed from the bone already, but the remaining bits would be supper for a few families.

'Where do they get the food?" Gino asked as his eyes followed the woman struggling with the large leg bone.

"The mutton is from a butcher's shop," Masina replied. "Florence is blessed with confraternities of honorable men who believe their path to paradise is opened by caring for the less fortunate. They arrange for shops to deliver unsold food to convents like this one, where it's distributed to the needy."

After they had unloaded the wagon, the women went into the building and distributed the food, so each woman got an amount in proportion to the size of her family.

Masina greeted the women cheerfully. "See me tomorrow. I have something to ease the itching," she said to a woman who was scratching at a rash on her arm. The women paid no heed to Gino until Masina introduced him. Her statement, "He has come here to offer work," froze the women with curiosity.

Gino said, "I'm seeking women to be mourners in a funeral procession." When his announcement elicited no response, he added, "You will be paid."

One woman spoke up. "My husband worked as a mourner. They paid him six denari. How much are you paying?"

"Six denari," Gino answered without hesitation.

"The same as for men?" the woman asked skeptically.

"The same," Gino stated, loudly enough for all around to hear.

A murmur went through the group, prompting another woman to ask her friend, "What will your husband say if you work and get paid the same as him?"

The first woman laughed. "He'll say I should do it every day."

The women asked questions: "When?" "Whose funeral?" And by the time Gino left, he had recruited a dozen mourners.

13

Monday, June 27

The sun was still low in the east, yet the morning air was already warm when Gino left his room and headed to Ercole's shop. The few people he saw were coping with the heat by plodding along the street. He decided Florence moved at a leisurely pace during the summer.

Ercole's wife greeted him when he entered the shop. She walked to the end of the counter and placed her hand atop a pile of brown and gray fabric. "He left this for you. There are three robes which your woman should be able to alter. The rest are lengths of cloth. This is all the material my husband could get quickly. He said to tell him if you need more." She flipped through the pile. "It looks like enough to make six or seven robes, depending on the size of the mourners."

Her comment let Gino realize the benefit of having women mourners: they were smaller than men. If there is enough to clothe seven men, it might be enough for eight or nine women, Gino reasoned. They chatted briefly, then Gino took the bundle and left the shop.

Gino carried the cloth to Fiametta's house. "Come in," she called in response to his knock. When he entered, she and another woman were sitting at a table busily sewing. "This is my sister," Fiametta said as an introduction. "I've heard Signor Beruzzi's condition has worsened. He may not be with us for even another week. I will need my sister's help if I'm to finish in time."

She eyed the bundle Gino was holding. "Here, put it on the table. The cloth I got from a nearby shop let us make five robes, and this looks like enough for ten more. Good. Good," she repeated as she flipped through the layers of cloth.

"Does it matter if the mourners will be women?" Gino asked.

"Women?" Fiametta echoed, her mouth open. "How big are they?"

Gino closed his eyes and tried to picture the sizes of the women at the convent. He opened his eyes and looked at Fiametta. "They're about your size except for one woman who is bigger."

"Bigger how? Taller"—Fiametta extended her arms out in front of her stomach — "or rounder?"

"Rounder," Gino replied, smiling.

Glancing at her sister, Fiametta said, "Let's save the large piece of dark gray cloth for her." Then to Gino, she explained, "Robes fit loosely. Since the women aren't short, we can make the robes to fit men and women. Only the one for the round woman will be different."

Pleased with his success at finding mourners and Fiametta's speed in making the robes, Gino set out for the funeral services building to report his progress to Piero Roselli. As he approached the funeral building, Gino heard shouting inside. "The signora wants red lilies, not these puny … whatever you call them," Piero bellowed. "Go find red lilies! Dozens of them!"

Gino hesitated with his hand over the door latch, reluctant to enter during Piero's tirade. Moments later, the door was pulled away from his hand. A visibly shaken man burst out of the office, nearly collided with Gino, and stormed off, muttering to himself.

The sound of Gino stepping into the office caught Piero's attention. He boomed, "What? What is it now? Have you come back to tell me of another problem?"

"It's Gino. Gino Liani."

Piero squinted at the figure silhouetted in the doorway. In a calmer voice, he said, "Come here where I can see you."

Gino crossed the room and stood next to Piero's desk. Piero exhaled forcefully. "He's been working for me for more than a year. He should know better than to bring these." Piero waved a hand at the small blue flowers scattered over the floor. "Who would want their church decorated with these?" Piero ran a hand through his hair, leaned forward, and said, "Tell me you have better news."

Gino raised himself to his full height and straightened his shoulders. "I've recruited twelve mourners. Fiametta has already made five robes, and she's working on seven more. Her sister is helping her."

Piero's eyes widened. "At last, here is somebody who's not a failure." He paused a moment to absorb the significance of Gino's report. "You found twelve mourners … in just two days." After another pause, he said, "Signora Beruzzi can afford the additional cost for Fiametta's sister. And we may need the robes soon because the priest has already given last rites to Signor Beruzzi."

Piero noticed Gino was still standing and motioned toward a chair. "Sit. Sit. There's something else you can do. The signora requested we serve cinghiale, wild boar, at the funeral meal. I told her no one could guarantee to have cinghiale, so she might have to serve goat." Roselli chuckled as he added, "But there would be more profit in cinghiale than goat. You had success finding mourners. Can you have as much success finding cinghiale?" A smirk came to Piero's face as realized he'd given Gino a nearly impossible task.

Wild boar roamed the vast forests of the Apennine Mountains foothills, but despite their large population in the woodlands, hunters rarely targeted the elusive and rugged animals because it was nearly impossible to kill a boar with a single arrow. Every hunter told stories of having glimpsed a boar charging through the forest with old arrow shafts jutting from their sides. It took more than a single strike to fell the powerful animals. Gino knew he could not dispatch a hunter into the forest and expect the man to return with a wild boar carcass.

Gino spent a restless night. He woke every few hours, leaving behind in a dream another fanciful scheme for getting cinghiale. By morning, he had pared down all the improbable ideas to one and set off for the mercato.

"Buon giorno, Taddeo. Is there news from my family?"

"Your father and I didn't talk at length, but he did say everyone is healthy and in good spirits." Gino nodded, pleased by Taddeo's report.

"I'm still working with Piero Roselli's funeral service business, and perhaps you can help me with another task. Signora Beruzzi wants to serve cinghiale at her husband's funeral meal. Signor Roselli has tasked me with finding the cinghiale. You visit many farms during your travels. If, by chance, you meet a farmer who has butchered a boar lately, Signor Roselli would pay him generously for a flank."

"There's only a small likelihood of anyone having a freshly killed boar, but I can ask," Taddeo responded.

***

Two days later, Gino met Piero Roselli and one of his men at the rear of the Beruzzi family parish church. At the lily-festooned altar, a priest prayed over the elegant hand-carved coffin. Facing him were relatives, friends, and business associates of the late Arnoldo Beruzzi plus twenty-two paid mourners.

Piero leaned toward Gino and whispered, "You didn't tell me the mourners you found were women."

"Is it a problem?"

Stroking his chin, Piero said, "I don't know. Hired mourners have always been men, but if the Beruzzi family accepts women mourners, word will spread and other families will want them too. If others are pleased with having women mourners, I'll use these women again at other funerals."

At the end of the ceremony, the paid mourners walked behind the bier to the cemetery. Wagons lined up outside the church to carry all the others to the burial site. Roselli sent his man to the cemetery to pay the mourners while he and Gino went directly to Palazzo Beruzzi to ensure the meal would be ready when the guests arrived.

Piero said, “It’s a miracle you could find cinghiale. You have a talent for arranging funeral services. You should stay with me rather than go back to the apothecary.”

Gino accepted the compliment with a polite smile, but never gave the suggestion serious consideration.

14

Wednesday July 13, 1345

Gino had not visited the apothecary shop in nearly two weeks. He missed the work, and he missed the possibility of seeing Gabriela. Standing outside, he felt the same apprehension he had when he first came to the shop looking for work. Every time the title of speziale came within reach, Fortuna placed an obstacle in his path. Soon he was to meet with the guild consuls. Will they approve my application, he wondered, or will the goddess Fortuna produce yet another barrier?

"I'm delighted to see you again, Gino!" Signor Roselli exclaimed when Gino entered the shop. "I don't think I can last another day by myself, constantly running between the apothecary and perfumery."

Gino said, "Gabriela could have helped you," then instantly realized his suggestion was inappropriate.

"It's true," Roselli agreed. "Gabriela's more capable than I'm often willing to admit. If it were just women buying perfumes …." He waved his hand dismissively. "But I won't let Gabriela be exposed to crass men buying elixirs."

Adopting a lighter tone, Roselli said, "My brother told me you were happy working for him, and you did well. He urged you to stay with him, so I wasn't certain you'd come back here."

"The funeral business is interesting, different from anything I've known before, and your brother is a fine teacher, but I never wavered from my goal of becoming a speziale."

"Then let's go see the guild consuls," Roselli said cheerfully. He locked the shop and the two men headed to the guild headquarters.

They waited only a short time before the senior clerk announced the consuls were ready to meet with them. Gino had expected the consul's office would be like a legal tribunal chamber, with robed officials on a raised platform looking down on applicants. To his surprise, the two consuls sat at a simple table in a small room. Both men wore stylish silk tunics, one light blue, the other cream colored.

They greeted Signor Roselli by name and bid him and Gino join them at the table. To Gino, one said, "I am Salvestro Trovato and my colleague is Arrigo Esposito. We are co-consuls of the Doctors' and Apothecaries' Guild. We understand you wish to register as a speziale."

Gino nodded and said simply, "Yes, signore."

Esposito said, "While doctors must undergo a rigorous process to gain admission to the guild, applicants to become registered speziali need satisfy only three requirements. They must be of high moral character with no criminal history. They must demonstrate skill in preparing medications. And finally, they must deposit a fee with the guild treasurer."

Trovato addressed Roselli using his given name. "Carlo, we understand you've witnessed Signor Liani preparing medications, perfumes, and elixirs."

"Yes, I have," Roselli replied. "Before coming to Florence, Signor Liani worked in an apothecary at a village in the Casentino Valley. He trained with a speziale who had himself once been a member of our guild. Gino impressed me with his competence when he came to my shop seeking work. Since then, he has learned to prepare perfumes and elixirs. His abilities and his care in serving others are admirable."

Trovato asked, "Can you also testify to his character?"

"I can, but Signor Liani also has testimony from someone who has known him much longer than I."

Gino handed a paper to consul Trovato. "This letter is from the priest in Poppi, the village where I lived until I came to Florence. He has known me since birth."

Trovato read the letter and passed it to Esposito, who read it and quipped, "I'm not sure my parish priest would give me such a strong recommendation. I think we can agree Signor Liani meets our character and skills requirements." Turning to Gino, he said, "The standard fee for speziale applicants is thirty florins."

Gino's jaw dropped. He had not earned even a fraction of that amount in his entire lifetime. Esposito smiled slightly at seeing Gino's reaction and continued. "However, the full fee pertains to applicants who intend to open their own shops. It is based on the risk a speziale might pose to his customers should he misbehave or err in preparing a formulation. Since you will work for Signor Roselli and not open your own shop, a lesser fee of five florins is appropriate in your case."

Gino's downcast eyes revealed he did not have even five florins. Roselli, who knew Gino had been sending money to his family, grasped Gino's arm. "I can pay the fee and we can arrange for you to repay me." He chuckled, "At least I'll know you won't leave to work for one of my competitors."

Gino had no words, but his glistening eyes showed his gratitude.

To Roselli, Consul Trovato said, "You can leave the fee with the clerk who will see it reaches the treasurer." Then to Gino, "Welcome to the guild, Signor Liani." Gino strutted out of the guild office proudly with his chest thrust out. Finally, he could officially call himself a speziale.

When he returned to the perfumery, Gino gazed at the urns. They seemed like old friends. He was there only a few minutes when two women came into the shop. Smiling broadly, one said, "Ah, Gino. It's good to see you again."

15

October 3, 1345

August had been a hot, dry month. Florentines felt relieved when the seasonal rains in September ended the long dry period and dispelled the summer heat. During the first rainy week, showers fell for three days. Children romped outside, delighted by cool raindrops dancing on their faces. Merchants and their customers greeted each other more cordially than they had during the heat of summer. But each of the following two weeks had seen four days of rain and three of gray overcast.

By early October, every day brought thick clouds and at least a light shower and often a downpour. The sun had gone on holiday. Children no longer played outside and rain kept from the streets all who enjoyed strolling through piazzas and along the riverfront in fair weather. The dismal weather tarnished everyone's attitude. Customers and vendors grumbled at each other with brash expressions. Those who had experienced past floods worried about what might yet come.

The rains continued into October. Water dripped from Professor Vianello's cloak when he entered the apothecary shop. He removed his cap and shook it, scattering droplets onto the already soaked floor. "Buon giorno, Gino. I may need a larger than normal measure of my elixir today. I'll be tutoring one of my better students later, and this streak of dreary weather has dulled my senses."

Gino prepared the elixir and, as he handed a mug to the professor, he said, "You were right about the water signs in the night sky. I haven't felt dry in weeks."

Vianello took a large swig. "Ah, my personal manna." He set the mug down, leaned forward with one elbow on the counter, and in a serious tone said, "When the planet Saturn moves into the star signs of Cancer and Leo, as it is doing now, it foretells of more than just rain. It augurs famine. I fear we have not yet seen the worst."

***

The following morning, Gino woke up shivering. He pulled the coverlet tight as a shield against the chilly morning dampness. On the farm, his mother had always risen before her children. On wintry mornings, she stoked the fire and had a steaming pot of broth waiting when Gino made his way to the kitchen. Now, those tasks were his alone.

The small hearth against the far wall of his room held only embers. He pulled the coverlet snug around his shoulders, climbed out of bed, crossed the room, and grabbed two sticks from a small bundle of wood. He placed them atop the embers and coaxed them into flame. Gradually, the fire dispelled the cold while Gino made a broth. Before dressing, he pulled the door open to probe the day. The fine mist falling from a dismal gray sky meant it was another day to don his hooded rain cloak, still wet from yesterday.

After downing the broth and a piece of chicken left from last night's supper, he felt ready to brave the day. Fearful the Arno might have pushed over its banks during the night, he walked to the docks, where he spotted several other worried men watching the fast-flowing water. The river had risen overnight, but it still had not overrun the docks.

An elderly man approached him. "Do you live nearby?" the man asked. "Everyone who lives near here is afraid of being flooded. We all come to watch the river," the man said. Before letting Gino respond, he gestured toward the sky. "This is nothing to worry about. This rain is hardly more than horse piss. Come with me and I'll show you what can happen when the sky opens."

He grasped Gino's arm, led him to a nearby warehouse, and pointed to a brown stain on the side of the building at shoulder height. "This is where the river reached twelve years ago. Twelve years. I remember it because I lost nearly everything in that flood. It rained without stopping for days. Heavy rain. Steady rain." He held a hand out into the mist and let the water drip from his fingers. "Not like this drizzle.

"The river rose so fast that my wife and I were forced up to the second level of our house. We were trapped there for two days. I called out the window for help, but the current moved so fast boats couldn't reach us." The man's voice cracked as he continued. "It was nearly a week before the water receded. When we returned to our house, most of our things had washed away, and what remained was ruined."

His head bent forward and his shoulders slumped as he relived the tragic experience. "I worked my whole life … and it was all swept away." Gino helped the man to a nearby stone bench and sat beside him for several minutes until the man calmed. When Gino rose to leave, the man said, "May you never know the pain I have faced."

Gino went from the riverfront to the mercato, curious whether Taddeo had any news from his family. He found Taddeo's cart not in its usual position but crowded together with the tables and carts of other merchants under the loggia at one end of the piazza. Customers complained and pushed each other as they squeezed through the cramped space. Other vendors were not fortunate enough to find a place under the shelter had fashioned canopies over their merchandise. In the exposed piazza, men stood in puddles, hunched forward to keep the rain from striking their faces.

Gino jostled his way through the shoppers to reach Taddeo. "At least you're keeping dry," he said, trying to cheer the merchant.

"Someone must have cursed me when I was a child. Why else would I be a merchant? Three times on the road this morning, I needed help to get my wagon freed from the mud. And I stopped more times than that to help others. If the rain continues, the road will become impassible." He gestured toward the customers. "Look at them. Women buy only what they need, not more. None are shopping with their eyes in this foul weather."

Gino handed Taddeo a hot cake and joked, "It was hot when I left the cookshop. I thought it would warm your body." Gino shrugged, "But I have nothing to warm your spirit."

"Your kindness is appreciated, my friend." Taddeo scanned the sodden carts scattered across the piazza. "I grumble, but I have less reason to complain than others. I met Wiener on the road this morning. He said some wheat farmers have already lost part of their crop to rain. His wagon wasn't as full as usual. He felt sure the millers will protest when he limits the amount of grain he can deliver to each of them, but he feels it just to share the meager load among all who depend on him."

In a shaky voice reflecting his anxiety, Gino asked, "Have you spoken with my father? Have his crops been affected?"

"He asked that I not tell you, but yes, he is worried. He showed me the field where he has cabbage. It's like a pond. Only a miracle will let the plants survive, and his other fields are too muddy to plant any winter crops. I'm sorry to say this, but if the rain continues, your family will have a hard winter. It's a blessing for you to be working in Florence because your family depends on the money you send them. And you being in Florence means one less person for the farm to feed."

Taddeo's words eased the guilt Gino felt for having left the farm. He walked away from the mercato, wondering what else he could do to ease his family's burden.

16

Friday October 7, 1345

Signor Roselli stirred apricot oil into an herb mixture to create a salve for one customer when a second man rushed into the shop. He wore a magistrate's attire, a black robe with a red sash. Roselli looked up briefly to greet the man respectfully, saying, "Buona sera, Messer Pagholi." Then he beckoned Gino to join him. Pagholi stood to the side politely, waiting until he could be served, but his nervous manner revealed his impatience. "Please attend to Messer Pagholi," Roselli said when Gino came into the apothecary from the adjoining perfume shop.

Pagholi handed Gino a slip of paper, a prescription written by a doctor. "It's for my wife," the magistrate explained. "Will it take long?"

Gino opened the medications folio and scanned the page that described the process for making the medication. "The ingredients must first be boiled; then after they are dried, they must be ground to a powder, so it will take several minutes."

Pagholi inhaled sharply. "I am needed at the Signoria," he said, voicing his thought aloud.

Gino suggested, "I could deliver the salve to your house when it is ready."

The tension in Pagholi's face eased. "I appreciate your offer. Can you bring it later, after the Signoria session has ended and I'm at home?"

Although Gino puzzled why the magistrate wanted the delivery delayed, he replied simply, "As you wish."

Pagholi thanked him for his kindness and hurried out of the shop.

Gino asked Signo Roselli, "Is Messer Pagholi a member of the Signoria?"

"No, but he's a highly respected and experienced magistrate whom the Signoria calls upon for advice in legal matters," Roselli explained.

When the apothecary closed for the day, Gino took the medication with him and made his way to the address Pagholi had given him, a three-level house in an affluent San Lorenzo neighborhood. He expected to be greeted by a servant; instead, Messer Pagholi, still wearing his magisterial robe, answered Gino's knock. Noting Gino's surprise, the magistrate explained, "Our house servant recently left for Pistoia to be married. She is a great help to me and my wife. We're eager for her return and hope her new husband finds work in Florence quickly." Gino held out the medication. Reaching for it, Pagholi said, "You are most kind." He reached into his coin purse. "Let me pay you for your trouble."

Gino held up a hand to decline compensation for delivering the medication. "I only hope the medication relieves your wife's discomfort."

"I'm sure it will help, but the doctor said she will need additional treatments every week until the soreness is completely gone."

"It will be my pleasure to bring another measure each week."

"No, I can't have you do that," Pagholi protested, and as Gino turned to leave, he called out, "Wait! I heard Signor Roselli say you lived on a farm before coming to Florence. Did I hear him correctly?" Gino's brow furrowed at the unexpected question. He nodded. "And your family still lives on the farm?" Pagholi asked.

"Yes, in the Casentino Valley," Gino replied.

"Please come inside if you can indulge me. Perhaps you can help me with a matter that has just arisen in the Signoria."

Messer Pagholi escorted Gino to an anteroom and motioned for him to be seated. "I'll return as soon as I give this medication to my wife."

Pagholi no longer wore his robe when he returned several minutes later. He carried a tray of fruit, which he set on a small table next to Gino. "Please forgive my lengthy absence. I wanted to be sure my wife applied the medication properly." The distinctive smell of his hands revealed he had applied the salve himself.

He sat facing Gino. "As I mentioned earlier, I could use your help to understand an issue being debated in the Signoria. One of their number owns a small farm where he grows wheat and he's lamenting the loss of a portion of his crop because of the prolonged rain. His distress is weighing on other members of the Signoria because it reinforces a prediction made by a respected professor who foresees famine in our future."

"Professor Vianello," Gino said.

"You know him?" a surprised Pagholi burst out.

"He comes to the apothecary every week for an elixir. The professor believes that the positions of planets and stars forecast future events. He's been observing the planet Saturn, and he said it's moving to a position that foretells famine."

"Do you believe him?"

Gino shrugged. "On the farm we let the moon tell us when to plant, but I know nothing of the planets and stars."

"The mention of a rotted crop along with Vianello's prediction has a few members of the Signoria on the verge of hysteria. They keep ranting about the famine of a decade ago, and they weren't relieved when I reminded them the great famine was caused by a period of extreme cold. They want the Signoria to institute extraordinary measures now in anticipation of another famine. I fear doing so will cause people to panic." Pagholi thought for a moment, then asked, "Have you heard from your family? Are their crops suffering?"

Gino's shoulders slumped. "Much of their late autumn harvest has been lost." He recalled his discussion with Taddeo. "If the rains continue this month and into November, they won't be able to plant a winter crop, meaning there would be no harvest in the spring. More than a year without a decent harvest would be a tragedy." Gino shuddered at the thought.

He continued, "A merchant who brings wheat from farms to the mills in Florence told me the lengthy rains have also caused substantial losses on the farms he visits. He said the losses are causing prices to rise. Millers complain to him about high grain prices and bakers are complaining to the millers about high flour prices." Gino paused again, then said slowly, as he formed the thought, "Grain farmers have the same schedule as vegetable farmers. This is when grain farmers sow their winter crop. If the rain continues much longer, they won't be able to plant in muddy fields. There's already a shortage of grain. If grain farmers can't plant a winter crop, there'll be no bread in Florence by springtime."

Pagholi clasped his hands together as he absorbed Gino's words. "You've given me much to consider. From what you've told me, I understand the next few weeks are crucial. If the rains continue, there could be a crisis." His brow furrowed. "The Signoria can't act in haste lest they create a panic; nor can they ignore an impending catastrophe. I would appreciate knowing of any further news from your family or the grain merchant."

"I'll see the grain merchant again before I bring the salve to you next week. Perhaps I'll have more news after I meet with him."

***

The next day. October 8, 1345

Since the third century, Florentines had embraced Saint Reparata as their patron saint. They gave their cathedral her name and annually on October 8 they held celebrations in her honor. Some people thought the heavy rains would force the festivities to be canceled, but the Florentine bishop declared otherwise. "Saint Reparata's faith let her endure horrific torture, so surely we can bear these rains," he announced.

The guilds required all shops to close for the day so workers could attend the events. Signora Roselli invited Gino to view the procession with her and Gabriella. Her husband and other men from his church took part by pulling a wagon gaily decorated with paper flowers. The heavens themselves paid homage to the saint by covering the sky with only thin clouds and suspending the rain. Gino found a shop with a recessed doorway where they could shelter should the monsoon resume.

While they waited for the Benedictine monks, the procession's traditional first unit, to appear, Gino said, "I'm confused. I understood Saint John the Baptist was Florence's patron saint, but people say Saint Reparata is the city's patron saint."

Gabriela laughed, "Florence is a big city. Big enough for two saints, and we enjoy having celebrations."

Signora Roselli said cynically, "Saint Reparata has been our patron saint since the city's earliest days, and she is revered by the people. But when the city grew, the bishops argued we needed a more important saint as our patron… and maybe it needed to be a man, not a woman."

Embarrassed, Gabriela implored, "Mother, you mustn't say such things."

Undeterred, Signora Roselli continued, "It wouldn't surprise me if, when the new cathedral is finished, the bishops will choose a different name and we will no longer have a Cathedral of Saint Reparata."

Suddenly, Signora Roselli pointed to a woman on the opposite side of the street and exclaimed, "Look! It's Sophia. I haven't seen her since she returned from Siena. I must speak with her." She hurried across the street, leaving Gino and Gabriela alone.

They stood silent and uneasy for a moment until Gino reached out and took Gabriela's hand. She shivered slightly, then turned so the folds of her dress hid their joined hands from the view of those assembled to watch the procession. Gino moved closer and inhaled her scent. She did not wear perfume. He told himself that none of the luxurious fragrances in the perfume shop could make her more appealing.

They stood silently with hands linked until Gino heard the procession approaching and saw Signora Roselli rushing across the street toward them. He brushed Gabriela's fingers lightly as he released her hand.

17

November 4, 1345

Ever since Gino had come to Florence, he, Taddeo, and Wiener had met every week or two at Wiener's favorite tavern for beer and to share stories. Wiener was usually sipping a beer by the time Taddeo and Gino arrived, so they were surprised to find their favorite table unoccupied when they made their way to the rear of the long, narrow room. They had both finished their first mugs of beer and signaled the barkeep for refills when Wiener finally entered the tavern. He stopped at the bar to grab two mugs, one in each hand, and said, "I have to catch up with you," as he placed the mugs on the table. He sat, took a swig, and stunned his companions by groaning loudly.

Laughing, Taddeo quipped, "You're late and you sound like a sick dog. I thought you liked rain, so you must take great pleasure in these downpours."

"Pleasure? No, not today. Three of the farms I visit routinely had no grain to sell … none … and the others had only meager harvests. The millers expect me to bring them a full measure every day, so I had to travel in this rain as far as Mugello, an extra hour each way to fill my wagon. Even there, at the far end of the valley, the few farms I found with grain to sell wanted nearly double the normal price. And when I delivered the grain, the millers blamed me for the higher price."

Taddeo nodded. "It's the same at the mercato. All the vendors arrive with wagons only half full, and the women who come early take everything, even the bruised vegetables they normally reject. By mid-morning, our carts are empty. Women who come then find nothing, and they scold us."

Gino listened quietly, wondering how well his family was coping with the poor crop yields. Taddeo regularly brought Gino news from his family, but Gino knew his father would not share his own pain with his son. If Gino wanted to learn the truth, he would have to visit the farm. He resolved to travel to Poppi on Sunday.

***

After leaving his friends at the tavern, Gino headed to Casa Pagholi. He had promised to tell Messer Pagholi of any news he heard from his merchant friends regarding crop failures. He expected the family's servant to answer his knock, but once again it was the magistrate himself who opened the door and led Gino to the anteroom. "Has your servant not yet returned from Pistoia?" Gino asked.

"Unfortunately for my wife and me, the girl's husband found work in Pistoia, so she won't be returning. I need to replace her, but the Signoria's business hasn't allowed me the time to look for someone." Pagholi waited until the two men were seated before asking, "What brings you here today?"

After Gino recounted the conversation he'd had with Taddeo and Wiener at the tavern, Pagholi said, "I've received other reports of shortages, but yours shows the situation is escalating." He clasped his hands together and closed his eyes briefly to digest the news. "We've experienced crop failures in the past, enough to know the devastation they cause," he said. "Women who can't find food at the mercato turn to begging, adding to our already overwhelming number of indigent families. As soon as wealthy families learn of shortages, they hoard, and hoarding pushes prices up beyond the reach of many."

Pagholi stood and paced across the room. "This is not good news, not at all, but I thank you for bringing it to me. The Signoria must act now. They can't create food, but they must summon the wisdom to find a solution."

***

November 6, 1345

Most Florentines were still at home dressing for church on Sunday morning when Gino headed out of his room into an icy drizzle. He crossed the city to a stable outside the Porta a Pinti gate where he had reserved a horse. By leaving at daybreak, he expected to reach Poppi and return to Florence in a single day.

Gino had considered getting gifts for his parents and his siblings, but many of the items prized by Florentines held little value for farm families. While fashionable Florentine men and women masked their smells with fragrances, Gino was certain no one in Poppi used perfume. Florentines decorated their houses with paintings. In Poppi, the ruling Guidi family might have paintings in their castle, but Gino had never seen paintings in a farmhouse. Ultimately, he opted to give money to his father rather than spend it on trinkets.

For someone not used to being on horseback, it was a long, uncomfortable ride, even though the rain had tapered off midway on his journey. Gino's spirits picked up when he reached Poppi village and his family's farm came into view. *He rode around the side of the farmhouse and dismounted near the barn, where he could shelter the animal from the rain.*

He recognized the voices coming from the barn as belonging to his brothers. "Laro! Fanto!" he called as he swung the door open. The startled boys, who had been helping their father with a wagon wheel, jumped up, ran to greet their older brother, and began peppering him with questions. Gino raised his hands to deflect their onslaught.

"Boys, there will be time for questions later. Tend to Gino's horse," their father directed.

Gino said, "There was steady rain when we left Florence, so it would be good to dry him. He also needs food and water."

Father set the wheel aside, crossed the barn, and hugged his son. After the boys had left, he gestured toward the wheel he and the boys had been repairing. "With the rain, we can't work in the fields, so we spend time here fixing what isn't broken. We've greased this wheel enough for a lifetime."

He led Gino outside and gestured to a barren field. "The fields are mud. If we tried to plant, the seeds would just wash away. We should have had a crop in the ground last month, but there haven't been three days together without rain. Now, it's turning cold, so even if the rain were to stop, any seeds we plant would probably rot." He put an arm around Gino's shoulder. "Enough of my whining. Come, let's go into the house. Your mother will be eager to see you."

Gino's mother was standing with her back toward the door, chopping vegetables, when they stepped into the kitchen. Gino inhaled the aroma coming from a large pot hanging in the fireplace and said, "I haven't had venison stew since I left for Florence."

His mother dropped her knife, whirled around, and shouted, "Gino!" Tears welled up in her eyes as she ran to him. For a minute she held him tightly, saying nothing; then she stepped back and ran a finger along his cheek. "You look good, Gino. You must be taking care of yourself." With a devilish grin, she asked, "Or is someone else taking care of you?"

"There is no one else, mother."

Suddenly, her reaction switched from joy to worry. "Is something wrong? Is that why you've come home?"

"I'm fine. I came because of the rain. Taddeo told me that none of the farmers can plant crops. I've been worried about you … all of you."

She pointed to the onions she had been chopping. "We dried and brined more food this year than in normal times." Gino tensed when she added, "Do we have enough to last until the next harvest? I don't know."

The sound of Gino's voice brought his sisters to the kitchen, where the entire family gathered around him to hear about his time in the city. Taddeo had given them the highlights, but they wanted to hear every detail about his work and life in Florence. They scrunched up their noses when he told them Florentine men wore perfume, and they struggled to imagine a church being four times the size of their San Fedele parish church. Gino's youngest brother said working for a funeral service seemed scary.

Gino assured his parents he was being treated well by his boss, Signor Roselli. He told them about Masina, the healer who rented rooms in the same house as his. When his mother asked whether he had met any women, he chose not to mention Gabriela and deflected her question by saying that work was keeping him busy.

After they exhausted every imaginable topic, Gino said he had a matter to discuss with his mother and father. His siblings rose to leave, and as they filed out of the room, he called to his oldest sister. "Lucia, stay with us."

He looked from one parent to the other, unsure of how to express his proposal. With his eyes locked on his mother, he began, "If father cannot sow seeds until spring, there will be no harvest until summer. You told me the food you've preserved may not last until then. It will last longer if there are fewer people to feed. It will last longer if you let Lucia come to Florence with me."

Startled by her brother's proposal, Lucia spun around to face Gino. Their mother jumped up and tramped to the far side of the room as if to distance herself from Gino's suggestion. "I've already lost one child to that city and you're asking me to lose another."

Her mother's protest caused Lucia to sit quietly, gazing down at the table, unable to look at either parent. Gino looked at his father. If he, too, opposed the idea, it would be pointless to pursue it further. His father said, "Ten years ago when cold weather made crops fail, families who could not feed their children sent their daughters to convents. This time might be as bad … or worse." His words made Lucia shiver.

Gino rose and went to stand beside his mother. Tears flowed down her cheeks. He put an arm around her. "You haven't lost me, mother. You won't ever lose me, and you wouldn't lose Lucia, either. She need stay in Florence only until the next harvest."

"How do you know there'll be food in Florence?" his father asked.

"Florence is a wealthy city. During the past famine, the one you mentioned, the city provided for all its people. I'm sure it will do so again."

Lucia worked up the courage to speak and looked up at her brother. "What would I do in Florence? I know no one there."

Gino returned to the table and sat next to his sister. "I've become acquainted with a magistrate. He's a powerful man who advises the Signoria. He and his wife had a house servant until the girl went away to be married. They're eager to find someone to take her place. Maybe you can work for them. If not, we'll find something else for you. Florence is a busy city filled with opportunities."

Gino's father went to his wife. They spoke briefly, too softly for Gino to hear. "Where would Lucia stay? With the magistrate?" his mother asked.

"I haven't thought about that. To begin, she can stay with me."

"You're her brother. You must keep her safe," their mother said with hints of both resignation and fear in her voice.

When it came time to leave, Lucia packed her satchel, said a tearful farewell to her family, and climbed aboard the horse with Gino. "Are you sure he can carry both of us?" she asked.

"He's a sturdy steed, but we'll stop midway to let him rest at Taddeo's house. Taddeo's wife will be happy to meet you."

18

Monday November 7, 1345

Gino awakened to the sound of footsteps. Mice, he thought, until he rolled over on his hard floor, rubbed his eyes, and looked up at his sister. "I'm ready to go," she said eagerly. "I don't want to spend the entire day in your room. There are clouds, but no rain, so today will be a good day for me to see the city and the shop where you work."

"No rain?" Gino echoed, still not fully awake. "How do you know? Have you been outside already?"

"Yes. I met the healer you told me about, Masina. She showed me where to dump the chamber pot. She invited us to join her for a mug of mead when you're dressed."

"I don't know …" Gino mumbled. Lucia was always ready to meet the morning as soon as her feet touched the floor, while it took Gino several minutes to become fully alert.

"Masina said she begins every day with mead. She's a healer, so it must be a healthful tonic," Lucia declared eagerly.

Gino splashed water on his face, dressed, combed his hair, and yielded to Lucia's persuasion by agreeing to accept Masina's invitation.

Masina welcomed her guests and bid them to sit. When she brought three mugs to the table, Gino said, "I'm not sure Lucia is old enough for mead."

Masina's eyes twinkled with mischief as she leaned in and asked, "How old are you, dear?"

"Fourteen years," Lucia said, frowning at her brother.

Turning to Gino, Masina said, "Bah. I had my first taste of mead in my twelfth year. At fourteen years, your sister is a woman, not a child. I was betrothed in my fourteenth year."

Grinning, Lucia took a swig, licked her lips, and took a second swig. She set the mug down slowly. "It tastes like fruit nectar, only different." She placed a hand atop Gino's and announced, with excitement in her voice, "This is my first day in Florence, and my good brother is going to show me the city and his apothecary shop."

Gino withdrew his hand. "I'm sorry to disappoint you, Lucia, but Monday mornings are busy times at the apothecary. Signor Roselli expects me to be there helping him. Your tour of the city will have to wait until later."

Seeing Lucia's disappointment, Masina intervened. "I have a shoe in need of mending. I'm planning to take it to a cobbler. If Lucia were to come with me, I could show her some of Florence's sights and then bring her to your shop."

Gino couldn't resist the yearning in Lucia's eyes. He leaned toward Masina and said, "A farm girl of fourteen years is not the same as a city woman of fourteen years."

Masina smiled. "I understand. I'll keep her safe."

Gino emptied his mug, kissed Lucia on the forehead, and left his sister with one of the few people in Florence he trusted.

***

It was mid-afternoon when Lucia bounded into the perfumery. Rarely had Gino seen his sister looking happier. She danced to the counter where Gino stood and launched into a detailed description of her day. "Masina brought me to the church you told us about with the paintings on the walls. Santa …"

Lucia glanced at Masina, who said, "Santa Croce."

"Yes, Santa Croce. And it is as big as you said, at least four times the size of San Fedele. I saw tall towers, many of them. Masina said they're houses. Why would anyone want to live in a house with so many levels? And we passed the Signoria Palazzo. Men in black robes with colored sashes were going in and coming out."

"It's called Palazzo della Signoria," Gino corrected, smiling at hearing his sister's delight in her new city.

Masina said, "I am expecting a woman for treatment, so I must return home."

"How can I repay you for your kindness to Lucia?" Gino asked.

"There is no need for repayment. I was delighted to spend the morning with your sister. She showed me the city through a young *woman*'s eyes." Gino noticed Masina had emphasized the word woman.

After Masina left, Lucia walked around behind the counter. "These must be the perfumes," she said as she started sniffing the row of urns.

Gino dipped a strip of cloth into one urn and dabbed Lucia's wrist with the wet cloth. She sniffed her wrist, said, "Now, I'm a Florentine woman" and strutted across the room.

Gino smiled, but cautioned, "Never let our mother hear you say those words." Turning serious, he said, "We need to find work for you while you're in Florence. Do you remember my mentioning magistrate Pagholi and his wife are seeking a new house servant? It's one job to consider."

Lucia took the perfumed cloth from her brother and dabbed it on her other wrist. She enjoyed her day free from chores, but she knew the dalliance had to end. "What are the duties of a house servant?" she asked.

"We could guess at them, but to be sure, we should talk to Messer Pagholi's previous house servant. She's in the city of Pistoia, about an hour's ride from here. Signor Roselli said I can take time this afternoon so we can go speak with her."

"Wouldn't it be easier to ask Signora Pagholi what duties she expects me to perform?"

"We could ask him and his wife, but I also want to be certain that you'll be safe working at Casa Pagholi. The only way to be sure is to speak with the girl who worked there before."

Two women entering the shop interrupted their conversation. Gino impressed his sister by remembering the perfume preferred by each woman. He let them sample a new fragrance made from flowers brought from Asia by the Venetians. Each woman took his suggestion and bought vials of the new perfume. After the women left, Gino went to the apothecary to tell Signor Roselli he was leaving for Pistoia. "You look the same age as my daughter Gabriela," Roselli said when he saw Lucia. His observation made Gino uneasy because, in Gino's mind, Lucia was a girl and Gabriela was a woman. "I'm sure Gabriela would like to meet you. Can you join us tomorrow for supper?"

"That's very kind of you. I'd like to meet your daughter. I don't know anyone my age in Florence." She laughed. "In truth, I've met only one other person in Florence."

Speaking softly to Lucia, pretending he did not want Gino to hear, Roselli winked and said, "You may bring your brother if you wish."

***

At the cathedral in Pistoia, Gino asked a priest if he knew where they could find the young woman from Florence who had been married in the cathedral the previous month. The priest told Gino her name and said she lived in a house outside the city near the carpenter shop where her new husband worked. Gino found the house easily, using the priest's directions. Exhilarated by her adventures on her first day away from the farm, Lucia rushed to the door and knocked. When the woman answered, Lucia explained she might be interested in working for Signor and Signora Pagholi and asked about responsibilities she would be expected to perform as their house servant.

The woman invited them inside, where she explained, "I did the cooking and cleaning. I never shopped at the market because Signor Pagholi is an important magistrate, so vendors come to his house. And Signora Pagholi never sent me to do errands myself. She always went with me because she said it wasn't proper for a young girl to go through the city alone. I'm in my fifteenth year, but still Signora Pagholi protected me as though I were a child."

Lucia's mouth fell open. "You're fifteen and you're married?" she asked incredulously.

The woman shrugged, saying, "My cousin was only fourteen when she was married."

Gino changed the subject abruptly. "Were you ever mistreated? Did Signor Pagholi ever behave inappropriately toward you?"

The woman stiffened. "No. No. Never. He was always respectful of me. I've heard stories of abuse from other servants, but never would Signor Pagholi treat me ungraciously. Never." She emphasized her feelings with a sincerity that convinced Gino his first impression of Pagholi was correct. "And Signora Pagholi couldn't have been kinder," the woman continued. "At times she even helped me with the cooking. She tried to teach me how to play the harp, but I must be lacking musical talent," the woman laughed. "I'd be fortunate to find such a fulfilling job here in Pistoia."

As Gino and Lucia rode back to Florence, Lucia said, "The work of a house servant isn't much different from the chores I did on the farm, cooking and cleaning." Minutes later, she mused, "I wonder whether Signor and Signora Pagholi will want me."

19

November 8, 1345

Gino had expected Lucia to be waiting in his room when he returned from the apothecary at the end of his workday. Instead, she came bounding out from Masina's office to greet him as he approached the house. His initial disappointment at her not staying in his room faded, knowing she had been with Masina rather than exploring the city on her own, as he had feared.

"Masina and I went to a birth," Lucia announced. Seeing his puzzled expression, she said, "A woman who comes to Masina for treatments gave birth to a son today. Masina and I went to help the midwife with the delivery. I was too young when our sisters were born to remember their births. Today I saw the birth of a baby isn't much different from the birth of a calf, except it was painful for the woman. Births never seem to be painful for cows."

"Sometimes birthing is painful for cows," Gino said, then shifting to a more important matter, he asked, "Are you ready to meet Messer Pagholi?"

"I think so," Lucia replied in an uncertain voice.

Gino reversed direction and headed toward Casa Pagholi with Lucia at his side. After a few moments, she asked, "Why do you address him as Messer rather than Signor?"

"Messer is an honorific title for magistrates and government envoys. Messer Pagholi is a senior magistrate. He presides over many of the city's most significant tribunals. Lately, though, he's spent most of his time advising the Signoria on how to resolve the food crisis, so he's been too occupied with work to hire someone to replace his house servant."

When they reached the casa, it was Signora Pagholi who answered Gino's knock. Her eyes widened in surprise at seeing Gino with a young woman. "Buona sera, signora," Gino said. He stepped backward, slightly behind Lucia. "This is my sister, Lucia. She just came to Florence. I know you and Messer Pagholi want to find a new house servant, and I thought Lucia might…"

Gino's voice trailed off enough for the signora to interrupt, saying, "Ah, I understand." To Lucia, she said, "Welcome, my dear. Come in." She led Gino and Lucia to the anteroom. Gino expected her to fetch Messer Pagholi; instead, she sat with them and said to Lucia, "Your brother told us his family lived on a farm in the countryside, but he didn't say he had a sister in Florence."

"I just came to the city yesterday," Lucia explained.

"We've heard the constant rain is a problem for farmers. Is that why you left the farm?"

"Yes, it's been a terrible struggle. We haven't been able to plant a crop because of the rain, and now it might be too cold."

"City life differs from farm life. Do you know the duties of a house servant?"

Lucia replied confidently, "Your previous house servant said she did the cooking and cleaning."

The signora raised an eyebrow. "You spoke with Filippa? Isn't she in Pistoia?"

Gino answered, "We went to Pistoia yesterday to speak with her. We wanted to find out whether Lucia's experience fits her for the chores you need done."

Looking at Lucia, the signora asked, "And does it?"

Lucia replied, "Ever since I was a little girl, I did some of the cooking and cleaning on the farm. I thank my mother for teaching me how to make a variety of meals. They may not be the ones you prefer, but I can learn."

Signora Pagholi smiled. "Come with me," she said as she stood. She led Lucia and Gino up a staircase to the kitchen at the house's top level. As they climbed, she quizzed Lucia on various cooking techniques. When they reached the kitchen, she pointed to a bucket on the floor. "We have fish at least one day each week. Our fish vendor brought these today. How would you use them to make a fish stew?"

Lucia reached into the bucket and pulled two grayling fillets from the water. "They've already been cleaned," she said with surprise. "When my brothers bring home fish, I have to clean them. Your vendor has already removed the innards, so to get them ready, all I have to do is take out the bones." She returned the fish to the bucket. "I know two ways to make fish stew: with vegetable broth and with cream. Which do you prefer?"

The signora smiled. "I've never had fish stew with cream."

Lucia said, "On the farm we always had fresh cream. Maybe cream isn't available in the city." She went to the pantry and studied the shelves. "You have parsnips and onions, so I could make a vegetable broth." Looking further, she said, "White wine. Carrots. Good." She picked up another item, rubbed it with her fingers, sniffed it, and said, "Smoked pig skin could be an interesting addition. Shall I start the broth now?"

Gino stepped forward. "You can't start now. Remember, we've been invited to supper by Signor Roselli."

Signora Pagholi shook her head. "I'm not expecting you to begin now. I just wanted to understand the extent of your cooking skills. Come, let me show you the rest of the house." Leaving the kitchen, she pointed to a bedroom across the hallway. "My brother-in-law owns a vineyard in the countryside. He and his wife stay in that room when they come to the city." She turned her attention to a second bedroom, a spacious room, nearly as large as Gino's room. "This would be your room."

Gino gazed at his sister. Her face glowed as she scanned the room. She looked like the same young girl to him, but as Masina had tried to tell him, Lucia was a woman ready to embark on her own course in life. He had told his mother Lucia would return to the farm in the spring, but he wondered whether those words might become only an empty promise once Lucia succumbed to the city's charms.

They descended to the second level, passed through the dining salon, and approached the study where Messer Pagholi was at work. He looked up when he heard them. The signora smiled broadly at her husband and said, "My dear Avito, this young woman is Lucia, our new house servant. She's an experienced cook who knows two ways…at least two ways, to make fish stew."

Avito leaned back and, while suppressing a smile, he folded his arms across his chest, and said in a stern voice, "

Did my lovely wife instruct you to greet me with a cup of wine when I return home from a tribunal or the Signoria?"

Lucia replied, "I'll make that a priority, signore."

They spoke as though she had already been offered and accepted the position of house servant. After a quick glance at Gino, Pagholi said, "Would I be correct in assuming you're related to Signor Liani?"

"He's my brother, signore."

"I appreciate being shown respect, but you needn't end every statement with signore." He beamed a smile at her. "Reserve accolades for when you see my spirit is low and needs to be lifted." Laughing, he added, "When I return home after a long day of meetings with members of the Signoria, you can greet me with a cup of wine and call me signore."

They discussed Lucia's duties and her compensation, a meager amount of money by Florentine standards because she was being provided with a room and food, but more than Lucia could have dreamed of. Signora Pagholi accorded her leave on Sundays so she could spend time with her brother. Lucia agreed to start work the next morning. As Lucia and Gino were leaving, Signora Pagholi said, "I look forward to tasting your fish stew with cream next week. I'm sure we can find cream somewhere in the city."

***

It was too early for supper with the Rosellis when Gino and Lucia left Casa Pagholi, so they took a leisurely walk through the Santa Croce district, a neighborhood Lucia had not seen. Noticing the bounce in

Lucia's step, Gino said, "You seem pleased with you new position as house servant."

"I couldn't be happier. I can already tell Messer and Signora Pagholi are wonderful people. They made me feel welcome, more like a helper than a lowly servant. The work—cooking and cleaning—doesn't differ from what I did on the farm. I'll have a generous wage and time for myself on Sundays. And I'll have a room of my own … with so much space. I never even imagined I might someday have my own room."

In a plaintive tone, Gino said, "I've been enjoying our time together since you've come to Florence, but now you'll be leaving to live at Casa Pagholi."

"I'll only be a short distance away. You can plan special activities for us to do on Sundays, and you can come to visit me at Casa Pagholi anytime." Lucia gave Gino a friendly poke. "But if you come in late afternoon, you might have to help me with the cooking."

Lucia stopped suddenly and pointed. "What's that curving wall?"

"It's the remains of an amphitheater built by the Romans."

"It was built by the Romans and it's still standing? I've never seen anything so old."

While Lucia gazed at the wall, Gino looked at her and touched a patch on the sleeve of her smock. "You need new clothes. When Signora Pagholi entertains her aristocratic friends, it wouldn't be proper for her house servant to be wearing a threadbare smock with patched sleeves. Tomorrow, I'll take you to a used clothing shop."

From the amphitheater, they went to the Rosellis' quarters above the apothecary shop, where Gabriela answered Gino's knock. "Gabriela, this is my sister, Lucia," Gino announced.

Gabriela flashed Gino a quick smile before taking Lucia's hand and leading her to the sitting room. "I've been eager to meet you since my father invited you. When did you arrive in Florence?"

Signora Roselli diverted Gino to the kitchen before he could follow the two women. She said, "We should give the girls a chance to become acquainted. Gabriela has few friends her own age."

Gino nodded slowly, acknowledging to himself Lucia's need to find friends in the bustling city. He chatted with Signora Roselli in the kitchen while attempting to listen with one ear to the conversation in the other room. He caught only snippets, but the rapid exchanges told him Gabriela and Lucia were bonding, although he couldn't imagine how a farm girl and a city girl could relate to each other.

Signora Roselli had arranged for her and her husband to sit at opposite ends of the table with Gabriela and Lucia along one side and Gino opposite them. She gave the women ample time to talk before calling Gabriela to the kitchen to help serve the meal. When all were seated, she said, "With the food shortages, it is getting more difficult every day to plan a meal. The butcher is the only shop able to maintain its stock. Rain hasn't kept hunters from finding game, so the butcher always has ample amounts of rabbit and venison."

"Are my eyes deceiving me or are bread loaves getting smaller?" Signor Roselli asked.

"Your eyes aren't deceiving you," his wife replied. "The baker claims he hasn't raised prices despite the grain shortage, yet he neglects to mention his loaves keep shrinking. Soon they'll be muffins," she said cynically.

Although the Rosellis knew about Gino's experience before he came to Florence, they were interested in hearing a woman's perspective on life in a small village. Lucia said, "I've only been in Florence for two days, but everyone I've spoken with has warned me it's not safe for unmarried women to walk through the city alone…even in daylight. In Poppi, I could go anywhere by myself, even at night."

Signora Roselli said, "Here in the city center where the streets are busy, it's safe, but there are outlying neighborhoods where I would not venture alone during the day. At night, even men avoid those neighborhoods."

Gabriela shot her overly protective father a look when Lucia explained she had taken a job as house servant at Casa Pagholi.

Toward the end of the meal, Signor Roselli said, "On Sunday, a visiting musician from Naples will perform at the guild hall. I've been told his music is popular with young people."

Gabriela and Gino looked at each other, puzzled by his statement. Was he suggesting his daughter had permission to attend the event without him or his wife? Surely he wouldn't expect the two women to be without an escort, so could he be intending for Gino to accompany them? Signora Roselli's smirk showed she wasn't surprised by her husband's suggestion. Seeing her mother's cue, Gabriela, eager for any opportunity to exercise her independence, said, "What a wonderful idea."

***

Sunday November 13, 1345

Lucia spun, letting the folds of her dress flare outward. "Wearing this dress, I feel like a princess," she said giddily. "Ercole claims it was made for the granddaughter of Beatrice Portinari. He said her name as though she were an important woman."

"Indeed, she was," Gino said. "Beatrice Portinari was Dante's guide in the Paradiso book of his Divine Comedy. Paradiso is a powerful story of faith. Someday I should read it to you or teach you to read it yourself." Watching his sister's joy made Gino smile. "Is this the first time you've worn the dress?"

"Yes, the first time I've worn this one. I wore the other two dresses from Ercole's shop while working at Casa Pagholi, but I wanted to save this one for a special occasion."

With a flourish, Gino held out Lucia's rain cloak. "Can you stop twirling and don your cloak, princess? I regret no carriage has come for you, so we must walk to meet Gabriela."

Light rain and the late autumn chill didn't blunt Gabriela's enthusiasm when Lucia and Gino called for her. "I've been looking forward to this outing for days. I can't remember the last time I went anywhere without my mother or my father. Probably it was the celebration at Easter with my cousin, but we weren't alone. My uncle went with us." She looked up at Gino and said despairingly, "You've met my uncle Piero. I felt like a dog on a tether. Uncle Piero kept a close watch on us, never letting us out of his sight."

"You should be honored he's so attentive to your safety," Gino said, half-joking. Gabriela replied with a glare. Lucia struggled to imagine how difficult it must be to have such a sheltered existence. In contrast, during the past week, she had been out in the city every day with Signora Pagholi. It wasn't the freedom she had in Poppi, but she got to visit shops and meet many of the signora's friends.

***

The Doctors and Apothecaries' Guild grand audience hall was rapidly filling when they arrived. With Gabriela and Gino close behind, Lucia threaded her way through the crowd and found a row with three seats together. "I wouldn't have expected a farm girl from a small village to be so assertive," Gabriela said quietly to Gino as she watched Lucia ease another woman aside. "I should learn from your sister."

The performer began with lively Neapolitan folk songs to get the audience's fingers snapping and toes tapping. Once he had their attention, he set his lute aside and recited a story about a cuckolded French prince. Tittering spread through the crowd when he began and turned to guffaws as his story became increasingly bawdy. At the story's end, he returned to music, this time playing a bowed instrument he called a rebec.

During the mid-show pause, a young man sitting near Lucia approached her and began chatting with her. Gino listened to be sure theirs was a polite conversation before taking Gabriela by the hand and leading her into the hallway. Other couples were also moving into the hallway in search of niches where they could be alone. Gino and Gabriela found a quiet spot in a small alcove. He ran a finger along her cheek, bent forward, and kissed her. "I'm surprised your father suggested we come to this performance without him or your mother."

"I'm certain it was mother's idea. She must have convinced father Lucia could protect my honor." Snickering, Gabriela added, "But surely father hadn't known the musician would tell the story about the dandy French prince."

When they saw other couples drifting back toward the grand hall, Gino said, “We should get back as well. I shouldn’t have left Lucia alone with a boy.”

“He didn’t seem like a *boy* to me,” Gabriela observed.

“That’s what concerns me,” Gino admitted. They kissed again and fell in with the other couples, returning slowly to the grand hall. Gino’s worry eased upon finding Lucia in her seat, chatting casually.

After the performance ended, Lucia and Gino walked Gabriela to her house. The concert’s afterglow kept them from feeling the stinging drizzle or noticing beggars lingering in the alleys.

20

March 7, 1346

At the end of his workday, Gino returned to his room, sat on his bed, and groaned as he pulled off his shoes. Every morning, the shoes went on easily, but it was always difficult to remove them after a full day of standing at the shop. He sat wiggling his toes against the cool floor when a knock came at the door. He padded across the floor in bare feet and pulled the door open. "Masina, how good to see you!" He stepped aside and motioned for her to enter.

"You won't be pleased to see me when you hear my news. I just returned from the convent at Santa Maria Novella. The shelters throughout the city are overwhelmed by desperate people coming to Florence from farms in the countryside where the rain is destroying their crops. They have no food to eat. The number of women seeking shelter at Santa Maria Novella exceeds the ability of the nuns to care for them and the capabilities of the confraternity to provide them with food." Gino motioned for Masina to sit at the table. He poured mugs of ale and handed a mug to her. Masina continued, "Ten more women came to the convent this afternoon. The nuns had to tell them there was no more room at the convent. There wasn't even enough food to give the poor women a meal. They couldn't stay at Santa Maria Novella, and the nuns didn't know of another shelter with space for them. I'm telling you this because one woman is from your village, Poppi. She's thin and pale, like a ghost."

Masina took a drink from the mug. "All the women were gaunt, little more than skin and bones."

"Did she say her name?" Gino asked.

"Someone called her Tomasia. I didn't hear her family name."

"I know her. She and her husband have a small farm near the river. I've known them as long as I can remember. How can it be she's seeking a shelter in Florence?"

Masina spread her hands to show she had no answer.

"I don't understand why she would be alone in the city. She has a husband and a little girl." A memory came to him. "No. I remember the girl died from a disease the doctor couldn't treat. What will happen to her if she can't stay at the shelter?"

"You know what will happen if she can't find a shelter," Masina said solemnly. "She'll become another beggar living in the streets like all the others."

Gino jumped up from the table, went to his bed, and struggled to put shoes onto his swollen feet. "I can't let her become a beggar. She's a good woman. She deserves better. Is she still at the convent?"

"She was still there when I left, but not for much longer."

***

A nun intercepted Gino when he arrived at the shelter. She held up a hand and said, "Men are not allowed inside."

"I'm here for Tomasia, the woman from my village, Poppi. She came today and was told there wasn't room for her."

"I'm sorry," the nun said with sadness in her voice. "We have no more space. All the women who came here today have gone." Anticipating Gino's question, she said, "She and the other women went toward the warehouses by the docks."

Ships transported fruit and vegetables from Sicily, North Africa, and the Levant to Pisa. Barges carried the goods from Pisa to Florence, where they were kept in warehouses until they could be distributed. Inevitably, some items were damaged during handling. Dockworkers provided a share of the damaged goods to the desperate women. Some men did so as acts of charity; others expected the women to repay them with favors.

Gino circled the warehouses at the waterfront; a dozen or more whey-faced women were receiving handouts from dockworkers, but Tomasia was not among them. He made his way to the waterfront, where he saw, in the distance, a frail figure sitting on a stone bench and peering into the river. The woman faced away from him, so he saw only her profile, but her hair, nose and the curve of her chin fit his memory of Tomasia.

As Gino walked toward the woman, a man approached her, held out an orange, and said something to her. They were too far for Gino to hear what was said. The man pulled out a knife, cut a slice, and handed it to her. She licked the juice dripping from the ripe fruit.

"Tomasia!" Gino called when he got close. She turned, and with her gaunt face looking directly at him, Gino could tell the woman was not Tomasia.

The man scowled at Gino, bent down next to the woman, and said, "There's more to eat inside. Come with me." He took her hand and raised her from the bench. As they walked toward the warehouse, he reached a hand under her dress and grasped her buttocks.

"Bastard. Taking advantage of desperate women," Gino said to himself, but as he looked toward the warehouse, he saw similar scenes repeated everywhere along the waterfront. One incident drew his attention. An older woman turned suddenly and slapped the face of the man pursuing her. He raised his hand as if to return the strike, but merely cursed her and stormed away.

Gino approached the older woman. "I'm looking for a woman who just came to Florence today. Her name is Tomasia." The woman's eyes narrowed suspiciously. Gino continued, "I was told she came here a short time ago from the convent at Santa Maria Novella. They had no space for her in the shelter. She's from my home village."

"I don't know anyone called Tomasia," the woman replied curtly.

"Where might she go from here?" Gino said, his voice faltering.

"To the streets. Men, women and children. All the same. If they can't get shelter, they live on the streets," the woman said in a mocking tone. "How can you be asking, fool? Everyone knows what becomes of beggars."

The woman walked away, paused, and called back over her shoulder, "Some who fear the streets camp in fields outside the city gates."

Gino sat on a stone bench along the river, gazing into the black water. He knew of at least six city gates, and he had seen clusters of beggars in several neighborhoods throughout the city. Tomasia could be nearly anywhere. Poppi was a small village where neighbors were almost like family. Here in Florence, she had no one. He made a solemn promise to find her.

21

Thursday April 14, 1346

When Gino first came to Florence, he, Taddeo, and Wiener had shared a jug of beer every week or two at Wiener's favorite tavern. The merchants enjoyed hearing how Gino was adjusting to life in the city, and Gino looked forward to hearing news about his family from Taddeo.

Those meetings of the three friends were disrupted when crop failures altered the merchants' normal routines. The farms no longer had enough grains and vegetables to fill their wagons each day. They were forced to travel to more distant farms, often spending several days gathering a full wagonload of produce to bring to the markets in Florence. Since the merchants were away from Florence for long periods, the time between meetings of the three friends at the tavern had extended from weeks to a month. Gino missed the companionship of Taddeo and Wiener, and he missed hearing news about his family. But today, the two merchants would be in Florence, and Gino was eager to meet them at noon.

***

Shortly after the apothecary opened, two men entered the shop nearly simultaneously. The first one, a short, broad-shouldered man with a ruddy complexion, voiced his complaint as soon as Signor Roselli came within earshot. He said both he and his wife suffered from constipation. "I was blocked for two days, and this morning on the pot I felt like I was shitting a tree trunk."

The complaint had become commonplace in recent weeks. Roselli tried to tell him everyone's diet had changed because of the shortage of vegetables, but the man wasn't interested in reasons, only in a cure. Roselli went into the preparation room to mix an extract from buckthorn bark with dried senna flowers brought from North Africa. Since the food shortage began, he had made the same curative for customers nearly every day, so he didn't have to consult the formulation listing. Constipation was merely one consequence of the food shortages. Every day, Roselli also treated customers for malnutrition and other more serious ailments.

There were no customers in the perfumery, so Gino came into the apothecary to serve the second customer, an elderly man with pale skin and a bony frame. He had one hand pressed hard against his cheek, causing him to mumble as he told Gino about a problem with a tooth. Gino explained he would make something to ease the pain, but the relief would be temporary, and the tooth might need to be extracted.

While Gino and Signor Roselli were in the preparation room, a boy of about twelve years entered the shop. The boy went unnoticed until the constipation-afflicted customer left the shop. Roselli observed the youngster was too clean and neatly dressed to be a street urchin or an apprentice at the nearby woolen mill. He guessed the boy to be the son of a local artisan, but when he greeted the boy, the youngster said, "I have a message for Signor Liani."

"He's busy now, but he'll be available in a few minutes," Roselli responded.

The boy stepped aside and waited until Gino appeared and showed his customer how to apply the salve to his aching tooth. After the man left, still pressing a hand against his cheek, Gino introduced himself to the boy, who announced, "Messer Pagholi would like to meet with you."

At first, the request puzzled Gino, but then he became concerned that there might be a problem with his sister. "Tell him I'll come to his house as soon as I leave the apothecary."

"He's not at home. He's at the Palazzo della Signoria and he requests you to meet with him now."

Gino glanced at Roselli, who had been listening, and said, "For him to summon you, it must be an important matter. Go," although neither man could imagine why Gino would be wanted at the Palazzo della Signoria.

As they walked, the boy explained he was one of the Signoria's clerks, but he didn't know why Messer Pagholi wished to meet with Gino. At the Palazzo, the clerk led Gino through the narrow wooden door that served as the main entrance. They moved through a short passageway to a narrow courtyard. Small rooms, their entrances covered by porticos, surrounded the courtyard on all sides. Gino had never been inside the Palazzo. He paused in the middle of the courtyard and looked up at the balconies jutting into the irregularly shaped space at the upper levels.

Gino followed the clerk up a stairway to the second level and into a chamber known as the Hall of the Two Hundred. It was a stark room with unadorned brown walls and little furniture other than seating for the Florentine Council. Banks of windows on two walls made the room bright enough to see the intricate details of the coffered ceiling. They passed through the hall to a small space where, directly ahead, flanked on both sides by stairways, was the small meeting room of the Signoria known as the Hall of the Eight. The clerk carefully pulled the door open enough so those in the room would be alerted to their presence, but not enough for it to creak and disturb anyone.

Gino stood behind the clerk, listening to the voices coming from the hall. He heard no levity and no arguments, only serious dialogue. They waited several minutes before someone in the room signaled them to enter. The clerk opened the door fully, entered the room, and stepped aside so Gino could move forward.

Of the six men sitting at a large oak table, Gino recognized only Messer Pagholi. All the men had haggard expressions and leaned wearily in their seats. Their fashionable silk tunics, once well-pressed and elegant, were wrinkled and stained with sweat. It was only mid-morning, yet they appeared to have spent many hours struggling with important matters.

The men neither introduced themselves, nor did they invite Gino to join them. He remained standing near the doorway. All eyes locked on Gino as a narrow-faced man with intelligent eyes sitting at the far end of the table leaned forward, clasped his hands together, and asked, "Are you Signor Liani?"

Gino could only assume his questioner and the others were members of the Signoria. Intimidated by that illustrious company, he swallowed to wet his dry throat. In a scratchy voice, he uttered, "Yes."

The narrow-faced man continued, "Messer Pagholi told us you know the merchants who bring grain to the city."

Fearing his mere association with the merchants might earn him the Signoria's wrath, Gino said, "I know one of them."

"We would like to speak with him. Can you bring him here?"

"I think so," Gino said, aware he'd be seeing Wiener soon.

The questioner dismissed Gino with the simple response. "Good. Do it."

As Gino turned to leave, Pagholi rose from the table, followed him out of the room, and said, "This must seem puzzling to you. Let me explain why you were called here. Members of the Signoria feel they must act to solve the acute bread shortage. Their plan involves enlisting the help of grain merchants. I remembered you know one of the merchants, and I told them you can contact him."

***

Gino returned to the apothecary, where he waited nervously for midday when he would meet his friends. When the sext bells rang at the nearby church, Signor Roselli closed the apothecary for a midday respite and Gino headed to The Spotted Dog tavern where he joined Wiener and Taddeo, who were already seated at a table in the rear. From his brisk step, his companions guessed he had something important to tell them. Flashing a broad grin, Wiener raised his mug and quipped, "Did you finally get your woman alone on a soft bed of leaves somewhere in the woods?"

Gino flushed red and snapped, "No. Certainly not." Regaining his composure, he clinked his mug against Wiener's and grinned. "And when I do, I'll surely not boast to you about it. And don't call her my woman. She's not. At least not yet."

Wiener retorted, "The way you danced in here, something must have stoked your ethos."

"Ethos!" Taddeo yelped. "I didn't know a humble merchant like you read ancient Greek stories. Where did you learn the word ethos?"

Wiener smiled at Taddeo. "You know well I'm unable to read Greek stories. Last year, a minstrel came to our village, and one thing I learned from his show was the word ethos. The minstrel portrayed is as meaning something like one's soul." Returning his gaze to Gino, he said, "So tell us, what has you all stirred today?"

"This morning, I was summoned by the Signoria." Gino rested his elbows on the table, leaned forward, and stared directly at Wiener. "They feel the food shortages must be addressed before starvation becomes widespread. Their plan needs the support of grain merchants."

"If they want to meet with grain merchants, why did they summon you?"

"Messer Pagholi had told them I know a grain merchant, so they directed me to bring you to meet with them."

Taddeo slapped Wiener on the shoulder and teased, "If you meet with them, you best be sure your head is still firmly attached when you come away."

"I don't think they intend to pressure you," Gino said. "They wish to form a business arrangement with you…you and the other grain merchants."

Wiener peered into the beer jug. "They've waited this long to take on the food crisis; they can wait until we empty this jug."

Gino fidgeted nervously, waiting while Wiener and Taddeo drank slowly and chatted at length about topics mundane compared to the urgent matter being addressed by the Signoria. After finally taking his last swallow, Wiener pushed himself up from the table and said, "I'm ready. Let's go see what fate awaits me with the lawmakers."

Gino led Wiener to the Palazzo della Signoria and into the courtyard. A knight standing guard at the staircase intercepted Gino and said he was not permitted on the upper levels without an escort. Gino scanned the small rooms surrounding the courtyard. Most appeared vacant, but he noticed a shadow sweep across the wall in one room. Inside, he saw the clerk who had taken him to the palazzo earlier. With the clerk as their escort, Gino and Wiener climbed to the second level. Upon entering the Hall of the Two Hundred, Wiener looked around and said cynically, "I've always heard the Signoria encircled themselves with marble statues and fine tapestries. Those trappings certainly aren't in this room. They must be hiding their valuable possessions elsewhere." The clerk's dark look went unnoticed by Wiener.

As before, they waited outside the Hall of the Eight until they were told to enter. Gino and the clerk stepped into the room and moved aside, while Wiener walked ahead toward the men seated at the table. He stopped only when a knight positioned at the far wall stiffened and moved a hand to the hilt of his sword.

Wiener adopted a defiant stance, his feet apart and hands pressed against his hips. The narrow-faced man sitting at the table turned his lips up in an amusing smile. "You can relax, signor. We didn't call you here to raise your taxes." The quip elicited snickers from his associates. "Your name?"

"I'm called Wiener."

"You're a grain merchant, Signor Wiener?"

"I am," Wiener replied, his voice flat.

"We know you and your fellow merchants have been forced to travel far to find grain because the rains have devastated crops throughout Tuscany. Information we've received says the harvest in Romagna has not suffered to the same extent as here in Tuscany. We're told there is grain to be had in the Po Valley."

The man waited for Wiener's reaction, which was as he expected. Weiner said, "Bringing grain from Romagna will be expensive and make bread prohibitively expensive. Even now, people blame us merchants for the high prices. They don't realize how much time we must spend searching for farms with unspoiled grain. The stench of rotting wheat is everywhere. I've been cursed and spat upon in the streets."

The man at the table spread his hands. "We are aware of the situation you are describing, but beggars are dying in the streets for lack of food, and workingmen can barely afford to buy bread. More will die if we don't act now. We're not asking you to absorb the cost of traveling to Romagna. We propose that we, the Signoria, hire you and your fellow merchants to bring grain from the Po Valley."

Wiener's tension eased. He lowered his hands and his shoulders relaxed. He bit his lip as he considered the proposal, then he spoke slowly as he formed an idea. "It will take time to travel to Romagna and return. If I take one wagon, the journey will yield only one wagon load of grain. It would be better to take several wagons. I'm a grain merchant. I know good grain from bad, the best grain for making bread, and how to negotiate with farmers. If I were to lead a caravan of wagons, each round trip to the Po could yield many wagon loads. The other wagon drivers need know nothing about grain; they could simply follow my direction."

The men at the table exchanged glances. "Do you know where to get wagons and drivers?" one man asked.

"Every stable has wagons, and there are many drivers eager for work, especially if they are being paid by the Signoria."

Another man explained, "The grain will belong to the city. You'll deliver it to granaries we will establish in every district of the city. We'll have the grain milled and allow bakers to withdraw the milled grain if they agree to sell loaves at the price we decide...a price that every working man can afford."

Wiener gave a quick nod, although he cared little about how the grain was distributed. He discussed payment with the men, squaring his shoulders and standing tall when they came to favorable terms.

A husky man at the table reached for a parchment and began writing. When he finished, he signed the paper and passed it to two other men who also signed it. Then he marked it with the seal of the Signoria. "This document says the treasury will advance funds for you to buy grain, and when you return from Romagna, the Signoria will pay the balance as agreed." The clerk took the paper and handed it to Wiener.

"When can you leave?" the husky man asked.

Wiener thought for a moment. "I need to plan a route and hire wagons and drivers." He held up the document marked with the easily recognized seal of the Signoria. "With this document, hiring won't be a problem. I should be ready to leave tomorrow morning."

As Wiener turned to leave, he glimpsed the knight across the room, paused, and said, "A caravan of grain traveling through the countryside would be an attractive target for bandits. You might wish to assign knights to accompany us to protect the grain." The men nodded in agreement.

Outside in the piazza, Wiener smiled broadly, pointed to a nearby tavern, and said, "Gino, my friend, the tavern is calling us to celebrate my good fortune with a fine wine."

Gino shook his head. "I wish you well, Wiener, but I've been away from the apothecary far too long. I have to return to the shop. Signor Roselli is surely wondering what happened to me. We can celebrate when you return from Romagna."

22

Tuesday May 10, 1346

"His medication used the last of our buckthorn bark," Roselli said to Gino as a customer left the shop holding a curative Roselli had made for him. "Every day, people come here with digestive problems because they eat only meat and fungi. They say they can't get vegetables."

Gino said, "I've not been able to get vegetables at the mercato either, but every Sunday I go foraging with Masina, the healer who lives near me. She looks for plants to use in her treatments, and I hunt for edible greens like borage and chicory. There are edible plants in many fields outside the city, but people don't want to eat them because they're tougher than farm-grown vegetables and they're bitter."

"Have you seen any buckthorn trees?

"I haven't looked for them, but buckhorn is a common shrub, so it probably grows around the edges of the fields. I could go look for some this afternoon."

Roselli listened to the rain sheeting against the front of the shop. "It's raining steadily, not a good time to go trudging through fields."

Gino laughed. "The deluge never stops. One rainy day is no worse than any other."

Roselli said, "If you could find buckthorn bark, we'd be able to help the customers who are sure to come tomorrow with digestion problems."

On his way out of the city, Gino passed other men striving to stay dry. The constant rain had driven them away from fashionable attire. Since water pooled in the fancy cappuzzo style hats favored by wealthy Florentines, even the city's aristocrats had adopted the simple muffin caps worn by peasants. In normal times, tightly woven wool cloaks afforded excellent protection from the rain, but even those soaked through after an extended exposure. Some men wore heavy leather boots, but Gino found wetness worked its way into any footwear, so he opted for simple leather shoes. To keep his head dry, Lucia had made her brother a hood he could attach to his rain cloak. To make it shed water, she had coated it with a thin layer of duck fat. He was amazed by her creation, which kept his head dry even after hours in the rain.

The steady rain continued as Gino passed out of the city through the Porta al Prato gate. Shortly, he came to a field spread with yellow dandelion flowers. Despite the rain, he wasn't the only person in the field. Ahead of him, two women were gathering dandelion and bellflower leaves. They wore no protective coverings, and their thin dresses were soaked, but they weren't deterred.

To his right, at the edge of the woods, Gino noticed a stand of buckthorn shrubs. He took out a knife and began scraping strips of bark from one stalk. A single stalk provided enough bark for him to fill his sack, an ample amount to treat customers for several weeks. He was about to leave when he spotted another woman. She wasn't in the field with the others; she was surveying the ground around a grove of larch trees where the field met the forest. Could she be gathering fungi? When he moved closer, he saw her collecting stems of wild asparagus. She shivered in the chilly rain. Closer still, he stood for a moment watching her, unsure whether the frail figure and gaunt face belonged to Tomasia. She turned when he called her name, and her mouth opened, but she said nothing.

"I'm Gino, Gino Liani from Poppi," he said and saw a glint of understanding in her eyes.

She stood, an asparagus stalk in one hand, and looked at him for a long moment before echoing, "Gino?"

He went to her. "I was told you came to Florence months ago, and I searched for you but couldn't find you. Why are you here? Why did you come to the city?"

In a quavering voice, she said, "The rain destroyed our crops. Nothing would grow. Three times my husband put in seeds and each time they were washed away. We had dried vegetables and meat, but they lasted only through the winter. We didn't expect the rain to last this long. No one did. At every meal, my husband insisted I take the larger portion. He ate practically nothing." Tears flowed and her voice sputtered as she spoke. "When we neared the end of our food, he was so weak he couldn't stand. He told me to take the rest and leave. 'Go to the city,' he said. He insisted. I had no choice."

"Was there no one in Poppi who could help you?" Gino asked.

"All the farms suffered from the rain. No one had any food to share."

Tomasia, like the other women, was soaked. Her thin dress gave no protection from the rain. Her hair was matted, and she was barefoot. "Did you find a shelter? Where are you living?"

"There," she replied and pointed to the woods. "I fashioned a shelter from fallen branches. Twice each week I go into the city to get bread from the granary. They give away stale rolls. But it isn't safe to stay in the city, so I stay in the woods."

Gino shook his head. "How dreadful. You can't stay like this. Come with me. I have a room where you can get dry." Tomasia clung to her fistful of asparagus as they made their way to Gino's room in the city. When they reached his room, he stoked the fire and gave Tomasia a blanket to wrap around herself so she could remove her sopping dress.

Even though Gino had a job, his money held little worth because the extreme scarcity, bordering on famine, meant there were few goods available for him to buy. He supplemented his market purchases with plants he found on his Sunday morning walks with Masina. He made soup for Tomasia from the plants he had gathered, and on a hunk of bread he spread a preserve he had made from wild berries.

Gino held out a cup of apple juice and asked, "How did you get to Florence?"

Tomasia grasped the cup with two trembling hands, took a sip, and said, “I came with a young couple from a neighboring village. A merchant coming to Florence gave us a ride in his wagon. The woman was so weak her husband had to help her sit upright. They said their baby had died because the woman had withered so much she couldn’t make milk to feed it.

“Hearing her story made me remember my daughter. She died last year of an illness the doctor couldn’t cure. She was such a pretty girl. I miss her so much. First, my daughter was gone; then my husband.” Her eyes filled with tears.

After a long pause, Tomasia took a drink, then said, “I didn’t know what to do, so I was just standing beside the road when a wagon came along. The merchant offered to let me ride with him. I didn’t know him. He wasn’t from Poppi. If he hadn’t let me go with them, I never would have made it.

“The closer we got to Florence, the more people we saw, all coming to the city. There were many wagons crowded with people; other poor souls were walking. The merchant stopped along the way to take three more into his wagon.” She crossed herself. “May the Lord bless his kind soul.

“Our wagon was full when we passed a man and a boy plodding wearily along the roadside. They had no satchel, no food, no water. The boy staggered, then fell. The man lifted the boy and tried to carry him, but the boy was too heavy. I saw resignation in the man’s eyes. He knew they wouldn’t reach the city.”

“Where did you go when you reached Florence?” Gino asked.

“The merchant took us to a shelter he knew of, but it was full. They told us of two other shelters, but they too had no space. We wandered through the city from one shelter to another, but all were full. The Santa Maria convent was the last.”

Their conversation continued until dark with Tomasia telling Gino of other families he had known in the village who had also abandoned their farms. Gino let her sleep in his bed, and he wrapped himself in blankets on the floor. Exhausted, she slept soundly while Gino had a restless night, wondering what would become of her.

In the morning, Gino was already dressed and preparing to leave when Tomasia awakened. "I must leave for work, but you are welcome to stay here," he said. "There's food on the table. If you need anything, ask Masina, the woman who lives in the room above."

"Thank you for your kindness, but it's not proper for me to stay with you. I must go."

Gino interrupted. "Where would you go? Not back to the woods." She didn't reply, and after a lengthy pause, Gino said, "I know someone who might help you. Stay here at least until I can speak with him." Again, she didn't respond, and Gino left for the apothecary, not knowing whether Tomasia would be there when he returned.

***

After work, Gino went to Casa Pagholi as he often did to visit his sister, and as usual, he found her in the kitchen preparing an evening meal. Every time he visited her, he thanked the Lord she worked for a senior magistrate whose position afforded him access to increasingly scarce food items. Gino could do little for his family members in Poppi, but at least he had helped his sister by bringing her to Florence.

Lucia's eyes went wide with astonishment as Gino told her about Tomasia. "Merchants who bring food to the casa have mentioned shortages, but I didn't realize the shortages were so bad. The merchants said nothing about people starving or shelters turning people away. They are the only outside people I speak with other than you and Gabriela. Signor Pagholi doesn't talk about business at home, at least not when I'm present. When Signora Pagholi meets with other women each week to play tric-trac, they always talk about pleasant topics. I've never heard them mention beggars or a food crisis."

Gino clasped his sister's hand in his and said, "We're fortunate. Messer Pagholi is an important person, so vendors come to his house with the finest goods available. And I have a job, so I can afford to buy items at the mercato, even though prices keep rising. Although lately, the few vendors who still come to the mercato have very little produce to sell. Customers at the apothecary have told me bakers have very few loaves of bread to sell because they can't get enough grain. A pastry shop near my house has closed. The owner told me there was only enough flour for bread. The Signoria has enlisted merchants to deal with the problem, but their solution won't come quickly."

Lucia touched her hand to Gino's arm and said, "I worry about our family."

Gino nodded. "I do too. Taddeo used to bring me news from them every day, but I haven't seen him for four days. The farms in the valley provide barely enough to fill his wagon, so he comes to Florence only once a week." After standing silent for a minute, Gino said, "I'd like to speak with Messer Pagholi to ask whether he can suggest how I might help Tomasia. Maybe he knows of other shelters."

As the house servant, it was Lucia's responsibility to receive callers and inform Messer Pagholi of their requests. She led Gino to the anteroom and said, "Wait here."

Messer Pagholi came into the room a few minutes later. He looked haggard; nonetheless, he smiled when he saw his visitor. Gino had misgivings about mentioning Tomasia's plight to someone who already bore the weight of the city's problems, but he needed the magistrate's help. He described her failed attempts to find space in a shelter to Pagholi, who responded, "Yes, the Signoria knows all the shelters are completely full. Several tower houses were abandoned many years ago when the families owning them were discredited and forced to leave the city. Today, the Signoria ordered two of the abandoned towers near San Tommaso church be made into shelters. They'll help, but only briefly. With so many people streaming into the city, I'm sure those towers will fill quickly." Pagholi shook his head in resignation. "The woman you spoke of should go there soon."

The two men discussed the worsening situation. Pagholi told of actions being considered by the Signoria, and Gino told how his merchant friends, Taddeo and Wiener, were finding it nearly impossible to get vegetables and grains from farms in the Tuscan countryside.

After leaving Pagholi, Gino returned to the kitchen, where Lucia handed him a parcel wrapped in paper. "The baker brings fresh bread every second day. He came this morning. This is old bread. It's hard, but if you wrap it in a wet cloth and warm it by your fire, it will soften."

***

Tomasia was sitting alone when Gino returned to his room. "A new shelter is being opened," Gino said as soon as he entered. "It's expected to fill quickly, so we should go there now to ensure that you can get a place." He handed one of his blankets to Tomasia. "Take this. I can get another." She wanted to resist, but instead she wrapped the blanket around her shoulders.

They walked to San Tommaso church across the piazza from the mercato. From the front of the church, Gino saw workers carrying a table into an old tower house on a nearby side street. He entered the building, with Tomasia following behind, approached the supervisor, who was directing the workers, and asked, "Is this the house being made into a shelter?"

"Yes, but it's not ready. We need to finish preparing it and give it a thorough cleaning. Come again tomorrow."

Gesturing toward Tomasia, Gino said, "This woman needs shelter now. If we help with the cleaning, can you give her a place?"

The supervisor scratched his head while considering the unusual suggestion. After scrutinizing Tomasia, he said, "She seems too frail to do any meaningful work."

Gino said, "I'll help with the cleaning. We'll both work until the building is clean."

Swayed by Gino's persistence, the supervisor said, "The nuns at the convent behind the church will care for the women in this shelter. Go tell them this one is to have a place because she's helping to get the building ready. Then come back here and I'll give you work."

Gino and Tomasia washed walls and floors until dark, when the supervisor declared the building was ready and Tomasia became its first occupant. "I'll come to see you tomorrow," Gino promised, as he left her.

***

The following afternoon, Gino returned to the tower house and waited outside while a young nun fetched Tomasia. Color had returned to her face, and she moved with strength absent the previous day. Her eyes brightened upon seeing Gino. Speaking softly, she said, "Already, there are ten of us in this house. There's only one room on each floor, so we must share. The woman sent to my room this morning was nearly delirious. She's not even able to tell me her name. I fed her broth because she couldn't feed herself. The nuns said if more women come, we may have four in each room." She fixed her eyes on Gino. "I thank you, and the Lord, for finding me and bringing me here. I pray our Lord blesses the other poor women who were begging at the warehouses, the ones who spent last night in the streets, with a savior like you."

Gino gave a humbled nod, then his eyes brightened. "I may have some good news, a place where you might find work."

After telling the nuns she would return, Tomasia accompanied Gino across the river to the Oltrarno district and through the Porta San Niccolò gate to the building housing Piero Roselli's funeral services business. Gino entered the office and moved close enough for Piero to recognize him. "Ah, Gino," Piero said cheerfully. "I knew you'd eventually become bored at the apothecary and return to me." He squinted at the figure standing beside Gino. "And you've brought someone with you. Good, I can always use more help."

Urging her forward, Gino said, "This is Tomasia. She's from my village. She just arrived in Florence and needs work."

"Come closer, let me look at you." Piero leaned forward to examine her, and announced, "She's skinny." He gave a dismissive wave, and said, "Don't be offended, signora; with this food shortage, everybody is getting skinny." He patted his pudgy stomach. "Even me.

"As I said, I can use more help. This food shortage is dreadful. At first, it was only people in the countryside who suffered, but now the beggars and poor here in Florence can't get enough food either. I have a charter from the Signoria to bury the ones who don't survive and every day there are more than the day before." Tears welled in Tomasia's eyes as she thought about her husband's fate.

Piero looked at Gino. "When you worked here, every funeral had a procession with mourners. Even the poor had family members to mourn their souls. Now, we bury beggars with no processions and no mourners. We put them into wagons and take them to unmarked graves in the cemetery. Once each week, the bishop says a mass for all the dead and nuns pray for them without knowing their names."

He turned to Tomasia. "The church says the bodies must be washed and wrapped in shrouds. Is that something you could do?"

"I washed my mother when she died. We believe the dead should be washed by someone close to them."

"Your mother was blessed to have you care for her." He bowed his head slightly. "But the indigent often have no one." He turned toward a side door and shouted, "Luigi!"

The thin man with the bent nose stepped into the office from the adjoining room. Piero said, "This is Tomasia. Starting tomorrow, she'll be helping to prepare the bodies."

Luigi glanced at Tomasia, grunted in the affirmative, and left the office.

***

Gino accompanied Tomasia back to the tower house. She said, "You've done more for me than I could ever repay. If it weren't for you, I might be in the river."

Gino responded, "We may all need help before this crisis passes."

As he turned to leave, he heard a nun inform Tomasia, "Another woman has been added in your room." Gino stared up at the towering structure and tried to estimate how many women will find a home there, and how many more will be without shelter.

23

September 1346

Since his acceptance as a member of the Doctors' and Apothecaries' Guild, Gino had attended the monthly guild meetings, but not always with the same enthusiasm. For him, the sessions attended by both doctors and speziali were frustrating because the doctors used those occasions to flaunt their superiority over the speziali. They pranced about in the flashy clothing they always wore in public, bright red caps and robes topped by ermine lined black cloaks. They used tenets of the guild charter to ensure doctors were the only ones elected as guild officers, and they made sure the speziali were barred from positions of power. Meetings controlled by the doctors had little value for Gino. In contrast, he always learned something at the meetings arranged solely for speziali.

After a day of serving the growing number of ailing Florentines at the apothecary, Gino and Signor Roselli walked to the guild headquarters and entered its bustling grand audience hall. Voices from animated groups of people echoed from the walls and the marble floor, creating a chaotic din. Roselli observed, "In these difficult times, it's encouraging to see such energy."

Gino glanced around and once again found himself to be the youngest person in the room. Although he'd been welcomed as an equal as soon as he was accepted as a guild member, he hadn't felt worthy of membership until he had repaid Roselli for the loan of his membership fee. Now, with his debt paid, he felt pride in walking among his colleagues and calling himself a speziale. He wandered through the room, catching snippets of conversation. Most were comments on how the food shortages had expanded their businesses. One man said gleefully, "It seems like everyone in my neighborhood is suffering with stomach cramps. I struggle to keep gentian in my shop. As soon as I get some, it's gone."

"Bastard," Gino said to himself. "All around people suffer, while your concern is only growing your business." Gino heard similar thoughtless comments in other groups. He meandered through the room until he heard someone talking about witchcraft. He drifted closer to listen.

The speaker proclaimed, "We're overrun with derelicts from the countryside. They have no skills useful in the city, so they become beggars ripe to be preyed on by the witches. The fools will believe anything." Some in the group listened attentively, while others nodded vigorously. The speaker continued, "Witches have always been among us, but in the past, they cast their evil spells in secret. Now they do Satan's work in the open." He glanced around to confirm he had everyone's attention, then said in a low voice as though sharing a secret, "I've heard the bishop has asked the Holy Father to send advocati from Rome to rout out the witches and rid us of them."

Another man joined the tirade. "The Bible says witches must be punished. Leviticus tells us witches shall surely be put to death with stones." Gino and a few others moved away, not wanting to lend their support to the denunciation.

The sound of a chime being struck stilled the banter and people turned their attention to a man at the lectern whom all recognized as the organizer of the speziali meetings. After welcoming everyone and announcing the schedule of future meetings, he introduced their guest. "Today we are to hear from Signor Volpato, a Venetian merchant who searches for curatives and medicinal plants in Asia and the Levant." The man stepped aside to let the guest move behind the lectern.

Volpato's bright green silk tunic with silver buttons and his large gold ring set the Venetian apart from the conservatively dressed Florentines. He scanned the crowd, smiled, and began, "I've spent my life seeking plants and herbs you good men can make into curatives." With a flourish, he held up a flower and said, "This is my latest find. It is called Esfand. When the flower is dried, seeds can be removed from the tiny pods at its center." He opened his other hand to reveal a cluster of dark seeds. "These Esfand seeds have been prized in the Holy Land for centuries for their magical and medicinal properties. Burning the seeds creates a fragrance that casts away illness and negative energy. I'm pleased to tell you I'm now able to make these marvelous seeds available to you," he spread his arms wide, "here in your wonderful city of Florence."

Volpato held everyone's attention as he described the ways Esfand was used in the Levant, and how Florentine speziali could use it to ease the pain of those suffering from malnutrition. When he had finished his presentation, he happily answered questions about the availability, price, and other properties of Esfand seeds.

Gino listened with skepticism. Only moments ago, he had heard women being castigated as witches for promoting their curatives; now the accusers gave rapt attention to a stranger professing to have seeds with magical qualities. He recalled the day in Poppi when a hunter came into Signor Morelli's apothecary shop with wolf bones said to have supernatural powers. Are mystical claims considered witchcraft only when they are made by others?

When the crowd finished questioning Volpato, the meeting dissolved again into small groups. Across the hall, Gino spotted one group of people gesturing wildly and spewing angry words. He moved closer. A muscular man with a large neck and thick bushy eyebrows snarled, "They broke into the granary last night and stole bushels of grain. Damn near an entire wagonload. The grain they took was *our* grain. People in our neighborhood might starve because of those thieving bastards."

"Who did it?" someone asked.

"I'll tell you who did it," the big man said, jabbing a pointed finger toward the questioner. "It's those derelicts who sleep in the alleys behind the church. They don't do shit all day except go to the church for free meals. Then they repay our hospitality by stealing our grain. They're probably selling it to buy ale."

Although Gino didn't know the agitated speaker, he summoned the courage to ask, "Are you sure it was them? Did anyone see them?"

The big man gave Gino an icy stare. "I didn't have to see them. I know it was them, and we need to make sure they can never steal from us again." He pounded a fist into his open palm.

"You could ask the Signoria to post guards at the granary," Gino suggested.

Another man spat on the floor and barked, "The Signoria doesn't listen to us. All we can do is speak to our member of the council, and he's a useless fool. I tried talking to him once. It was like talking to a stone. If we want something done, we need to do it ourselves. We can't depend on those worthless lawmakers."

The big man grinned. "Tonight. We'll show them tonight." Shouts of support came from the crowd.

A voice from behind Gino called out, "They're probably the same ones who robbed the butcher shop. They broke the door open in the middle of the night and took food that belongs on *our* tables." Cries for action grew louder.

Two men came alongside Gino and grasped his elbows. "Your opinions aren't welcome here," one man said as they pressed Gino's arms backward to force him away from the group. As he turned to leave, another man hissed and drove his fist into Gino's back. The blow sent Gino stumbling forward and crashing into a table. He moaned as pain shot upward to his shoulders, and he clutched the table to keep from falling. For several minutes, he leaned against the table until his vision cleared and he felt able to walk. Petty theft and looting brought on by high prices and scarce goods is one more problem the Signoria is ill-equipped to solve, Gino thought as he limped away.

***

At the apothecary the following morning, Gino was serving a man buying perfume for his mistress when another man charged into the shop. The newcomer announced, "Did you hear about the brawl in San Lorenzo last night?" Before Gino could respond, the excited man said, "Locals attacked a group of derelicts. I was told a dozen or more were injured in the brawl, and six were beaten so badly they had to be taken to the hospital. Two of them were locals." He paused, and when Gino remained silent, he said, "I heard the locals who went to the hospital work at an apothecary in San Lorenzo. Do you know them?"

Gino rubbed the tender spot on his back and swallowed hard. "No, I don't know them."

24

Wednesday October 4, 1346

Gino was mixing a new batch of the popular Jasmine Rose perfume when Professor Vianello swept into the perfumery. "Buona sera, Gino. How is my favorite speziale today?" Cupping a hand near his mouth and speaking in a softer voice, he joked, "I shouldn't speak so loudly or Signor Roselli might hear me. I wouldn't want him to feel rejected. He's a good man too, a good speziale."

"You're in an especially cheerful mood today, professor."

"I have two new students. They're brother and sister."

"A girl," Gino said with surprise. "Do you tutor many girls?"

"She's the first since I came to Florence, although I did tutor girls when I was in Padua." Vianello gave a short laugh. "This one wants to learn poetry and her brother wants to learn about ancient Rome. Their father owns a woolen mill; he wants me to teach them about commerce. Every father hopes his children will follow him, although often a father's expectations for his children are laced with false hope."

"Are you versed in poetry, ancient Rome, and commerce?" Gino asked.

Vianello snickered. "Enough to school these young people."

"With such diverse interests, pleasing all three of them could present a challenge," Gino suggested.

"Yes, it will, and I'm looking forward to it. I get little satisfaction from teaching people only what they want to learn. I feel more accomplishment when I can enlighten people beyond their own narrow interests." Vianello waved a hand in the air playfully. "I'll feel success when I have the boy reading poetry and the girl eager to visit Rome."

"And both wanting to manage their father's business?" Gino queried.

"Bah." Vianello gave a dismissive shrug. "Neither child has the desire or ambition to manage a woolen mill. I've already told their father they may gain an interest in his business when they're older, but not now, and he's prepared to wait."

Gino filled a mug with the professor's special elixir and set it on the counter. Upon observing Gino's sluggish movements and flat speech, Vianello asked, "Is something weighing on you?"

"Taddeo, the merchant I told you about, has joined the procession of wagons going to Romagna for grain. I haven't spoken with him for nearly two weeks. I miss talking with him, and I miss hearing news of my family he used to bring me after visiting their farm." Gino was struck realizing he had said *their* farm rather than *our* farm. Was he dissociating himself from Poppi village and his family?

Vianello took a swig of the elixir and said, "Ah, this is just what I need to fortify me so I can compose a lesson about the poetry of ancient Rome." He set the mug down and looked at Gino. "I can't give you news of your family, but I do enjoy stimulating conversation. There's a tavern in Piazza San Lorenzo. Join me there later; we can share a pitcher and swap stories."

***

Gino walked to Piazza San Lorenzo after ending his day at the apothecary shop. Across the piazza, he spotted a sign with the word tavern and the picture of a blue duck above the doorway of a narrow storefront. He had just reached the tavern when he heard his name being called and turned to see the professor behind him. The two men entered the tavern together.

Vianello set a silver coin on the counter, prompting the barkeep to fill a pitcher. The men took mugs and the pitcher to a table across the room from the only other occupied table. "What was the most recent news from your family?" Vianello asked, his tone quiet and serious.

"Like everyone else, they're praying for the rain to stop, so they can plant. If they can at least plant a winter crop, it won't give them enough to sell, but it would keep them fed until they can plant a full crop next spring. Men in the valley say this is the first time they can remember rain destroyed both the spring and fall harvests. Most farms in the Casentino Valley lost more than half of their crops. Some lost everything. There is nothing they can do other than ask God to stop the rain, so the crisis will end in the spring."

Gino's last comment made Vianello shake his head. He ran a finger slowly along the rim of his beer mug and said in a serious tone, "I fear the crisis may not end in the spring."

"Why? Have you seen another sign in the sky?" Gino asked.

"No, not another one, but the full prophecy of the last sign hasn't been fulfilled."

"Those wandering stars … I mean planets … are far away. Maybe their movements aren't always meant for us," Gino said in hopeful desperation.

"It's true the planets are far away, but they're not disconnected from us. All objects in the heavens move around the Earth on spheres. The moon is on the nearest sphere. The sun is on a more distant sphere, and Mars, Jupiter, and Saturn are each on their own spheres beyond the sun. But all the spheres move around the Earth. We are at the center. This was determined by the great Greek astronomer Ptolemy. When Mars, Jupiter, and Saturn come together as they did last year, it foretells of more than merely two seasons of rain." Vianello refilled his mug, took a long drink, and said, "But this is our first time drinking together. Let's not spend it talking of ill omens. Tell me about Gabriela. When will you be seeing her next?"

Gino's shoulders slumped. "I don't know."

"You care for her?"

"Oh, yes, and she cares for me. I'm certain she does, but I can't be the one to find reasons for us to be together."

Puzzled by Gino's comment, Vianello asked, "Does Signor Roselli know your feelings? Does he approve?"

"Signora Roselli knows, and she approves. At least Gabriela tells me her mother approves. But Signor Roselli has stature. He owns a reputable business and will surely want his daughter betrothed to a man of means. I couldn't approach him to ask for Gabriela because I have nothing to offer. I live in one small room near the river. Whenever the rain goes on for days, I pray my room doesn't flood." Gino looked away and down at the floor. "Signor Roselli would never let his daughter … his only daughter … live like a lowborn. And I couldn't ask her to live like a lowborn either."

"Don't be discouraged. Wives can be persuasive. Signor Roselli may open his heart if his wife favors you."

Before Gino could respond, two burly men came into the tavern. Their boisterous voices drew everyone's attention. Their workingmen's smocks were stained with tannery dyes. Each one got his own pitcher from the barkeep and carried it to a table behind Gino. They dropped roughly onto chairs and continued their loud conversation. One bellowed, "It didn't take the advocati long to find witches. They've only been in Florence four days and they already uncovered a widow who calls herself a healer and a rector who was sending women to her for her magic potions."

"The advocati wasted no time because they're members of the Dominican order sent all the way from Rome. Dominicans defend the church like a pack of wild dogs. I wouldn't want them hunting me. The witch's trial will be held next week. Do you think she'll be stoned?"

"Stoned or whipped, and not only her, but the rector, too." A smirk appeared on his face as he said, "The church always applies its punishments in public so we can watch, and you can be sure the priests will be there watching too." He laughed. "They enjoy brutal entertainment as much as us."

"This witch and the rector won't be the end of the search. The Dominicans won't wait until the trial of their first catch before they look for more victims. I heard they're already hunting another witch in the Santa Maria Novella neighborhood."

The two men laughed raucously, then switched their loud harangue to a different topic. No longer able to carry on their own conversation, Gino and the professor finished their beers quickly and left the tavern. Outside, Vianello said, "Next time we must find a quieter retreat." Gino nodded while his brow furrowed with worry.

25

Thursday October 5, 1346

Tired after a busy day at the apothecary, Gino trudged home. He spotted Masina a distance ahead, walking toward the house where they both rented rooms. She was with another woman whom Gino did not recognize. The woman's simple peasant clothes let Gino guess she was coming to Masina for treatment of an illness.

Suddenly, two boys dashed out from behind the house the women had just passed. One boy cocked his arm and hurled a rock that struck Masina's back. She turned. "Witch!" the boy shouted.

Gino raced ahead. The second boy raised his arm. Gino saw the rock in his hand. As the boy's arm arced forward, Gino grabbed it; the boy lost his grip, spilling the rock harmlessly to the ground. "She's a witch," the boy whined as he squirmed to free himself from Gino's grasp.

"No, she's not a witch. She's a healer," Gino barked.

"My father said she's a witch," the first boy insisted. "He said she makes evil potions and the advocati are coming for her."

"Your father is wrong. She makes curatives to help sick people, not evil potions. Now go and never let me see you troubling her again. She's a good woman."

The boys slunk away, Gino watching them until they were out of sight. When he turned back to face Masina, the other woman had gone. He walked with Masina and when they reached his room, he said, "Come inside. I have something to tell you."

Gino poured two mugs of lemon water and set them on the table. He said, "Yesterday, I heard two men saying the advocati sent by the Holy Father in Rome have already arrived in Florence ready to find and punish witches."

Masina took a sip of the cool liquid and said dispassionately, "I've heard the same."

"The men claimed the advocati have already detained a healer and a rector. They've accused the woman of witchcraft and scheduled her trial for next week."

Masina's nose scrunched with concern. "Did you hear the woman's name? I must know her. There are only a few of us healers in the city."

"No, I didn't hear her name, but someone said they're searching for another witch in the Santa Maria Novella district. They could be looking for you!" Gino said forcefully. Masina shrugged but said nothing. Gino continued, "Two days ago, I saw a man and a woman leaving your office. I thought you kept yourself safe by treating only women."

"I did when all the women I treated were locals. They appreciated my need for secrecy, but the migrants don't understand. When they're sick and need treatment, I can't turn them away even when they come with their husbands or children. I try to tell them, but …"

Loud thundering of footsteps on the stairway leading to the second level of the house stifled Masina's words. "Those are her rooms. Up there!" a voice outside shouted.

From above, they heard pounding on a door, followed by an emphatic demand by a throaty voice. "By authority of the Holy Mother Church and His Holiness Pope Clement, we order you to open this door." Again, there was pounding on the door. When no one responded, the same voice commanded, "Open it!"

A single hard thwack and the splintering of wood preceded the tromping of three sets of boots storming into Masina's room. From the sounds, Gino and Masina could tell what was happening above their heads. "She's not here," one voice muffled down through Gino's ceiling.

"Look for her writings, for parchments with spells. Look for any signs she's practicing the teachings of Satan," the throaty voice ordered. After the men rummaged through Masina's room for several minutes, a thin voice said, "There's nothing incriminating here."

"Search the rooms on the lower level," the commanding voice directed.

Gino heard footsteps outside approaching his room. He realized quickly there was no place to hide Masina. "Get behind the door. Hurry," he mouthed.

She had barely scurried across the room when there was a hard rap on Gino's door and a voice outside demanded the occupant to open the door per order of the Church and His Holiness. Gino pulled the door open enough to see a monk clad in the white robe of the Dominican order. "We're looking for the woman who lives in this building," the monk announced.

"There's no woman here," Gino replied. He swung the door fully open, flattening it against Masina. "You may look if you wish." He stepped to the side with his back pressed hard against the door to keep it from moving and gestured for the monk to enter.

The monk took a step into the room, looked around, and, seeing no one, asked, "Who lives in the other room on this level?"

"I don't know. I'm new here," Gino lied. "People stay in these rooms only a short time. I don't know who is there now."

Believing Gino knew nothing, the monk turned and left. Gino pushed the door closed. The sudden relief caused Masina to gasp. She took a few quick breaths and said, "Thank God he didn't stay. I couldn't have held my breath much longer."

Moments later, they heard the monks entering Masina's treatment room. Gino beckoned Masina to a narrow crack in the stone wall separating his room from her treatment room. They pressed their ears against the crack and listened to the sounds coming from the other room.

"This is where she does Satan's work," a voice said. "Look at these urns. They hold the powders she uses to make her evil potions. Take them, all of them. We'll use them as evidence at her trial, then we'll burn them...after we burn her," he snarled.

Satisfied they had enough proof to convict the witch, the men left the room. The leader ordered one of his subordinates. "Stay in her room on the upper level and when she returns, bring her to me."

After the monks had left, except for the one pacing across Masina's room, Gino and Masina sat quietly at the table for several minutes, each contemplating Masina's next action. Finally, speaking softly to be sure his words wouldn't carry to the room above, Gino said, "You can't stay in Florence. You wouldn't be safe anywhere in the city because too many people can identify you. I'll take you to my family's farm in Poppi. You can stay there until you find another place."

Masina held up a hand. "I can't go there. Your family is already struggling with barely enough food for themselves. They can't take on another burden."

"There's no other place for you to go," Gino insisted. "You can at least stay on the farm for a short time. My father can help when you decide where to go, maybe to another big city, Bologna or Venice."

Masina had no alternative to suggest. Then, thinking of what she would leave behind, she pondered, "Who will help the women if I leave?"

"You've done all you can for them. Now, you must think of yourself. You can find a new city. Everywhere there will be women who need help." Gino stood and paced across the room, thinking. "There's one monk in your room, and others scouring the city looking for you. Our challenge is to find a way for you to get out of Florence. Can you ride a horse?"

Masina laughed. "I've never ridden a horse and I'm not a young girl who could learn to do it. I wouldn't get very far before I'd fall."

"A wagon then. We can hire a wagon."

Resigning herself to Gino's plan, Masina said, "I have money in the Bardi bank, so I can pay to hire a wagon."

Gino shook his head. "But if you go to a bank, you might be seen by the advocati."

From the pouch fastened at her waist, Masina withdrew a small metal disc marked with the seal used by her dead husband when he had established his account at the bank. She handed it to Gino so he could go to the bank and make a withdrawal from the account. She told him to withdraw enough to sustain her and to buy bread to take to his family. "Buy the big loaves," she said, "not the little ones the city forces bakers to sell for a few denari. Get as many loaves as you can carry." Gino donned his cloak and told Masina to stay quiet and keep the door locked until he returned.

The sun had set by the time Gino returned. Masina released the door latch when she heard a knock and Gino's whisper. "You took so long. I was worried," she said.

"I had to tell Signor Roselli that I couldn't be at the apothecary tomorrow."

She noticed Gino's bag wasn't filled with loaves of bread, and asked, "Weren't you able to buy bread?"

"I bought three loaves … the big ones … and put them in the cart I hired. It's waiting for us at the stable." He opened the bag he was holding and pulled out two garments. "These are clothes for you to wear. I got them at a used clothing shop owned by a friend." He held up a hooded cloak and a pair of men's leggings. "It would be safest for you to leave here dressed as a man. I have a smock you can wear with these."

Masina giggled. "You want me to dress as a man? Are you trying to liken my departure to the spicy tales told by French troubadours? I've heard them recite stories of criminals escaping their pursuers by donning false clothes."

Gino joined her laughter. "In their tales, do the escapees always succeed?"

"Often they do," she said as she took the leggings from Gino and held them in front of her. "What unholy garments you men wear. Do they itch?"

"Often they do," Gino replied with a grin.

They waited until the bell at Santa Maria Novella sounded matins, the call to midnight prayer, before leaving Gino's room. The thin crescent moon gave barely enough light for the two male figures to pick their way through the streets to the Porta al Prato gate and to the stable beyond. They prayed there were no muggers prowling the same streets they were traveling. Having taken a few wrong turns crossing the city, rather than risk getting lost, they remained at the stable until early morning light before setting out on the cart. Bales of hay stacked beside the stable gave them a place to stay the night. They settled into the hay bales with their cloaks pulled tight against the cold. When the first rays of dawn shone in the eastern sky, they climbed onto the cart and began the journey to Poppi.

Using Florence's high stone walls as their guide, they followed a road outside the city to the Arno River. Gray clouds and tiny patches of blue sky had become faintly visible when the cart reached the end of the river valley and began climbing into the foothills. The few farm wagons heading in the opposite direction, toward the mercato in Florence, were only partially filled. None carried the heavy loads they had in past years when crop yields were bountiful.

Neither Gino nor Masina spoke much during the long ride through the wooded highlands. When they reached the end of the hills, with the Casentino Valley spread out before them, Masina asked Gino to pull the cart to the side of the road. She climbed down and dashed behind a stand of low trees. Minutes later, she returned wearing her dress. "Ah, freedom," she said with a smile as she tossed the leggings into the cart.

Gino noted the nearby farms as they descended into the valley. October was the time when farmers should have been harvesting zucca and late-year cabbage, but Gino saw activity at only a few farms. When they neared Poppi village, he gazed intently toward Tomasia's farm. He knew in which fields her husband had grown aubergines and melons, but he saw no sign that any crops had been planted in the past season. As he had feared, the farm looked abandoned.

Gino's father and his brother Laro were unloading wood from a wagon when he reached his family's farm. Almost disbelieving his own eyes, Laro shouted, "It's Gino!" when he saw his brother. As the cart drew closer and Laro could examine Masina's face, he thought, surely, she can't be Gabriela, the young girl Taddeo told us about.

The commotion drew Gino's mother, sisters, and brother Fanto from the farmhouse. Gino embraced every member of his family, then introduced Masina. "She's a healer, a selfless woman, who's been forced to flee from Florence because the advocati are determined to brand her as a witch."

With bitterness in her voice, Gino's mother said, "The advocati never upturn a rock without seeing evil under it." Then, in a sympathetic tone, she said to Masina, "Come inside, my dear. You must be tired after the long ride from Florence."

Sitting at the table with his parents, Gino described how the advocati had broken into Masina's rooms and confiscated her medicinal herbs. He explained she couldn't remain in Florence and needed a place to stay until she could decide on her future course. After hearing her plight, Gino's mother clasped Masina's hand and declared, "You can stay with us for as long as you need."

His father leaned back, rubbed his chin, and posed, "You're a healer?"

Masina merely nodded, but Gino elaborated. "She's treated dozens of women, maybe more than a hundred, for longer than I've known her. We've foraged together for medicinal plants in the fields around Florence, so I know many of her curatives are the same ones we make in the apothecary."

His father, still forming an idea, said. "There hasn't been a speziale in Poppi since the apothecary became a lawyer's office. The village ... the entire valley ... could benefit from having a skilled healer."

Gino asked, "If she were to stay in the valley, would she be beyond the reach of the advocati?"

"I've known the abbot at San Fedele since before you were born. He's never yielded to false claims of heresy or witchcraft," his father replied and reiterated his wife's offer for Masina to stay with them; then he suggested an alternative to her staying with his family. "One of the vacant houses in the valley might be available and afford you greater privacy for treating your clients."

After sharing a meal with his family, grateful for his mother's familiar food, Gino helped his father and his brother Laro gather firewood until mid-afternoon, when he climbed onto the cart for the lonely ride back to Florence.

26

Sunday December 10, 1346

Sundays were normally the one day each week when Lucia had time away from her duties as house servant at Casa Pagholi. This Sunday was the rare exception when Signora Pagholi needed Lucia's help to prepare for a special event.

Signor Pagholi's guild, the Magistrates' and Notaries' Guild, planned to hold a special celebration to commemorate its members' generous contributions to the convents whose shelters had kept thousands of poor Florentines and migrants from the surrounding countryside from starving during the food crisis. They, like their fellow guilds, religious confraternities, and wealthy aristocrats, had a proud long-standing tradition of caring for the city's needy. In an uncharacteristic move, the guild consuls had called upon members' wives to arrange the celebration for the next Sunday. The consuls assigned duties to each woman, and delighted Signora Pagholi by giving her the responsibility to provide the musical entertainment. She would need Lucia's help later in the day to prepare for the musician's audition, but she gave Lucia time in the morning to attend mass with her brother.

Since moving to Florence, Gino had tried to attend mass at a different church every Sunday as a way of familiarizing himself with his new city. He found parish priests reflected their personal priorities in their sermons. Some centered-on sin, evil, and the devil; others charged their flocks to care for the sick and helpless; while others told stories from scriptures and the Bible. As much as he appreciated hearing the variety of sermons, Gino found it even more interesting to observe the reactions of the other churchgoers. Fire and brimstone sermons made people stiffen with fear. He had seen other appeals bring forth compassion and understanding.

Gino led Lucia from Casa Pagholi toward the river to Santi Apostoli, said to be the oldest church in Florence and founded by Charlemagne. They stood amid the small flock when the priest approached the pulpit. "God hears you," the priest proclaimed. "He listens to your prayers. Your prayers," he repeated, "beseeching Him to end the deluge causing this terrible food shortage. And He will do what you ask…what we need. By His action, the holy season of Christ's birth we are about to enter, and the new year beyond, will be bountiful."

Gino watched the people nearby. All were listening with rapt attention. Some were nodding. A few elderly women kissed the rosary beads they were holding. The sermon echoed the predictions of men in taverns who had expressed similarly favorable outlooks, claiming the rain couldn't possibly continue much longer. Everyone hoped their propitious forecasts would prove correct, but despite the widely shared optimism, Gino found himself unable to dispel Professor Vianello's grim prediction of a future fraught with suffering.

Gino and Lucia returned to Casa Pagholi after mass. Signora Pagholi had heard accounts of twenty-year-old Francesco Landini, a musical prodigy who composed his own works. She wanted to hear him play before asking him to perform for the guild, so she had invited him to audition at her house. She was also curious to see the instrument he played, a small portable organ known as an organetto.

Signor Landini arrived shortly after Gino and Lucia had returned from mass. An aide carried Landini's instrument and guided him into the casa's reception room. The young musician with shoulder length black hair and a thin face settled in a chair, smiled, and said, "Unless someone already told you, I imagine you're surprised to learn I'm blind. It's the result of a childhood illness. Fortunately, eyes are unnecessary for making music."

Signora Pagholi introduced her husband, Gino, and Lucia, then she explained the nature of the guild event. "*Perfetto*," Landini said. "The secular songs I play should be appropriate for your event; I don't play religious chants." He began by playing a popular caccia that everyone recognized. With the instrument balanced on his knee, the fingers of one hand danced over the keys while his other hand, out of sight behind the instrument, pumped the bellows. While he played, Signora Pagholi's eyes brightened; obviously delighted by his performance. When he finished, he said, "I like to play songs where the music is accompanied by voices. I recently composed a ballata you might enjoy. It's a lovely song, but it needs two voices. I can sing one part. Is there someone who could sing the second part?"

When no one volunteered, Gino said, "Gabriela Roselli has a wonderful voice. I've heard her sing with her church choir."

"She doesn't live far," Signora Pagholi said; then she and Lucia coaxed Gino to fetch Gabriela.

When Gabriela answered his knock, he explained the reason for his unexpected presence. "How delightful," she gushed and grasped Gino's hand. "Let's go."

Gino stood firm. "Are your mother or father able to accompany you?"

"They're away. They won't return until late." She tugged on his hand and repeated, "Let's go." They trotted down the stairs hand-in-hand. The short distance to Casa Pagholi marked the first time Gino had ever been alone with Gabriela. Although they were merely walking in daylight on a busy street, Gino felt his heart beating faster.

Landini played a variety of traditional songs and his own compositions, so the audition lasted longer than anyone had expected. Landini took pleasure in teaching Gabriela his compositions as much as she enjoyed singing them. After they had sung only a few songs, Signora Pagholi felt certain the musical entertainment for the guild event should include both Francesco Landini and Gabriela Roselli. She would ask her husband to get Signor Roselli's permission for Gabriela to attend the event.

As time wore on, Gino became increasingly fearful Gabriela's parents might return home before her. She would be shamed if her parents learned she and Gino had been together without a chaperone. He endured teasing from Gabriela and his sister, but ultimately he persuaded Lucia to accompany them when Gabriela returned home.

27

Tuesday May 2, 1347

The priests were wrong, as were the men in taverns who swore sustained rains happened only once in a century. After the wettest winter in many years, steady rain started falling in March, a month earlier than the traditional beginning of spring rains. With hardly a break throughout the month, cold hard rain fell day upon day, mixed with hail on many nights. As it had the year before, the wet weather continued through the planting season, April into May. Laughter and joy were rare in the countryside and in the city. Dismal conditions had dulled everyone's spirits.

In early May, Gino eagerly awaited his meeting with Wiener and Taddeo, whom he hadn't seen in nearly two months. He entered the Spotted Dog tavern, removed his cloak, and ran a finger along the underside of the fabric. Water had soaked through the dense wool pile, leaving the cloak's inside nearly as wet as its outside. Little wonder his tunic felt moist.

He carried a pitcher of beer to a vacant table, filled his mug, and waited for his friends to join him. Soon Wiener arrived, but without his usual wit. He grunted a perfunctory greeting as he sat and raised a mug to his lips. After taking a long drink, he dropped both elbows onto the table, leaned forward, and groaned, "This is turning out to be another piss-poor year."

Gino raised a glass to signal his agreement. His expression turned to puzzlement when Wiener voiced what sounded like an illogical comment: "Genoa is putting pressure on Venice."

"They've been feuding with each other for years, so what prompts you to remark on it now?" Gino asked.

"Venice has been feeding its people with grain from Sicily," Wiener replied. "Now, Genoa is blocking Venetian ships from reaching ports in Sicily." Before Gino realized the implications of that statement, Wiener added, "Since the Venetians are being denied access to Sicily, they've turned to Romagna as a source of grain."

"The same place where you…" Gino began, before Wiener interrupted him.

"Exactly! The same farms where we've been getting grain for the past year. And if Venice taking a share of the grain isn't bad enough, this damned rain has halved the harvest yields at those farms. We just returned from the Po Valley, where many of the farmers who had been selling grain to us said they'd already sold their stores to Venetian merchants."

Wiener took another drink, then slammed his mug down forcefully enough to draw the attention of men at other tables. "And I'm the one who gets blamed for the meager hauls. The granary managers cursed me because I couldn't deliver them a full measure. I should look for other work," he grumbled.

"Does the Signoria know about the Venetians?" Gino asked.

"I doubt it, and I'll not be the one to tell them. I've already taken enough abuse. You can go tell your friend Signor Pagholi. At least he won't hold you responsible."

Gino was half standing, preparing to leave, when Taddeo entered and growled, "This entire world is going to shit." He dropped onto a chair and said, "I might just sit here drinking until I empty every barrel in this tavern." He leaned forward, his head in his hands, and stared at Gino. "I'm sorry to be the bearer of disturbing news, my friend."

Gino said, "It couldn't be worse than Wiener's news."

Taddeo ignored Gino's comment. "I just returned from the Casentino Valley. I couldn't find a single farm with a crop in the ground. Many looked abandoned." Taddeo took a deep breath, then added, "Including your family's farm."

Gino stiffened. "That can't be," he protested.

"I saw no one at their farm. The house was dark. I knocked, but no one answered."

"They could have been visiting someone," Gino said, sounding more desperate than hopeful.

"I looked in the barn and some of your father's tools were missing. Would he have taken his axe if he were just visiting someone?"

The muscles in Gino's neck tightened; his mouth went dry. He felt his heart pounding. "Where could they have gone?" he asked, although he knew Taddeo couldn't have an answer. Taddeo simply spread his arms and shrugged.

Without another word, Gino donned his cloak and walked out into the rain. He didn't feel the cold droplets striking his face or the water soaking into his shoes as he splashed through deep puddles. He walked for several minutes without a clear destination in mind until the sound of a church bell cleared his thinking. It was too late in the day to ride to Poppi, but he vowed to go there in the morning, leaving at daybreak. All he could do now was relay Wiener's news to Messer Pagholi.

He pulled the bell rope at the rear entrance of Casa Pagholi and was greeted by his sister. He had decided not to tell her what Taddeo had said about their family being missing. There was no reason to worry her unless he could confirm Taddeo's claim. Even then, he might not tell her, as the news would only make her distraught. Lucia smiled at her brother and urged him to hurry inside. "Quickly. Come in here where it's dry. You look like a wet dog … and you smell like one." Gino stepped inside and removed his cloak. Lucia joked, "I just baked sweet rolls for supper. Is it their aroma that drew you here?"

"I wish your baking was my reason for coming, but I have some troubling news for Messer Pagholi. Is he at home?"

"I'll tell him you want to see him. You can wait in the reception room."

Gino went to the reception room and gazed out a window waiting for the magistrate, but it was his sister who came into the room. "Messer Pagholi is in his study. He asked me to bring you there." Gino had been to the study previously and could have gone there alone, but Lucia fulfilled her duties as house servant and escorted her brother to the room on the second level.

Pagholi looked up when Gino entered. "I understand you have news for me."

Gino repeated the information Wiener had given him about the Venetians taking a quantity of grain from Romagna. Pagholi closed his eyes, stroked his chin, and said, "This could be a disaster; our granaries have only a one-week supply of grain." He pointed at a chair. "Sit. Let me think."

For several minutes, Pagholi said nothing other than mumbling a few words, as though talking to himself. Finally, he opened his eyes and proclaimed, "I might have a solution. Genoa may have a grievance against Venice, but they have no quarrel with us. If Venice can't take Sicilian grain, the grain should be available for us." He continued speaking, but now to himself. "We'll need ships to sail from Pisa, an entire fleet of ships. The Genovese will have no reason to harass Pisan ships flying Florentine standards."

Pagholi stood. "I must go inform the Signoria." He rested a hand on Gino's shoulder. "Thank you for bringing me this news so quickly. The Signoria needs to act without delay because it will take time to assemble a fleet of ships." Pagholi rushed from the room, leaving Gino sitting in his study.

After he heard Pagholi leave the house, Gino climbed the stairs to the third level, where he found his sister working in the kitchen. She said, "It seems there was an urgency to your meeting."

"Yes, we've lost our sources of grain in Romagna. Messer Pagholi has gone to meet with the Signoria to devise a plan for bringing grain from Sicily."

Lucia glanced at the pot on the fireplace and surmised, "If he's gone to meet with the Signoria at this hour, I may need to delay supper. Their sessions are never brief."

Seeing Lucia brought Taddeo's bad news to the front of Gino's thinking. He embraced his sister, kissed her on the forehead, and told himself again he would not share Taddeo's news with her. They chatted at length about more pleasant matters, and when Gino finally turned to leave, Lucia handed him one of her freshly baked sweet rolls. "I'm sure this will go well with whatever you make for your own supper," she said.

28

Tuesday May 2, 1347

Gino sat with a mug of ale in his hand, watching the flickering flames in his fireplace as he had often done on the farm with his brother Fanto when they were youngsters. They had delighted in watching the fire, eagerly waiting for twigs to crackle and shoot dazzling sparks into the air. He recalled fondly those good times when his family was together and safe. Now, if Taddeo's observation was correct, his family was missing.

Gino continued watching until the last flame had died, leaving only embers before climbing into bed, closing his eyes, and trying to sleep. But sleep didn't come easily. One minute he felt cold and pulled the coverlet around him. The next minute he was too warm and pushed the coverlet aside. He turned over again and again, struggling to find a comfortable position. He fell asleep only to be awakened by a frightful dream of Taddeo shouting, "No one was there! Your family is gone!"

Eventually he found a few hours of fitful slumber. Had he been sleeping soundly, as he often did, he wouldn't have heard the bells at Santa Maria Novella, but on this morning the ringing of lauds at dawn woke him.

Gino dressed and combed his hair. He had had no appetite the previous evening, so he'd not eaten the sweet roll his sister had given him. He took the roll and his rain cloak and set out across the city to the apothecary, where he left a note for Signor Roselli, before continuing to a stable near the Porta al Croce gate. Thick gray clouds blocked most of the early morning light, but Gino knew the main roads well enough to find his way.

The owner wasn't at the stable when Gino arrived, so he roused the stableboy, who had been posted as the overnight guard and should have been awake. The groggy youngster managed to saddle a horse, although he wasn't alert enough to collect the hiring fee, and Gino was too distracted to remind him.

Gino saw no one as he rode away from the city to the foothills. In normal times, the road would have held a stream of farm wagons heading to Florence; now there were none. He considered stopping at Taddeo's house to warm himself by the fire and dispel the morning chill, but he decided not to disturb Taddeo or his wife at the early hour. Shortly after passing Taddeo's house, he pulled out the sweet roll Lucia had given him. His first bite reminded him that even as a young girl, his sister had been a skilled cook. She had learned well from another excellent cook, their mother. The first meal Lucia had ever prepared on her own was a honey chestnut breakfast flatcake. She had insisted on collecting chestnuts in the nearby forest, grinding the nuts into flour, and mixing the batter by herself. She only needed help in cooking the cakes because she was too young to lift the heavy iron pan.

The tasty roll merely whet Gino's appetite, making him wish he had brought with him more than just the roll. There were no inns along the road, so he would have to wait until he reached Poppi before getting something else to eat. When he came within sight of the Casentino Valley, he stopped at the same place where Masina had asked him to stop the wagon so she could remove her leggings when he had spirited her away from Florence. Was she still somewhere in the valley treating needy women, or had she gone to another city? Riding through the valley, he realized how Taddeo had concluded the farms were deserted: he saw no one. He tried to fool himself into believing it was too early for people to be out working in the fields or tending their animals, but long experience told him farmers always began their chores at first light. The absence of people was telling.

Gino dismounted when he reached the dirt track leading to the Liani farm. There were only two sets of wagon tracks on the path leading to the farmhouse. He assumed they were made by Taddeo's wagon, heading to the farmhouse and returning. He walked ahead, studying the ground as he went. Although rain would have washed away older tracks, prints should still have been visible from his father's wagon when the family went to church or when his father and brother Fanto went into the hills to gather firewood. But there were no tracks other than those made by Taddeo's wagon.

At the house the door was latched, as Taddeo had said. Gino pushed the door, but it wouldn't open. Its latch had failed or jammed. He rapped on the door and called out, but got no response. Peering in through a window, he saw no signs of anyone was inside. Moving around to the side of the house, he looked through a kitchen window, yearning to see his mother making soup or mending clothes. All he saw was a dark, empty room.

In the barn, just as Taddeo had said, the rack where his father's axe was normally kept was empty. From another rack, Gino took a heavy blade used for scraping leather and returned to the house. He wedged the blade between the door and the jamb and tried to pivot the blade to release the latch, but the blade didn't extend far enough to reach the latch. Leaving the blade in place, Gino returned to the barn to search for another tool. On a worktable, he spotted an awl with a long, thin shank, long enough to reach the latch.

Using the blade to pry open the latch, and the awl to lift the mechanism, he carefully opened the door. The house smelled musty, as though it had been shut for a long time. The massive stone fireplace capable of holding heat for days was now cold. Utensils and his mother's favorite cooking pot, the one large enough to hold soup for the entire family, were missing. The only clothes left behind in the bedrooms were old, torn garments, the ones they wore when doing the dirtiest jobs on the farm.

Gino sat at the table in the kitchen, staring at the far wall. "Where could they have gone?" he asked himself. "Why didn't they tell me they were leaving?" He repeated, "Why didn't they tell me?" then realized they couldn't have told him. They didn't know where he lived in Florence or how to contact him. Taddeo was the only person who could have delivered a message to him, and Taddeo had stopped going to the Casentino Valley because the farms there had no produce to sell.

He tried thinking of places where they might have gone. When the apothecary in Poppi had closed, his parents were convinced he would find work in Florence. Since they believed Florence offered opportunities, it's possible, he surmised, they might have gone there as well. He wondered, could we possibly be living in the same city without seeing each other? Florence is a big city, but is it big enough that we could spend weeks, maybe more than a month, moving through the same city without crossing paths? It didn't seem likely. Arezzo was another place they could have gone. It was nearby, but it was only a small town and wouldn't offer his father many prospects for work.

He walked to the river's edge, little more than a stream compared to its appearance in Florence. A drifting tree branch held his gaze until it passed beyond the farm boundary. My parents might have told a neighbor where they were going, he thought. His mother had always been close to the woman who lived on the adjacent farm. Returning to the farmhouse, he noticed his horse grubbing at a small patch of weeds, looking for tender shoots. The steed looked nearly as despondent as Gino felt. From the barn Gino retrieved a bucket partially filled with animal feed. Watching the animal devour the oats, Gino remarked, "Your needs are more easily satisfied than mine." After the horse had its fill, Gino mounted and rode to the nearby farm. There were no wagon tracks or hoof prints on the path to the farmhouse and when he reached it, he found it too was vacant.

If the farms are all vacant, someone in the village center might have information, he hoped. When he reached the village, he found two shops that had been in Poppi for as long as he could remember: the candlemaker's shop and the metalworker's shop. Both were closed. Apparently, the farm crisis had affected not only farmers but also those who served the farmers. It had always been common to see people shopping in the village center, but now Gino saw no one. Finally, he came upon one shop still operating, the butcher shop. The bearded, muscular man slicing a pork belly raised an eyebrow when Gino entered his shop and said, "Gino Liani, I never thought I'd see you again."

"It's been nearly two years since I last came to the village," Gino said. "I'm pleased to see your shop is still open. Others haven't fared as well."

"Bah, these are difficult times," the butcher groaned, then gestured to the meat resting on the block in front of him, and said, "But people must eat. I'll be here as long as animals roam the hills, and hunters bring carcasses to me."

Gino said, "I've come to Poppi looking for my family. They aren't at the farm. Might they have told you where they went?"

The butcher shook his head. "They didn't tell me anything. When your folks stopped coming here, I just assumed they'd left, like all the others."

More discouraged than ever, Gino continued exploring the village. The lawyer's office, which had replaced the apothecary, was dark and lifeless. The windows were boarded up, leaving him to wonder whether the closure was temporary or if the lawyer had joined the mass exodus. He stopped at two more shops, but neither shopkeeper could give him any helpful information.

There was no one else in the village for Gino to ask. He sank down onto a rock outcropping and gazed mindlessly at a swirl of dust drifting along the street, blown away by a steady breeze. The dust disappeared like the pillars of his life; his family and the town he knew had vanished. A slight movement of Gino's foot startled a small bird hopping along the ground. His eyes followed the bird's flight as it winged skyward and headed toward the San Fedele Abbey bell tower.

"The abbot," Gino said as he stood. His father and the abbot had been friends. The abbot was his last hope of finding anyone who might know where his family had gone. He walked his horse past the remaining shops and continued to San Fedele Abbey at the end of the road. He waited impatiently on a bench in the garden until the monks' prayer session ended. Another person might have appreciated the pungent scents of jasmine and lavender permeating the garden, fragrances Gino knew well from his work at the perfumery, but his mind was too preoccupied to notice. Finally, a novitiate approached him. The young monk had a round, boyish face and reminded Gino of his youngest brother, Laro. "Have you come to this abbey recently?" Gino asked.

The monk, conscious of his youth, squared his shoulders and tried to stand tall. "I was sent here two months past from the Abbey of Chiaravalle in Piacenza."

Gino asked, "Is the food shortage as severe in Piacenza as in this valley?"

The novitiate's eyes brightened. He appreciated Gino's serious question, which was unlike remarks often made to him by some monks at the abbey who treated him like a child. "The shortage is less of a problem in Piacenza because farms there grow rice," he replied. "Rice is more tolerant of wet soil than wheat or barley. I brought a few rice grains with me. We sowed them in the garden and the plants are growing well. Would you like to see them?"

"Perhaps later. I'm here to see the abbot."

"Yes, of course. The abbot's office is …"

Before the novitiate could finish, Gino stood and said, "Thank you. I know how to find his office."

The abbot greeted Gino warmly, saying, "I heard you've found success in Florence. The Holy Mother must be looking on you with great favor because few people are faring well in these troubled times."

Gino bowed his head slightly and said, "I've been blessed."

"As has your sister, Lucia. I understand she's also in Florence and working for a very important magistrate." Gino wondered how that information had reached the abbot, but he didn't ask. The abbot shifted in his chair as he recalled, "You are the one who brought a healer to our community." Then, laughing, he said, "Your father told me she was being hunted as a witch in Florence. We've certainly seen no evidence of witchcraft here. Since coming here, she's done God's work treating the sick."

"Is Masina still in the valley?"

"Oh, yes. Many have left, but not her. She has stayed."

"My family is among those who've had to leave. Perchance, you've heard where they've gone?"

"Your father came to see me, to tell me they could remain no longer. Leaving was a hard decision for him. He loved his farm and this village, as did your mother. On the day they left, I went to their farm to bless them and their wagon, asking God to let it carry them to a better future. It was heartbreaking to see them, and all the other families leave. Your mother and your sisters were in tears. Your brothers were resigned, but I could see in their eyes they were fearful. They all knew the time had come, but knowing didn't make it less painful."

"Did they say where they were going?"

"To Pisa. Your father said he has a cousin in Pisa who's a carpenter. He hoped to find work with his cousin."

"His cousin," Gino echoed, and rubbed his chin. He had only the vaguest recollection of hearing his father mention a cousin in Pisa. "Did he say the cousin's name? Or where he could be found in Pisa?"

"No, he said neither, but Pisa isn't a big city like Florence." The abbot showed a weak smile. "How many carpenter shops can there be in Pisa?"

The abbot told Gino what had become of his family, but the journey to Poppi had left Gino with unanswered questions. He couldn't take a week away from work to journey to Pisa searching for his family. Was there another way to contact them? To find whether his father had found work? To know whether they were safe? What should he tell his sister? Would it distress her to learn her family had left the farm without knowing they were secure in a new life?

29

Monday October 8, 1347

The Signoria had arranged a celebration when the first barges carrying Sicilian grain had arrived from Pisa. Hundreds of Florentines had gathered along the riverfront to watch the procession of four huge barges approach the city dock and wait their turns to unload. People who had only days before complained and criticized city officials, chatted amicably with strangers and cheered the speeches made by members of the Signoria, the merchants who had organized the grain purchases, and even a barge captain. Interspersed between the speeches, musicians and jugglers entertained the crowd.

As he stepped up to speak, one member of the Signoria, a banker by trade, stared a hard eye at a rival banker who had argued vehemently for Florence to lend support to Venice. "Thank the Lord," the speaker began, "we Florentines had the wisdom to remain neutral in the feud between Venice and Genoa. The Genovese fleet is blocking the ships of Venice and its allies from ports in fertile Sicily. Our neutrality has allowed our ships sailing from Pisa to bring this grain and fresh produce from Sicily without encountering opposition." He finished to the applause of all except his rival, who spat on the ground and thrust his hand upward in an obscene gesture. "They waited until hundreds starved in the streets before doing anything," the man barked loudly enough to be heard by those around him. Although Florentines hadn't yet been nourished by the Sicilian grain, they believed their worst days were behind them; the food shortage was nearing an end, and Florence could look forward to a glorious future.

The Signoria's meticulous planning ensured that the first grain shipment bypassed warehouses and granaries entirely. Dockworkers unloaded the barges directly into a line of waiting wagons ready to carry their loads to grain mills. Bakers throughout the city had been directed to stoke their ovens and be prepared to receive wagonloads of flour, as much as they could use. No longer would Florentines go hungry.

***

The celebration of the first grain arrival had occurred months ago. Now the euphoria of that auspicious day had faded, but its promise had been fulfilled. Counters in bakery shops held loaves of bread and fancy pastries. Grandmothers sat beside the river, feeding crusts of stale bread to hungry birds. Peasants who had streamed into the city began returning to the countryside, hoping to revive their interrupted lives.

October brought cool air to Florence. Cool, but not clean. Through the heat of summer, Gino had become inured to the city's smells, but cool October days reminded him of one difference between Florence and Poppi. Gino enjoyed walking, and on autumn mornings in Poppi with its crisp air, he had relished long walks from the farm to the village center. But in Florence, his walks were shorter. In the mornings, going from his house to the apothecary, he often chose a route along the river because breezes from the western highlands seemed to follow the river and dispel the city's offensive odors.

***

One clear morning, he stopped near the docks, surprised to see a barge approaching. Two men aboard stood with poles in hand, one at the craft's fore end and the other at the rear, guiding the vessel to the dock. The one at the front had a young man's bearing. He stood straight and handled his pole with firm, forceful movements. His associate had slumped shoulders and the paunch of an older man. Laborers came out from a nearby warehouse ready to unload the craft. The barge must have left Pisa at daybreak, Gino thought, for it to have already made the journey to Florence.

Gino locked his eyes on the man at the near end of the barge. He looked familiar. Gino quickened his pace as he moved toward the dock. When the barge reached the dock, the men set their poles aside, jumped onto the dock, and fastened ropes to secure the craft. As they did so, they were turned so Gino couldn't see their faces clearly.

Finally, the near man stood and gazed past the warehouses toward the city center, giving Gino a clear view of his face. "Fanto!" he shouted. His brother swiveled to find the person who had called his name.

"Gino!" the younger brother responded. The two men rushed toward each other and embraced.

"You've grown so tall and so strong," Gino said as he grasped his brother's bicep. He ran a finger over the scraggly stubble at Fanto's chin. "These whiskers don't make it easy to recognize you either. "

Fanto teased, "I've always been tall and strong, dear brother, and if you've forgotten, it's only because your memory has lapsed since we've last seen each other."

"I was told the farm had been deserted and when I went there, all of you were gone. The abbot at San Fedele told me you went to Pisa, but I had no way to contact you."

"We wanted to tell you we were leaving, but we had no way to contact you either. We didn't know where you were in Florence." Fanto spread his hands in resignation. "It was awful. The rain just wouldn't stop, so we couldn't plant anything. Nothing would grow. As the months wore on, our stores of dried vegetables and smoked meat dwindled, so we couldn't stay on the farm. Father thought about taking us here, to Florence, but he heard that other farmers who had come here ended up as beggars. Since there's no work for farmers in the city, he decided we should go to Pisa."

"The abbot told me father has a cousin who owns a carpenter shop."

"Yes. Everyone calls him Legnoso. He's a big, cheerful character who's always laughing. He welcomed us immediately and put father to work in his shop making furniture for ships. Shipbuilding is a hectic business in Pisa. Legnoso gave Laro a job too, sweeping the shop floor. Our young brother is no longer a child."

"How are mother and the girls?"

"They're well. Mother works at a shop making and repairing sails. She says sewing sails is easier work than making clothes."

"I'm relieved to hear all of you are well. Lucia and I have been worried. Father made the best decision by taking you to Pisa. Hundreds, maybe a thousand, people came to Florence when their farms failed, and most couldn't find work. Now they're beggars living in the streets. Hundreds had starved before grain and produce was brought here from Sicily." Gino leaned back and appraised his younger brother. "You appear to be thriving as a barge captain."

Fanto laughed. "I'm not a captain, just a deckhand. These river barges," he said, pointing, "don't have captains. The person at the rear is the steerman. He's the barge master. I just help with the poling when we come into a dock." He placed a hand on Gino's arm. "Until this week, I'd been working on barges in the canals around Pisa. This is only my second time in Florence ... and who should be here to greet me but my brother? I can hardly believe it. Are you doing well, dear brother?"

"I'm doing well, as is Lucia. She works for a kind mistress who treats her like a daughter."

"Mother will be happy to hear God's mercy has protected her children. Every night, she prays for the Lord to keep you safe." Flashing a grin, Fanto asked, "Are you betrothed yet?"

"No. Gabriela and I are close, but her father may have other plans for her." Eager to change the subject, Gino said, "Since you're a recent visitor to Florence, let me show you the sights. There's much to see, and we can visit Lucia. She'll be delighted to see you."

Fanto turned so he could view the barge. "I'd love to spend more time with you, but the dockworkers were quick at unloading the barge and now they've almost finished loading the goods for us to take to Pisa, so I can't stay. Maybe in the future I can arrange for a visit." The brothers embraced again before Fanto returned to the dock. Gino watched Fanto re-board the barge and continued looking downriver until his brother vanished around a curve.

***

Two weeks later, October 24, 1347

The usual din filled the guild hall when Gino entered. He immediately spotted a group of the guild's younger members, none more than ten years older than he, with whom he had socialized at prior meetings. "Gino!" one of them called as he approached. "Maybe you can help us. We're looking to pursue a different activity on Sunday and thought hunting might be a pleasant diversion."

Gino laughed. "You're all city dwellers. What do you know about hunting?"

One man jested, "I know we'll need a bow and arrow."

"An arrow?" Gino probed firmly. "You'll need more than one arrow." Still laughing, he added, "And maybe more than one bow."

"All the more reason we need your guidance," the man responded. "You're a country boy. You must be an expert hunter."

"What do you intend to hunt?"

"There are wild boars in the woods," another man replied, "and I like the taste of cinghiale."

Laughing so hard that he verged on tears, Gino said, "If you go into the woods where there are wild boars, they'll be the hunters and you'll be the prey. If you really intend to go hunting, you had best start with a less fierce creature, like a squirrel."

"I've never eaten squirrel. What do they taste like?" the man asked.

"Exactly like boar, except they're smaller," Gino joked. The other men, who had eaten both boar and squirrel, laughed raucously.

The room quieted when one of the guild's two consuls approached the lectern. He had previously served as guild secretary; following tradition, he was elevated to consul in the recent election. Gino recognized him as the owner of the apothecary shop Gino had passed while walking near the Santa Croce church on his first night in Florence.

After calling the meeting to order, the consul explained the need to plan an event for All Saints' Day. Only recently had the guild paid heed to All Saints' Day, and some members felt it inappropriate. They believed only churches, not guilds, should celebrate religious holidays. Other members cited the silk guild's contribution to the building of the new cathedral, claiming the patronage had earned the silk guild great favor with the public. The consul allowed a brief debate before quelling the opposition and securing support for his proposal.

When the formal meeting ended, Gino wandered around the hall, eavesdropping on conversations. Most were casual exchanges, but one group seemed centered on a disturbing topic. A man whom Gino held in high regard said, "It's a sickness never seen before. It shows as dark swellings on necks and in armpits." Those around him listened in awe. "The treatments they tried were ineffective, and all those who contracted the disease died within days. "

A doctor clad in his distinctive red robe said cynically as he walked past, "They must not have competent doctors."

"How is it spread?" someone asked.

"No one knows, but it's spreading fast," the authority replied. "It was first detected only one week ago and a bargeman today said already large numbers in the city have been affected."

Moving closer, Gino asked, "Where is this sickness?" expecting to be told the name of a distant land.

"Pisa," the authority answered. His response made Gino shiver.

30

Tuesday January 29, 1348

At guild social events, Gino had met the sons of other speziali, men his own age who invited him to join their bocce competition. Even though he couldn't match the skill of men who had played the game since they had learned to walk, he enjoyed the sport and welcomed the camaraderie. The games were an uplifting respite from the depressing conditions detailed by patrons at the apothecary. Lucia often accompanied him to the games to cheer his modest attempts and his rare victories. At first, he appreciated having her there, but he grew ambivalent when the men started paying attention to her and she acknowledged their interest. When pressed by Masina, Gino had been forced to admit Lucia was old enough to be married, but she was also his younger sister; in his mind, a girl who still needed his protection.

The speziali and their families were amicable, but many of the guild's doctors were arrogant prigs. At guild meetings, they rarely even gave a nod to a passing speziale. They paraded around the guild hall flapping their bright red cloaks as though they were giant birds. The worst among them carried the same pompous attitude to their medical practices. They gave no information to patients. If asked, they shared only the Latin name of a patient's ailment and sent him to the apothecary with a note in cryptic Latin.

Others, though, honored the creed of rendering the best care to those in need. One of them, Doctor Guarino, occasionally came to the apothecary for curatives, so he could administer them to patients himself and observe the effects. “People are not all the same. What cures one person might do little for another,” he had told Gino.

Shortly after Gino began working at the apothecary, Signor Roselli had confided to him, “Of all the doctors who send patients to my shop, the one I respect the most is Franco Guarino. Whenever anyone in my family is sick, we consult him, no one else.”

Roselli wasn’t the only person who appreciated Guarino’s skill. Wealthy aristocrats from other districts frequently came soliciting the doctor’s services for themselves and members of their family. With one exception, he told them he couldn’t attend to more patients, so they should find a doctor in their own neighborhood. The exception was a boy of thirteen years whose condition had grown worse despite having been treated by two other doctors. Guarino diagnosed the boy’s condition and prescribed a successful remedy. Now, years later, the boy had grown, married, had a child of his own, and moved to Guarino’s neighborhood so his son could have the best medical care.

Frequently, the doctor asked to have preparations delivered to his office, a task Gino relished because visits to Guarino’s office were always learning experiences. Gino admired the doctor’s dedication, and Guarino appreciated Gino’s ambition and curiosity. He’d often encouraged Gino to apply to the university’s medical school, telling him, “You’d make a fine doctor and you’re still a young man. It’s not too late for you to attend the university.” Gino accepted the compliment, although he had neither the academic training nor the financial resources to comply with the doctor’s suggestion.

Guarino was a rugged man with a ruddy complexion and a well-trimmed beard. In his office, he dispensed with his red hat and black robe and pushed the sleeves of his red cloak up to his elbows. He was examining a patient when Gino entered the office. The man sat on a bench, his arms dangling limp at his sides. His face tensed with pain, and he moved sluggishly in response to Guarino’s directions.

“This is the preparation you requested,” Gino said as he held up a cup containing a thick green liquid.

"It's for a patient who's coming later, so for now put it there," Guarino said, pointing to a side table. "Come here and feel this man's head. He's warm," the doctor instructed. Gino touched a hand to the patient's forehead and pulled away quickly. The man's head was hot, not moist with sweat, as it might have been from heavy labor, but hot and dry. Guarino said, "He has a headache." The man nodded in agreement. "And look at this," the doctor said as he pulled the man's hair aside, revealing a darkened lump on his neck.

The darkened lump matched a symptom of the disease said to be devastating people in Pisa — Gino closed his eyes for an instant while he spoke to God: "Please Lord, not my family." — but the reports from Pisa had not mentioned headaches and overheating. Perhaps this ailment was different.

Guarino said, "The problem appears to be an excess of yellow bile, an unusual condition at this time of year. Yellow bile is usually a problem in the summer. But I must be certain." He handed the patient a cup. "Piss into this."

The man pulled up his tunic and held the cup. After a minute of grimacing, he said, "I can't make it happen. It only comes when it's ready."

"Many patients say the same, but there's a way to make it happen," Guarino said as he placed his meaty hand on the man's bladder and pressed down, alternating between increased and decreased pressure. "Now lean forward." The patient grunted and a moment later, a pale-yellow stream flowed into the cup. When the cup received its last drop, the liquid had reached nearly to the rim.

Guarino lifted the cup to his nose, taking care not to spill its contents. "This is the most certain way to tell which of the humors is out of balance," he said to Gino. He inhaled. "As I thought, an excess of yellow bile," he said and handed the cup to Gino.

Gino sniffed. Unsure, he sniffed again and guessed, "It smells salty... and sour, like fermenting oats."

"An excellent observation for one with no training. All urine smells salty, but in this one the salt odor is stronger than normal and the scent you called sour is especially telling. There are other indications too. Urine tells all the body's secrets. With practice, you could learn to detect more than just the sour smell."

To the patient, Guarino said, "Go to the apothecary with Signor Liani. He'll prepare a mustard compound to let you expel the excess yellow bile and a laurel berry spread to relieve your headache. You'll be fine in a day or two."

Two Days Later

Doctor Guarino grumbled to himself as he plodded into the apothecary with his red cap askew and the sleeves of his wrinkled robe rolled halfway to his elbows. He laid his large hands on the counter and leaned forward to meet Signor Roselli's face. Gino came into the apothecary from the perfumery when he saw the big man enter the shop. Guarino said, "I expected Stefanelli to come to my office again yesterday so I could adjust his treatment, but he never came. Today his house servant came instead. The distraught young girl couldn't get intelligible words out. Her sobs made it clear Stefanelli's condition had deteriorated, so I closed up shop and accompanied her to his house."

Gino noticed Guarino's distress and moved a chair close to him. The doctor nodded his appreciation for the kind gesture and lowered his bulky frame onto the seat. He said, "Stefanelli has two boys. I've treated both since they were infants. The oldest is now in his tenth year. When he saw me, he said, 'My father is sick, and it smells bad in the house. Our mother said we shouldn't go inside.' My nose is proficient at detecting even the weakest scent, so I didn't need to enter the house to know his comment was truthful. Standing outside in the open, I could smell the bad air leaking out from the house.

"When the house servant heard me tell the boys to remain outside, she froze in her stead. Only by cajoling could I get her to follow me into the house. She stopped by the door and merely pointed to Stefanelli's bedroom. In the darkened room I could make out the figure of his wife standing by his bedside, sobbing. When I pushed aside the window covering to have enough light for an examination, she said Stefanelli had complained the light hurt his eyes. It must have been an old complaint, because the man I saw had his eyes closed and said nothing when a shaft of light fell upon his face. In just the two days since I'd seen him last, he'd withered. His wife said he hadn't eaten."

Guarino looked up at Gino. "Your mustard paste was effective. It forced him to expel yellow bile, as it should have. A bucket next to his bed was half filled with vomit."

"Did the laurel berry cure his headache?" Gino asked.

"I can't say. He didn't complain of a headache, but nothing he said had meaning. He only babbled incoherent words. His head was hotter than it had been when he was in my office. I had his wife bring a towel soaked with cool water and placed it on his forehead. In minutes, the towel was hot and needed to be replaced. Twice more, I replaced it before I left his side with instructions for his wife to continue changing the towel.

"The room reeked like a dead animal. Initially, I thought the dreadful stench came from the vomit, but when I examined the lump on his neck, I saw it had doubled in size and burst open, splattering creamy pus onto his bedclothes and the bed linens. Two new small lumps had formed on the back of his neck. I stripped him and the bed and rolled the coverings into a ball, taking care to keep the pus splatters to the inside. I carried the ball out of the bedroom, pressed it into the house servant's hands and ordered her to burn it. She shuddered, but had no choice other than to take the stinking ball from me. She held it at arm's length away from her body and turned toward the fireplace until I shouted at her to burn it outside." Guarino raised his hand, palm upward, in a symbol of resignation. "I couldn't blame her for being frightened; it was a devilish experience. I'd been through it before, but it was an unimaginable ordeal for the poor girl. When I saw the terror in her eyes after she burned the clothes, I couldn't ask her to empty the bucket. I emptied it myself."

Guarino stood, walked across the room, and turned back to face the two speziali. "Everything we doctors have learned from the time of Aristotle says the treatment should have cured him, but it didn't. He'd gotten worse…far worse…in only two days. I told his wife I was coming here to get treatments for the lumps, but his condition had deteriorated so quickly I also told her to summon a priest. It pained me to concede her husband was nearing the end. She swooned and would have collapsed to the floor had I not caught her. I took her to a chair and quickly checked her forehead for overheating and her neck for lumps. Thank the Lord she had none of Stefanelli's symptoms."

Roselli pressed the issue, "Two people came here today seeking treatments for headaches, but neither mentioned overheating nor lumps."

Guarino explained, "The lumps are easily hidden by hair, so they might not be noticed without a careful examination."

Roselli asked, "Do you think Stefanelli is afflicted with the same disease plaguing Pisa?"

"His wife said he hasn't traveled to Pisa or anywhere else. He manages an iron smelter outside the city. She has no notion of how he might have contracted the disease."

Roselli said, "The lumps sound similar to those reported in Pisa."

"Reports from Pisa mention blackened lumps, but the reports are incomplete. They don't mention headaches or overheating, and we don't know what treatments they've used. For Stefanelli, I want to try using onion to draw the poisons from the lumps."

"Onion paste," Roselli repeated as he headed to the preparation room.

Guarino thought for a minute, then said, "I'd also like to try using turmeric."

Gino raised an eyebrow. "I've never heard of turmeric to extract poisons, but I can combine turmeric with oil to make a paste."

"It's a little-known treatment for skin problems, but I'd be remiss if I overlooked anything that might help."

Roselli returned from the preparation room and handed Guarino a cup containing an onion slurry. Moments later, Gino returned with a cup containing an orange-colored paste made from turmeric. "Do you think Stefanelli's wife has the strength to summon a priest, or should I?" Gino asked.

"I don't believe she can even stand."

Gino and Guarino left the apothecary. The doctor made his way to Stefanelli's house, while Gino headed to the neighborhood church.

***

Later, when the priest came to Stefanelli's house, Guarino said, "He's gone, father. It happened so quickly."

"Then it's too late to administer last rites, but I can still offer a prayer for his soul," the priest said as he continued ahead to the bedroom.

The doctor looked at the grieving woman and observed, "She can't be alone. There must be someone who can be with her."

The oldest boy said, "I have an aunt who lives in the Oltrarno district. She's my mother's sister. I can get her."

After the boy left, Guarino slumped down in a chair and held his head in his hands. "Never have I been so helpless," he said to himself. "How many more will follow this poor man?"

31

February 11, 1348

Shortly after the shop opened in the morning, the sound of the door creaking caught Gino's attention. An elderly man, whom Gino had never seen before, pushed his cane ahead of him and limped into the perfumery. A stooped white-haired woman clung to his arm, supporting him or perhaps being supported by him. He hobbled to the counter, with the woman shuffling along beside him. With a smile, Gino greeted the pair, who stood barely taller than the counter. "May I help you?"

"We want perfume for my wife," the man croaked.

Gino gestured to the row of urns on the shelf behind him and directed his attention to the woman. "As you can see, we have an abundant selection of perfumes. Do you have a favorite fragrance, or would you like to sample our most popular perfumes?"

The man replied, "We're looking for a perfume strong enough to overpower the bad air."

Gino's mouth dropped open. "What?"

The man coughed. Saliva mixed with blood leaked from his mouth and hung on his lower lip. His wife reached up with a cloth already stained pink from his spittle. The man looked up at Gino and repeated his request slowly, as one might to a child. "We need a perfume to dispel the bad air."

Gino had heard people claiming bad air caused the pestilence. The claim lacked proof, but its adherents cited circumstances to support their belief. They argued the famine of the past two years had swelled the city's population with refugees from the countryside, many of whom have become beggars. The refugees lived in alleys with no sanitation, urinating and defecating anywhere. They slept on piles of refuse and ate rats and other vermin. Gino had to admit he avoided walking near those alleys because the stench was intolerable.

"I'm sorry, but I don't know which perfume might be best at displacing the bad air," Gino responded.

"Then I need all of them. Mix them all together."

"Are you sure?" Gino asked skeptically. "I'm not sure how the mixture might smell. It might not be pleasant."

"I don't care about the smell as long as it keeps her safe." He coughed again. This time, the saliva dribbled to his chin before his wife wiped it.

Gino took a few drops from each of the fifteen urns and combined them in a vial. After adding the last drops, he sniffed the vial. It had the sour odor of a peat bog after a rain, he decided, and handed the vial to the woman. She wet her finger with the liquid and dabbed it under her nose while displaying no reaction to the scent. Expecting the man might want a scent to protect himself, Gino asked, "Something for you, signore?"

The man took the blood-stained cloth from his wife's hand and held it up for Gino to see. "Look at this." He shook his head. "Nothing in this shop can help me."

No sooner had the elderly couple left the shop than they were replaced by two women, also unfamiliar to Gino. Most women who came to the shop were the wives of successful business owners or the servants of wealthy aristocrats. Judging from their clothing, these women labored in a workshop or a woolen mill. They stood a distance away from the counter and glanced around the shop as though it didn't meet their expectations of a perfumery. Finally, one asked, "Are you the person who sells perfume?"

"Yes, I am," Gino replied. "Were you expecting someone else? Signor Roselli is in the other part of the shop. I can fetch him if you wish."

"No. No," the woman stammered. "We thought perfumes would be sold by a woman."

"Perfumes certainly could be sold by a woman, but I've been the perfumer in this shop for three years." Gino gestured toward the row of urns. "I've prepared all these fragrances. Jasmine and Rose are the most popular, but if you're looking for a distinct scent, I'm sure we can accommodate you."

"What is the most pungent scent?" the second woman asked.

Although surprised by her unusual question, Gino answered, "Gardenia has the strongest scent. The perfume is made from flowers imported from North Africa." Gino went to the urn containing gardenia perfume, dabbed a few drops of the liquid onto a cloth, and handed the cloth to the woman. "This is gardenia," he said.

The woman sniffed the cloth, said, "It is potent," and handed the cloth to her friend.

Next, Gino wet a cloth with rose perfume and handed it to the woman. "This is rose. Like most other perfumes, rose has a much more delicate scent than gardenia."

"Gardenia certainly is much stronger," the woman agreed after sniffing the second cloth. "If gardenia is the strongest, it's the one we want."

"A vial for each of you?"

"Just one. We'll share it. If it works, we'll come back for more."

Unable to contain his curiosity, Gino asked, "What do you mean, if it works?"

"The foul air is killing people more and more every day. Yesterday, we lost two women who worked the looms at our shop. Today, two more good women were taken before their time. We need a smell strong enough to protect us," the woman explained as she dabbed the liquid onto her cheeks close to her nose.

Throughout the morning, other women came to the shop in groups of twos, threes, and fours, to buy gardenia perfume. *People are panicking,* Gino said to himself as he mixed up a new quantity of the suddenly popular heavy scent.

In mid-afternoon, a man entered the shop. He had leathery skin, calloused hands, and a jagged scar dangerously close to his right eye. Gino felt certain the man hadn't come to buy gardenia perfume. In a tight voice, the man said, "I need to protect my wife and children from the pestilence." He sank down into a chair. "A family in the house next to mine died from the sickness. Three days ago, they were all well and happy. This morning, all five bodies were taken from their house. I saw one girl before they covered her with a cloth." He shuddered. "Her face was misshapen so badly I hardly recognized her." He slapped a hand against the counter. "In just three days, this horrible sickness took them all."

He exhaled forcefully, took a moment to recover his composure, then stood. "I refuse to let my family be stricken. There was a woman living in my neighborhood who sold amulets, potions, and incense, but the church threatened her. They called her a witch and forced her to leave the city. If she hadn't been driven out, I would go to her, but since she's gone, I'm hoping you can help me."

In a sympathetic tone, Gino said, "We don't sell potions."

"I'm not looking for a potion. I want incense to cleanse the air and banish the sickness hanging in it. Can you make incense?"

Speziali didn't make incense, nor did apothecary shops sell incense, but Gino had watched Masina make incense before she, too, had been driven from the city by false accusations of witchcraft. She had made her incense from the plants she and Gino had gathered in the fields surrounding Florence. Masina's creations ranged from mild sweet scents to strong, harsh odors. "I can make incense, but I can't guarantee it will overcome bad air or protect your family from the pestilence."

"Make it strong enough to fill my house and block out the poisonous air."

Gino considered the compounds available to him in the apothecary shop and settled on cinnamon. "It will take several minutes."

"I'll wait," the man said firmly and sat back down.

Signor Roselli had heard the conversation while he was in the other room. He came into the perfumery to watch as Gino ground several pieces of cinnamon bark into a powder and added oil and a few drops of water to create a thick paste. With his fingers, Gino formed the paste into two cones, a large one and a small one. Recalling Masina's process, he heated the cones until the paste solidified. Signor Roselli watched intently and when the incense had dried, Gino handed a flint to Roselli, who lit the small piece. Gino beamed, pleased his attempt was successful as a thin smoke spiral rose into the air from the smoldering cone. In little more than a minute, the smell of cinnamon permeated the shop. Gino gave the man the large cone and repeated his caution, saying cinnamon might not be an effective protection against the pestilence. His words went unheeded.

Over the next few days, word spread. Other men came to the shop for cinnamon incense and women came for gardenia perfume. When Professor Vianello came for a mug of his elixir, Gino asked the man, whose opinion he respected, "Professor, do you believe all the deaths are caused by something in the air? Hundreds every day. Is it possible?"

Vianello inhaled deeply and his eyes twinkled. Clearly, Gino was not the first person to have posed similar questions to him. "There is no evidence … none at all … to show air is to blame for the countless deaths," Vianello said firmly. After a pause, he waved a finger, saying, "Nor is there evidence to prove the very air we must breathe for life has not turned malignant. Eventually, we may learn the cause of this pestilence, but for now, no one can say for certain." While Vianello consumed his elixir, Gino filled a vial with gardenia perfume. Later, he would take it to his sister.

32

Sunday February 24, 1348

For the second time since he had come to Florence, Gino crossed the river to attend mass at San Salvatore, a small church at the extreme southern edge of the Oltrarno district. Those attending the morning mass included families living in the parish, lumbermen who had been logging forests in the nearby hills, and a few other lone men like Gino. He recognized a man whom he had spoken with on his previous visit to the church, Antonio, a carpenter near his own age. Other people were still arriving when Gino took a position at the rear of the nave. Whenever he entered San Fedele in his home village, it had taken minutes for his eyes to acclimate to the church's dim interior, but no such adjustment was needed in brightly lit San Salvatore. Like the large, well-attended churches in the city center, its altar was adorned with candles, while tall candelabras placed along the side walls further brightened the church's interior.

Gino noticed family members stood close to each other, but each family group spaced itself away from the others. The lumbermen clustered together near the front of the church, close to the altar. They formed the single largest group. Everyone, Gino included, studied the people nearby, fearful someone close by might show symptoms of the sickness: flushed faces, lumps, or darkened areas on the neck or arms.

While waiting for mass to begin, Gino listened to snatches of conversation. Men raised their voices enough to speak with other men, probably neighbors with whom they had sat elbow-to-elbow in a crowded tavern months ago, and now wouldn't get within an arm's length of each other. Women felt it imprudent to speak above a whisper in church, so they merely smiled at each other across the void.

Gino heard some families were absent from mass because they were mourning the death of family members. In one family, it was said, both the mother and father had succumbed, leaving behind three youngsters. No one knew what had become of those children. Stories circulated of entire families having been claimed by the sickness. Most surprising were reports of families fleeing the city to escape the pestilence. For the past two years, people had streamed into Florence from the countryside to seek salvation from the famine. Did the departure of these families mark a turnaround, the beginning of an exodus?

Although the lumbermen were far from him, he sensed hostility in their guttural outbursts. Many had left wives and children in the city while they logged in the hills. Death rampaging unchecked though the city threatened their families and they reacted with anger. They wanted something more tangible than bad air—possibly someone—to blame for the misery.

A small bell sounded when the sacristy door opened, and a priest emerged, followed by two altar boys. When they reached the altar, the priest spread his upraised arms and delivered the opening blessing. Near the midpoint of the service, the priest stepped to the pulpit to deliver his sermon. "We are all God's children," he began. "God loves us … all of us. He wants us to love Him, to heed His word, and to obey Him. Our Lord would not cause His children to suffer without reason." Shifting from a tempered tone, the priest boomed, "This pestilence has been inflicted upon us because we have offended Him. There can be no other explanation."

Shaken by the indictment, people glanced furtively at those around them as if they were all co-conspirators in a plot against God. "What could we have done to deserve this punishment?" they asked themselves.

Pleased his words had stunned his flock as he had intended, he continued, "We have sinned against God, and only by ending our sinful ways can we expect Him to end this scourge. You may not be an adulterer or a fornicator, but ask yourself, are you committing the sins of envy and pride?"

One lumberman's face reddened. He bellowed, "My wife was a good, holy, God-fearing woman. She committed no sin worthy of this damnation; yet she suffered a horrible death. She cannot be held to account for this misery."

The outcry froze everyone. The priest gripped the lectern so tightly his knuckles turned white; his fingernails dug into the wood. Another lumberman shouted, "My son was barely old enough to walk. He was an innocent child. What sin could he have committed? But he was struck down."

Family groups moved farther away from the bellicose woodsmen, who began grumbling in support of their comrades. A third man called out, "I wear my best smock when I come to church." He pointed to its threadbare sleeve and its soiled shoulder. "This is my best! Look at it! It's frayed and spotted. How could anyone who dresses like this be accused of being prideful?

"Do you know who is prideful?" he asked and raised an arm angled toward the priest. "The priests! Look at them. They don't wear frayed vestments. Before the new bishop came, the priests in this diocese wore plain linen vestments. But now, linen isn't good enough for them. They all wear expensive silk." The eyes of all the parishioners shifted to the priest.

The man continued, "The bishop refused to serve communion from a pewter chalice. Now all chalices in the diocese are silver … all except the one used by the bishop. His is gold." He spread his arms wide. "My wife spends nights in the dark to preserve her lone candle, while this church and others are lit up like brothels."

He swept his gaze around the church to make eye contact with everyone. "For two years, when rain destroyed the crops, we all struggled to find food for our families. Beggars starved in the streets. But do you know of any priest who went hungry? None of them went to sleep with pangs of hunger. They made sure their bellies were filled."

He pounded a fist into the palm of his other hand. "Have you crossed the river to see what's being built at the center of our city? A new cathedral. We might need a new cathedral, but must it be grandiose? The plan they got from the first architect wasn't grand enough, so they cast him aside and hired a new architect. Now it's rumored even his plan isn't impressive enough, so they may look for yet another architect.

"If this terrible disease has been unleashed upon us by the sin of pride, it is the bishop and his minions who brought it upon us." He ended his tirade in a booming voice, saying, "We need to make the bishop stop his prideful ways and walk in the humble shoes of Saint Francis. I say we go to him now." He strode the length of the nave and out the door, followed by the other lumbermen.

The shocked parishioners moved aside to let the woodsmen pass. Their eyes followed the departing men until the church door closed, then they all turned slowly to face the priest. Without completing his sermon, he stepped away from the pulpit and continued the mass. Everyone noticed the tremor in his voice as he offered the Eucharistic Prayer.

At the end of mass, Gino stood to the side as people filed out of the church. "Are people in Florence so different from those in Poppi?" he wondered. In Poppi, whenever misfortune struck, the villagers rallied to help each other. He recalled when he was five years old, the house on a neighboring farm had caught fire. The burning house was a distance away, but standing outside his own home, he could see the flames and smell the smoke.

He remembered the episode but suppressed the memory of his reaction when his father had said, "I pray no one is inside the house." Terrified someone might die in the inferno, young Gino had run to his room, dived onto his pallet, and buried his sobbing face in the bed covering. His fear had ebbed only when his mother had come to his room, sat with him, and held his hand. The horrible fire wasn't Gino's first encounter with death. He had become sensitized to tragedy years earlier as a toddler, but that incident was too deep to be recalled.

Gino's conscious memory skipped from seeing the flames to the following day, when his father took him to the scarred farm, where all the men of the village gathered to rebuild the house. Even as a child, he had helped. The villagers always rallied together, no matter the cause. But Florentines, it seemed, found misfortune to be an excuse for pointing blame. Advocati had blamed Masina for being a witch. Customers at the apothecary blamed bad air for the pestilence. And now lumbermen blamed the bishop.

Antonio the carpenter broke Gino's concentration, saying, "You picked a momentous day to return to San Salvatore."

Gino managed a laugh. "Do you mean to tell me mass isn't this exciting every Sunday?"

"No, today was an exception. People who live in this neighborhood worry about the sickness, of course, but I've never heard them blame the bishop. The unruly ones were the lumbermen who've been cutting trees on the Bellosguardo Hill. Our carpentry shop buys wood from them, so I've talked with them, and I can understand their distress. They're away from their homes for weeks at a time without knowing whether the sickness has affected their families."

Gino pondered, "What will come of it when they confront the bishop?"

***

When the loggers neared the river, one man pushed to the front and spoke to the leader. "I think we're too few to influence the bishop."

The leader scowled at him. "You want us to turn around?"

"No, not at all. But we need to increase our number. Other members of our guild are logging near San Miniato. Julio is a fast runner. If he tells them what we're doing, they might join us."

The leader's scowl turned into a grin. Following the suggestion, he dispatched quick-footed Julio to recruit more lumbermen, and after crossing the river, he bade his men wait in Piazza Santa Croce. Growing impatient, some men entered the church. Seeing its new colorful frescoes further stirred their conviction that God would find the opulence of churches and the affluence of priests offensive.

Julio returned with over two dozen men trailing behind him. "Some of these men are stone cutters," he announced to the leader. "They believe as we do."

The expanded band marched through the city to the bishop's residence. A young monk responded to the shouts of the men and the leader's pounding on the door. "We demand to speak with his excellency," the leader exhorted.

In a tremulous voice, the monk responded, "He's not here."

"Where is he?" the leader pressed.

"I don't know. He left the city. I don't expect him to return soon."

Unsatisfied, men pushed past the monk and stormed into the building. "You can't do this," the monk pleaded, his voice cracking with desperation as he tried to stop them.

Moments later, a shout came from the kitchen. "These are silver plates. The bishop eats on silver plates!"

And from a different quarter of the house. "He sleeps on silk sheets … and wears silk night clothes."

The leader instructed the men to gather all examples of the bishop's extravagance. Carrying armloads of silk, silver, and other luxuries, they paraded to the river. Standing at the middle of the San Trinita bridge, they threw the bishop's belongings into the river. The leader proclaimed, "Pray our actions here satisfy the Lord so He will end the pestilence." The men cheered as the bishop's belongings sank out of sight.

33

Thursday February 28, 1348

Every morning before going to the apothecary, Gino kept vigil along the river near the docks, hoping to see his brother Fanto. Several months ago, Gino chanced to spot Fanto on a barge bringing goods from Pisa, but the two brothers had had only a few minutes together before the barge left on its return journey to Pisa. Fanto had expected to return to Florence frequently and said he would arrange for a longer visit, but his optimism proved untrue. Fanto had not returned to Florence during the intervening months when a deadly sickness had descended on Pisa, the same plague now raging through Florence. As time moved on, Gino became ever more desperate to learn whether his family had been stricken.

He pulled his cloak tight, trying to keep the frigid droplets spraying off the river from stinging his face as he watched a barge moving upriver stop short of the dock for the teamster to unhitch the animals pulling the craft upstream. Once the barge was untethered from the horses, the steerman poled the craft the remaining distance to the dock. The slow river current in mid-winter made propelling the craft an effortless task. When it reached the dock, the steerman threw a rope to the dock workers, who fastened it to a stanchion and began unloading the barge. From his vantage point, Gino could tell the man poling the barge was not Fanto. He slumped in disappointment.

He looked downriver, hoping a second craft might follow a short distance behind the first. Seeing nothing but smooth water, he sulked away from his post at the river and trudged uphill to the central market for a brief visit with Taddeo before heading to the apothecary.

When Gino first arrived in Florence, the central market had been crowded with vendor carts every morning. Eager customers had jostled each other and squeezed through narrow spaces to get the best of the fruits and vegetables. During the past two years, while rain had devastated crops on nearby farms, there were days when the market had no vendors. With no Tuscan produce available, the city survived on limited quantities of goods brought from Calabria and Sicily and distributed from government stockpiles.

Now vendors were returning to the market, but they took precautions to protect themselves from the pestilence ravaging the city. Because no one knew how the disease spread, they tried a variety of safeguards. If bad air carried the disease, as many believed, they did not want to share air with anyone who might be contaminated, so they positioned their carts well away from each other with vendors standing on one side of their cart and customers on the opposite side. No one wanted to touch another person who might carry the sickness, so they completed transactions with minimal contact. Rather than handing money to a vendor, customers took the items they wanted and set their payment on the cart. Women who had once come to the market with friends now came individually. They didn't linger to chat, but left promptly once they had filled their baskets. The market, once a vibrant place, was now a solemn reminder of tragedy.

Gino found a place to stand where he wouldn't hamper Taddeo's customers, but he would be close enough to Taddeo's cart for the two men to converse. "You have a good quantity of fine-looking apples," Gino observed.

"They're from an orchard in the Chiana valley. The orchards suffered only minor damage from the rain. Some vegetable farms have crops in the ground, but nothing will be ready to harvest until spring, so I've shifted my trade to the orchards."

"I haven't seen Wiener in months. Is he still bringing grain from the Po Valley?" Gino asked.

"I don't think so. When the Venetians started competing for grain, Wiener petitioned the Signoria to increase their bid price. He tried to convince them to outbid the Venetians, but the Signoria refused and instead began importing grain from Sicily. For all I know, Wiener may have returned to Austria." Taddeo took a moment to serve a customer, then said, "I passed through the Casentino Valley two days ago. Many of the farms there are still idle." He added softly, "There was no one at your family's farm. The house looks the same as when the family left, and the fields are barren, as I expected."

Gino allowed himself a momentary distraction by gazing at the ground and watching a bug struggling to cope with a tiny morsel dropped from a shopper's basket. At length, he said, "They may still be in Pisa. Every morning, I pass by the river hoping to see my brother on one of the barges. Even though I haven't seen him in months, I'm still unwilling to concede he might never return. But if he hasn't returned to Florence by now …" Gino let the thought hang.

Taddeo asked, "Have you asked any of the other men on the barges about him? If he still works for the barge company, one of them might know him."

Gino's eyes went wide. He stomped a foot on the ground. "Damn! What a damn fool I've been. Why didn't I think to ask them? Of course, one of the barge captains might know him."

Taddeo laughed. "Don't feel bad. You can't think of everything."

Gino bought three apples and headed to the apothecary, still chastising himself for being shortsighted.

***

The following morning, Gino rushed to the waterfront, eager to speak with a barge captain. He watched a craft tie up at the dock, and as the dockworkers began unloading, the captain went behind a warehouse to relieve himself. Gino headed to the warehouse, careful not to interfere with the unloading, and waited for the captain. When the captain returned to the dock, Gino said, "I'm trying to contact my brother, who works for the barge company. His name is Fanto. Might you know him?"

Without breaking stride, the captain gave Gino a sideways glance and replied in a gravelly voice, "I don't know any Fanto. Does he work on the canals?"

Gino walked with the captain into the warehouse, where the man helped himself to a mug and a jug of water. "I don't know if he works on the canals. I saw him months ago when he came to Florence on a barge. He came only once, and I haven't seen him since."

The captain emptied the mug and poured another. "If he works on the canals, I wouldn't come upon him. I'm always on the river." He belched and headed back to the barge, which was already loaded with goods destined for Pisa. Gino stood outside the warehouse, watching the craft float downriver, around a bend, and out of sight.

***

On each of the following three mornings, Gino headed to the river hoping to meet a barge captain who knew his brother, and each time, the man poling the barge was the same one he had already questioned. On the third day, he was about to leave when he looked downriver and noticed the sun glinting off shiny boxes stacked on a second barge headed to Florence. As the barge drew closer, Gino could tell the swarthy man with muscular arms wasn't his brother, but it was another person he could question.

After docking his craft, the steerman strolled along the riverfront eating a pastry he had brought with him. Gino caught up with him when he stopped to feed a pastry crumb to a small dog following him. "Fanto? Yeah, I know him. He's a tall fellow with sandy hair," he replied to Gino's query.

Gino's heart rate jumped. "He's my brother. It's been months since I've seen him ... since before the plague struck Pisa," Gino gushed.

The man resumed walking, swallowed another bite of his delicacy, then said, "I worked with Fanto briefly when we were poling large barges together. It takes two men to maneuver the large ones. I remember him saying something about having a brother in Florence, but I haven't seen him since he was assigned to a canal barge."

"My whole family is in Pisa, and I've been worried because I've heard nothing from them since the plague began ravaging that city." In a pleading tone, Gino asked, "Is there any way you could find Fanto and ask him about our family?"

The steerman chewed the last of his pastry except for a final crumb, which he dropped to the dog, who swallowed it and, seeing there was nothing more, trotted away. The man reversed direction and headed back toward the barge. "I can try."

The sun felt warmer and the breeze more refreshing as Gino walked to the apothecary, hopeful he might soon reestablish contact with his brother, even if only through an intermediary. As he walked past the old bridge, he glanced down at the stone masons rebuilding the piers and was reminded of his father.

Although his father spent most of his time tending crops, the man had many talents. He had used stones to expand their smokehouse; he had repaired wagons, plows, and other farm equipment; and he had built wooden tables and chairs. Surely, he must be prospering as a carpenter in Pisa.

***

The next two mornings, Gino arrived at the riverfront well before the first barge appeared. He paced back and forth impatiently, waiting for a craft to appear at the bend in the river. On both days, the captain of the first barge was the man who didn't know Fanto. Gino grew ever more impatient when no other barge followed closely behind. The first day, he waited as long as possible and had to run across the city to reach the apothecary before the church bells sounded terce. He had already turned to leave on the second morning when a second barge captained by the swarthy muscular man came into view. As he ran to the dock to intercept the steerman, Gino knew he'd be late for work, but the prospect of hearing news from Fanto outweighed the consequences of being delayed.

Gino stood expectantly as the man came toward him and said, "I spoke with your brother." The man paused and locked eyes with Gino. "There is news, but it's not what you wish to hear. I'm sorry to tell you, the sickness took your mother." Gino shuddered. The man continued, "Fanto said many who worked with her making ship sails were stricken. She was one of the first."

Gino fell to his knees with his hands over his face. The steerman said, "You're just hearing this now, but Fanto said it happened at the beginning of the year. The rest of your family was spared."

Images flashed through Gino's mind of his caring mother. He envisioned her picking him up, carrying him to the house, and bandaging his scraped knee when, as a toddler, he had fallen from a tree. He flashed through other memories ending with the time, just before he left for Florence, when he saw ambivalence in her eyes. She wanted him to go, but she also wanted him to stay.

The steerman bent down. "Are you all right?"

Without responding, Gino slowly raised himself up, turned, and plodded away, his shoulders slumped, his head down.

By mid-morning, Signor Roselli knew something was wrong because Gino had never missed work without notice. Had he succumbed to the sickness, Roselli wondered. At day's end, he closed the apothecary and made his way across the city to the Santa Maria Novella district. Roselli knew the street where Gino lived, but he didn't recall which house was Gino's because all the houses lining the street were similar. He wandered the street asking people if they knew Gino until a woman pointed and said, "A young man lives there. He's quiet and polite. Maybe he's the one you're looking for."

Roselli rapped on the door the woman had indicated. "Gino, are you in there?" He pressed his ear to the door, listened, and heard nothing. Again, he banged on the door. "Gino, it's Carlo Roselli! Open the door!" he shouted. This time, he heard shuffling inside. The door eased open. A blank, gray face topped by tangled hair looked out at Roselli. One sleeve of Gino's wrinkled shirt showed stains from wiping his eyes. His cloak lay in a heap on the floor. He was barefoot.

With his eyes downcast and his voice trembling, Gino said, "My mother died. The plague took her."

Roselli remained silent. In his experience at the apothecary, he'd encountered grief often, and likened it to a collapsing dam: first, only a trickle appeared; then suddenly a flood burst forth. He waited. Slowly, Gino raised his eyes to meet those of his mentor and he erupted. "I got word from my brother Fanto. The plague took her in early January. I didn't know until now. I couldn't even go to her funeral."

Roselli guided Gino to a chair. Gino held up the knitted wool cap clutched in his hand and murmured, "She gave me this when I left the farm. It's all I have from her. She was a wonderful woman. Everyone loved her. Even though she was miles away in Pisa, I always felt she was here with me. I thought about her every day." Gino went silent for several minutes, then looked directly at Roselli and said, "How am I going to tell my sister?"

Roselli didn't answer the question. The only way he knew to console people was to deflect their thoughts. "Did the message say anything about the rest of your family?"

"He said they are well."

"Then you must take comfort knowing they've been spared. The Lord's watchful eye must be on them."

"But how will they get on without mother? She bound us all together."

Roselli said, "To you, her death just happened, but she died in early January, so your family has been getting on without her for two months. Surely it's a struggle for them, but they are learning to cope, and in time, you will as well."

From personal experience when his own mother had died, Roselli had learned grief is best conquered through the support of family and friends. He would invite Gino to supper with his family, but tomorrow, not today. First, Gino must deal with the painful problem of reporting the death to his sister. "You'll agonize until you tell your sister. This is a time for you both to be together. I'll go with you. Put on a clean smock and brush your hair." Roselli picked Gino's cloak off the floor.

Gino shared memories of his mother as the two men walked to Casa Pagholi. When they reached the house, Gino grasped Roselli's arm and dismissed him, saying, "Thank you for bringing me here. I can tell Lucia."

"Take time for yourself if you need it," Roselli said. "Come to the shop when you are ready." As he turned to leave, he added, "I'll ask my parish priest to say a mass for your mother and we will keep her in our prayers."

With so many being stricken each day, Roselli understood her name would be but one of many recited during the mass. Only the wealthiest Florentines could afford to claim a mass solely for a departed member of their family.

Gino's sister answered the bell at the servant's entrance of Casa Pagholi. In her usual exuberant energy, she bubbled, "Dear brother, what brings you here at this hour? I haven't begun cooking, so it can't be the fragrance of my delicious meals."

Gino moved her to a bench in the rear hallway and sat beside her. "I have terrible news." He placed a hand on her arm. "I got word from Fanto … our mother has died."

Lucia, overwhelmed by disbelief, gazed at Gino, her eyes soon filled with tears. He wrapped his arms around her and let her cry until the sobbing slowed before he continued. "It was the pestilence."

"When?" she uttered, tears streaming down her cheeks.

"Nearly two months ago."

After several minutes, her tears stopped, and Lucia's thinking cleared. "Did Fanto say anything about our sisters? Did he say who's taking care of them? They can't be left alone."

"I didn't speak with Fanto myself. A barge captain brought me a message from him, but it said only that everyone else was well. If the captain can deliver a letter to Fanto, we can ask who is caring for the girls."

From a sitting room on the second level, Signora Pagholi heard disturbing sounds coming from the level below. She came to the hallway and saw Lucia and Gino holding each other with tears streaming down Lucia's face. She walked to them and, in a voice filled with compassion, asked, "What is troubling you, dear child?"

Gino looked up at her and said solemnly, "I received a message from our brother saying the plague has taken our mother."

Signora Pagholi wrapped her arms around the two siblings. Looking at Lucia, she asked, "What can I do for you? Do you need time to go to Pisa?"

Before Lucia could respond, Gino said, "She's worried about our sisters, Ciosa and Fiora, but the plague is still strong in Pisa, so it wouldn't be good for Lucia to go there."

"They're too young to be left alone," Lucia sniffled.

Gino said, "If one of the barge captains can deliver a letter to Fanto, maybe we can find out who is taking care of them."

Signora Pagholi called to her husband, who was working in his study. When he came into the sitting room and his wife explained the situation, he said, "There's no need to ask a barge captain. Florence has couriers who carry official correspondence. I can arrange for the courier who travels to Pisa to bring a letter to your brother and pen your brother's reply." With complete disregard for proper house servant behavior, Lucia rushed to Messer Pagholi and embraced him.

Signora Pagholi invited Gino to spend the night at the casa. He declined, trudged back to his house, and climbed into bed, clutching the knitted wool cap in his hand.

Gino carried the sorrow of his mother's death like a barb or stinger lodged in his flesh, haunted by not knowing whether she had received last rites or whether he would ever visit her grave. At the apothecary, he had spoken with many people who had suffered the loss of family members, and only a few of them had healed from their tragedy. Some tried to hide their pain, but most felt their sorrow as deeply as he did.

He spent the day in his room, leaving it only twice to relieve himself. His mother appeared whenever he closed his eyes, and even in the dim candlelight, with his eyes open. He ate only a chunk of stale bread softened in a dish of water. "I should have gone to Pisa to find them," he berated himself. "I could have held her hand and told her how much I loved her. Her other children were with her at the end and I was not."

34

Wednesday March 12, 1348

Many wealthy business owners and aristocrats fled Florence, heading to their villas in the countryside and to the homes of relatives in small towns. Whether bad air or something else produced the sickness mattered not to them. Their only concern was to escape its grasp. In the past, when they left the city for an annual holiday at the sea or in the mountains, they traveled in a carriage followed by a wagon containing the clothes and accessories they needed for a comfortable stay of one or two weeks. But fleeing from a seemingly endless scourge required more extensive preparation. Although they were leaving in spring, they also packed clothes suitable for the heat of summer and even heavy cloaks for autumn's cool nights. They prayed the plague would subside before winter. Affluent business owners crowded into a single carriage with their wives and children — mistresses were left to fend for themselves — and stuffed their belongings into one or two wagons trailing behind. Florence's wealthiest families traveled in multiple carriages trailed by a procession of wagons filled with the luxuries they refused to live without.

Every morning, compulsive gamblers gathered at Porta alla Croce, the gate exiting to the southern hills. As soon as they spotted a carriage coming toward them from the city center, they made bets on which frightened family it carried. They used the elegance of the carriage and the number of wagons behind it as guides to make their wagers. Processions having three or four wagons produced the most opportune bets because they might carry any of Florence's prosperous merchants. No bets were made when the longest procession, three carriages trailed by seven wagons, paraded out of the city. All the gamblers agreed it held the patriarch of Florence's largest banking family, accompanied by his wife and three daughters. The gamblers watched with envy as the carriages moved slowly past them. They peered into the vehicles, eager to see whether the third carriage carried the banker's mistress.

People always fled the city early in the day. Once the parade of carriages had thinned, the gamblers turned their attention to another form of entertainment. They moved to Piazza San Firenze, where they wagered on another condition brought on by the plague. In normal times, men didn't start drinking at their local taverns until late afternoon. But now days, weeks, then months of plague had driven men to the taverns earlier and earlier, and the number of men seeking solace in wine and beer grew. They queued outside taverns before the doors opened, so owners responded by advancing their opening times. Many taverns would open for business in the early morning and stay open until near midnight, when church bells sounded matins. Since the owners had so little time to sleep, some dozed on bedding stretched out on their tavern floors.

The gamblers chose San Firenze as the location for making wagers because the piazza was ringed with taverns. A few hours after sunrise, when church bells sounded terce, the gamblers went from tavern to tavern and counted the patrons in each. They bet not only on the total number of men in all the surrounding taverns, but also on which tavern had the most patrons, and which had the fewest. The winners saw no reason to hold on to their gains. Better they should reap enjoyment from their booty before the plague took them. Some emptied their purses on beer at nearby taverns, while others sought female companionship at a favorite bordello.

En route to the bordellos, the gamblers often came upon folks heading to morning mass. A year ago, weekday masses drew only a handful of elderly women. Now those women were joined by men and younger women who made time to attend mass before work to beg God to deliver His children from the terrible adversity. For the elderly women, mass alone was insufficient. They came again each afternoon to pray a novena.

Guilt or shame always sent the gamblers across to the opposite side of the street to avoid encountering the churchgoers.

***

Four men had already queued outside, waiting for Signor Roselli to unlock the door, when Doctor Guarino arrived at the apothecary. Guarino recognized them all. Two clutched prescriptions he had given them the previous day. He stood to the side while Roselli served the early arrivals.

After the others had received their medications, Roselli greeted his friend. "It gets worse every day. Some come here asking for treatments to protect them from the sickness. Those who are already afflicted plead for a cure, and I can't help any of them, the well or the sick. And if I'm besieged like this, I can't imagine what it must be like for you."

Guarino shrugged and dropped into a chair. "We've trained them to believe we have the knowledge to cure their ills; then when the worst comes along, as it has now, we tell them we can do nothing to rid them of the disease."

Roselli nodded his agreement. "It pains me to tell them all we can offer is herbane or hemlock to relieve the pain. Yesterday a man came begging for something for his son. The man was in tears. He said the boy couldn't move and was just lying in bed, moaning. I've heard similar stories before, and each time my helplessness makes me angry. When I told the man there is no cure, he implored me to give him something to end his son's suffering."

"What did you do?" Guarino asked.

"I gave him belladonna and cautioned him to give the boy only a drop or two. I warned him a larger dose would act as a poison. He thanked me profusely and clasped the vial with both hands as he rushed from the shop." After a pause, Roselli added quietly, "He understood what I was telling him. I blackened my soul and set him on a path to stain his own."

"If your soul is blackened by advising him how to end his son's suffering, then take comfort in knowing your soul is no darker than mine," Guarino said. "I have done the same. I believe my decisions fit my oath to eliminate suffering, and I can only hope our merciful God shares my view."

"Those who are themselves afflicted are desperate," Roselli said. "One man pulled up his tunic to show me the swellings at his groin. When I told him there was no cure, he lunged toward me with his fists clenched, threatening to beat me."

"What did you do?"

"Gino heard the commotion and ran from the perfumery. The man moved around the counter and rushed toward me with his fists raised. Gino had an urn in his hand. He jumped in front of the man, raised the urn, and drenched the man with rose perfume. Gino shouted at him, 'We can do nothing for you! Now leave!' The startled man looked down at his soaked tunic, then up at Gino's scowl. Without another word, he dropped his hands to his sides, turned, and sulked out of the shop."

Roselli leaned on the counter, drained by reliving the experience. Guarino placed a consoling hand on Roselli's arm and said, "We live in difficult times, Carlo, more difficult than some men can bear."

Roselli said, "Yesterday, my priest told me he trembles every time he is called to deliver last rites. He can't bring himself to anoint the dying by touching their foreheads and hands, so he sprinkles holy oil on them and signs the cross above them. He prays God will accept his actions as fulfillment of the sacrament.

"It must be even more difficult for you, Franco. You're called to the homes of those in such misery they can't even rise from their beds. Yet you go, despite knowing you can't make them whole. Few men have your courage."

Guarino laughed. "Courage? No, I'm not courageous. I cower every time I set foot inside a house reeking with the stench of death. Only a fool would not be afraid. I visit their houses, but not for the dying because they're never even aware of my presence and there is nothing I can do for them. When it's time to surrender their souls to the angels, no medical treatment can save them."

Roselli asked, "If you can't help them, why do you go to them?"

"My purpose is to treat the other members of the family. I test their urine because imbalances in humors make people susceptible to the disease. Balancing their humors can help those not yet affected stave off the disease. I know of houses where all but one person has perished. They all breathed the same air, so the one who didn't contract the disease must have had his humors in balance."

Roselli said, "Priests say the disease finds those who dwell on death and despair. They tell people to avoid such thoughts by spending time in gardens and engaging in cheerful conversation."

Guarino scoffed. "Their advice might have merit, but how can anyone think cheerful thoughts when a dear one is dying in the same room? If I were to tell family members not to keep a constant vigil with the dying, they wouldn't listen. I was called to the home of a long-time friend who had been stricken. I told his wife to keep her distance and not touch him; then, as I was leaving and barely outside the bedroom door, she dropped to her knees at his bedside and cradled his hand in hers. She was in good health when I saw her; yet she lived not another five days, so perhaps the priests are correct when they say dwelling on despair can unbalance the humors.

"I've taken to wearing gloves when I visit the sick. My mother always wore gloves when she labored in the garden to protect her hands from thorns. She claimed the practice originated with the ancient Romans. Am I being foolish by expecting gloves to shield me from the disease? Perhaps. I've certainly been ridiculed by my colleagues who swear the disease travels through the air in particles like dust. They say it's foolish to believe sickness can be transferred by touching someone. I have a few friends who wash their hands with vinegar after contacting sick patients, but they won't admit to doing so for fear of being mocked."

Doctor Guarino shook his head, then continued. "Do you recall the arrogant bastard at the last guild meeting? The one who kept proposing changes to the guild charter?"

Roselli replied, "He proposed limiting the number of speziali in the guild."

"Yes, he's the one. He fled the city, but before he left, he tried to convince other doctors to leave. He said we have no cure, so why expose ourselves by going to the homes of the sick where the bad air is concentrated? I can't refute his argument because, in truth, many doctors have died after visiting plague victims. I test myself often to be sure my humors remain balanced, but I also credit the goddess Fortuna for shielding me."

Roselli said, "I see Gino has also taken to wearing gloves when he serves customers."

Guarino grinned. "You can blame his behavior on me. He's wearing them at my suggestion." He and Roselli listened for a moment to Gino conversing with a customer in the perfumery, then Guarino asked, "Is he still troubled over the death of his mother?"

"Yes, he is. Deep inside, the move from the farm to Florence left him with a lingering guilt, as if he'd abandoned his family. He sent them money trying to assuage his conscience, but in his mind, he could never do enough. He had hoped to reunite with his family someday, and now his mother's death means they can never be all together again. I've tried to distract him. I invited him to supper several times, but each time he declined. And having no cure for this plague troubles him as much as us. I don't know what it will take to overcome his despair."

35

Wednesday April 2, 1348

Wearily, Gino left the apothecary at the end of a day dealing with difficult customers and nearly collided with Piero Roselli, who managed the funeral service. Twitching nervously, Roselli asked, "Is my brother inside?"

"Yes, he is." Gino replied, pushed the door open, and followed Piero into the shop.

Waving his hands in the air excitedly, Piero blurted, "There are too many bodies. Hundreds yesterday and more today. I have every carpenter in the city making coffins, and they can't make them fast enough." He gulped a few shallow breaths. "And there's no space left in the cemeteries."

Carlo Roselli put a hand on his brother's shoulder. "Sit, Piero. Calm yourself." He waved at Gino and said, "Piero needs a drink … some water," then waited until his brother had taken a few gulps before asking, "What can be done?"

Piero threw his hands in the air. "I don't know. The laws say bodies must be buried in coffins. I can't get more coffins, and I can't change the laws."

"Yes, there are laws," Carlo echoed slowly as he considered the implications of his brother's dilemma. "And no one can expect you to change the laws, so the lawmakers are the ones who must solve the problem. Tomorrow morning, we'll go to the magistrates' court and inform the lawmakers of *their* problem. We'll go to the court together."

Carlo eased his brother toward the door. “Now, you need to unburden yourself. Come with me. Let’s share a bottle of wine. A drink will make you feel better.” He waved a hand at Gino. “Join us. You’ve also had a trying day. The people of this city are becoming fanatical. I heard a fool complaining to you because we don’t have an elixir to cure the plague, so I know you, too, will benefit from a glass of wine.”

Although Gino felt no cause to celebrate, he accepted Roselli’s invitation. As they climbed to Roselli’s home above the shop, Carlo said, “Let’s agree to have no discussion of business problems, just friendly conversation. In the morning, we can deal with the thorns.”

Signora Roselli’s eyes widened at seeing her brother-in-law and Gino in the entryway. Carlo kissed his wife and said, “Joanna, these men need something to help them recover from a hard day. Please show them to the sitting room while I fetch a bottle of wine.” A minute later, carrying two bottles of wine and a tray with four wine glasses, he rejoined the others.

“Two bottles of wine,” Joanna remarked. “It must have been an especially strenuous day.”

“It was, my dear. But the day is finished, and we’ve agreed not to mention business again until morning.”

They sat in awkward silence for a few moments wondering what they could talk about if not business, or the even more unwelcome topic of the ever-expanding plague, when Carlo heard a faint musical refrain drifting in from another room. “Gabriela, come here!” he shouted.

Gabriela came around a corner and peered into the anteroom. “She’s learning to play the lute,” Carlo announced to the other men. To Gabriela, he implored, “We need cheerful music to relieve us from the weight of the day. Bring your lute and play a song for us to lighten our mood, dear daughter.”

Her face reddened. “Father, I’m just learning. I couldn’t possibly play for … your guests.”

“Oh, I know you can. I heard you practicing *La prossima primavera*. You played it beautifully. Please play it for us, my treasure.”

Gabriela glanced at her mother, who signaled her encouragement with a quick nod of her head. Moments later, Gabriela returned with her instrument and said, "I learned this song from Maestro Landini. It sounds wonderful when he plays it on the organetto. I've just begun practicing it on the lute."

Laughing, her father said, "We won't punish you if you don't play perfectly. Indeed, we won't even know if it isn't perfect."

Gabriela frowned as she began playing and singing. Her father and her uncle focused on watching her fingers as they floated across the strings. Gino hardly noticed the instrument. He lost himself in the curve of Gabriela's chin, the candlelight sparkling in her amber eyes, and her honey-brown hair bouncing on her shoulders every time she turned her head. Signora Roselli glanced to the side to observe Gino transfixed on Gabriela.

The plague had kept Gino and Gabriela apart for months. Gino looked at her as though he were seeing her again for the first time. At one time, he had dared to dream about their future together. Now, the plague had made his life uncertain.

As soon as she finished playing, Gabriela pronounced, "I made mistakes." Frowning at her father, she said, "I told you I wasn't ready."

Smiling and clapping, her uncle Piero said, "I didn't notice any mistakes. It was wondrous. I'm not a musician, but I can't imagine it sounding better on an organetto. The feathery melody seems perfectly matched to the lute. And you have the voice of an angel. Your music brings light to the blackest time."

Again, her cheeks reddened. Seeing her discomfort, Joanna said, "These men have had a tough day. Come to the kitchen and help me make a tasty treat for them."

After they stopped talking about music, the men struggled to keep depressing topics from entering their conversation. The agenda of the next guild meeting, the sermon at last Sunday's mass, the high prices of food, all began as innocuous topics but were soon distorted by mention of the plague. When they finished the second bottle of wine and the plate of *caponata di melanzane* Joanna had served them, Gino and Piero rose to leave. Gino agreed to mind the apothecary in the morning, while the Roselli brothers conferred with a magistrate.

***

The office of civil magistrates was nearly empty the following morning when Carlo and Piero Roselli entered the reception area. A lone clerk greeted them. "We have an urgent matter to discuss with a magistrate," Carlo stated.

"Do you have an appointment?" the clerk asked.

"No, we don't have an appointment, but if we don't meet with a magistrate immediately, no bodies will be buried in this city. They'll begin piling in the streets."

The clerk's eyes widened. "One moment," he muttered and rushed away from his desk and through a hallway.

"Appointment, bah," Carlo chided. "I knew the prospect of bodies in the streets would get his attention."

When the clerk returned, he sputtered, "The magistrate on duty will see you. Come with me."

He led the Roselli brothers to a well-appointed room where an official in a black robe trimmed with a magenta sash sat behind an ornate wooden desk. A marble statue of an ancient Greek personage stood atop a pedestal in one corner of the room, paintings covered two walls, and a side table displayed a silver candelabra against a third wall. But the room held no chairs for visitors. Carlo and Piero were forced to stand like supplicants petitioning an omniscient power. "What is this about bodies not being buried?" the magistrate asked gruffly.

"There are laws stipulating how burials must be done," Carlo began.

"I know the laws," the magistrate growled.

Unperturbed by the hostile response, Carlo continued calmly. "Every carpenter in Florence is making coffins for us, but they cannot make them fast enough. We need a waiver of the statute so we can bury bodies without coffins."

"I can't issue a waiver. Only the Captain of the People has the authority to rescind statutes."

"Then you need to bring this matter to the captain's attention immediately. Yesterday, the number of bodies collected exceeded the supply of coffins. Today… right now… carts stacked with bodies are lining the city streets."

The alarmed magistrate lost his aggressive bravado and jumped up. "Come with me."

Midway along the hallway, he knocked on a door, poked his head into a room, mumbled something to the person inside; then he pushed the door open and beckoned the others to follow him. The austere room was smaller than the magistrate's office, with neither paintings nor a silver candelabra, but with four chairs for visitors. Behind a modest desk sat the Captain of the People, the official with supreme responsibility for civil matters.

Attempting to suggest he had uncovered the problem and devised a solution himself, the magistrate declared, "There aren't enough coffins for all the dead. You need to suspend the statute requiring bodies to be buried in coffins."

"You see no problem in burying the dead without coffins?" the captain asked.

Having no answer himself, the magistrate paused to give the Roselli brothers the chance to object. When they did not, he said, "No," with a tremor in his voice betraying his uncertainty.

The captain blithely raised his hand, palm upward, and instructed the magistrate, "Very well then, the requirement to use coffins is hereby suspended. Have my decision entered into the records."

Satisfied with himself, and believing the problem had been solved, the magistrate smiled broadly and turned to leave when Carlo Roselli said, "Excuse me, Captain, but there are other problems as well."

The startled magistrate shuddered and tried to hide his embarrassment with a sheepish grin. The captain folded his hands on the desk and looked up at Carlo, who said, "There aren't enough shrouds."

"Surely you can find people to sew shrouds," the magistrate blustered.

"Sewing isn't the issue. The law says shrouds must be made from tightly woven wool, but the woolen mills able to make suitable fabric stopped operating when their owners fled the city."

The magistrate sneered, "Are you suggesting bodies be buried with no coverings?"

This time it was Piero Roselli who responded. "No, certainly not. Doing so would be indecent. We suggest making shrouds from linen, the same fabric used to make bed sheets. We have ample quantities of linen."

"Do you see a problem with linen shrouds?" the captain asked the befuddled magistrate.

"Uh … I don't know …. I suppose not."

"The requirement mandating shrouds be made from tightly woven wool is hereby suspended," the captain declared and looked from Piero to Carlo. "Is there anything else?"

Carlo said softly, "The cemeteries are full."

The captain understood this was a condition he couldn't eliminate with a simple edict. "Hmmm. This is a more difficult problem," he muttered and folded his hands on his desk as he analyzed the situation. He rocked side-to-side on his chair. "You said there are hundreds of bodies every day?"

"Yes," Carlo confirmed.

"So, in a week there could be more than a thousand and if the plague continues for another month …"

Carlo injected, "We assume it might continue even longer."

"Holy mother of God," the magistrate blurted when he realized the magnitude of the problem. He sank down onto a chair like a shriveling plant deprived of water.

The captain said, "I don't have the authority to designate public land as a cemetery. Only the Signoria can apportion land, and they rarely move swiftly. It could take them a week or more to agree on which land should be chosen. Furthermore, the dead must be buried in consecrated ground, and I can't sanctify land. Consecration is a matter for the church. If we were to wait for the Signoria to designate land and the bishops to deem it worthy, there might be thousands of bodies awaiting burial. We would have a disaster." The Roselli brothers nodded. The captain said, "Clearly, we need another solution." He thought for several moments before his face brightened, and he swiveled to face the magistrate. "Have the clerk summon the papal envoy and tell him I require his presence immediately."

While they waited, the captain quizzed the Roselli brothers. "As I recall, the law requires coffins be sealed to contain the stench of decaying bodies. Without coffins, how will the odors be contained?"

Piero replied, "The provision calling for sealed coffins was adopted to keep odors from offending people in church during funeral services. Now, with so many deaths every day, bodies are taken directly from houses to the cemetery. They are never brought to church. Our carters record the names of the deceased so they can be remembered and blessed at a later funeral mass. The law also stipulates bodies be buried at a depth of at least two *braccie* which is deep enough to keep any odor from escaping after the bodies are covered with earth."

The captain scanned the three men, letting his eyes linger longest on the magistrate. "When the envoy arrives, I will speak with him. Say nothing unless I ask you to comment."

***

A man wearing a white bishop's robe with a purple cincture rushed into the room. "The papal envoy is in Rome. Your messenger said you needed to see him immediately. I am his secretary. What do you need of the envoy?"

"Thank you for joining us, Your Excellency. Do you have the authority to make decisions in the envoy's absence? Will the bishops heed what you tell them?" the captain asked.

"I am entrusted with the envoy's seal, so I speak for him. The bishops will accept my word."

Without introducing the other men who were in the room, the captain gestured toward the sole vacant chair. "Please sit down. An urgent matter requires your attention." He described only the need for additional space to bury the dead. He didn't mention the shortage of shrouds or coffins because those problems were caused by Florentine law, which he could suspend.

When the captain finished framing the problem, the secretary said, "For souls to rest with the Lord, the deceased must be buried in consecrated ground."

The captain smiled thinly, pleased the secretary reached the conclusion he had expected. "As you say, they must be buried in consecrated ground." He leaned forward and locked eyes with the secretary. "And the only remaining consecrated spaces in the city are the lands surrounding the churches."

The secretary's mouth dropped open. "Are you suggesting the dead be buried outside churches?"

The captain smiled thinly. "Interring saints in crypts within churches has been a long-standing and respected tradition." He added firmly, "In our current crisis, I see no alternative to burying the faithful in the holy ground outside."

"Which churches?"

"Maybe all of them." To emphasize the extent of the problem, the captain called forth the Roselli brothers. "These men supervise the carters who collect the dead, hundreds every day. Their experience predicts thousands more will succumb in the coming weeks. As you might imagine, it will not be possible to dig thousands of individual graves."

The secretary sat immobilized by the gruesome picture as the captain continued. "In Roman times, legions buried their fallen comrades together in mass graves. We have no choice but to do the same."

The secretary bolted upright in his chair and exclaimed, "We are not uncouth Roman warriors. Burying our dead in mass graves would be barbaric!"

The captain rose from his chair, leaned against the edge of his desk near the secretary, and said in a low voice, "I share your anguish. Commingling bodies will not honor the dead as we would wish. But our first consideration must be the sanctity of souls. Only by interring all the bodies, thousands of them, in consecrated ground can their souls be at peace with the Lord."

The secretary gripped his pectoral cross tightly, his knuckles showing white. After a moment of silence, he said, "You are telling me something I already know. Preserving souls must be our prime concern. This is a dark day, and I can only pray God forgives us, and those who judge our actions will understand how we came to this loathsome decision." He rose slowly. "I will tell the bishops what must be done."

36

Wednesday April 9, 1348

Gino went directly to the perfumery, avoiding the apothecary and foregoing Roselli's usual morning greeting. Customers who came to the perfumery were served by a somber man, not the cheerful Gino they had known. Gino studied them, looking for clues in their speech and movement to find those who were suffering from a tragic loss, as he was. He discovered the ones who grieved moved with precision, as though their every motion mattered because it might be their last. They spoke with carefully chosen words.

The stream of women asking for gardenia scent had diminished from its peak the previous month. So many of them who believed the fragrance could protect them had already died. Every day when he came to the shop, he asked himself, have the others come to realize we have nothing, no perfumes or medicinals, to shield them from the plague?

A woman who had regularly come to the shop with two friends entered the shop alone. She deposited a vial on the counter and asked Gino to refill it with gardenia scent. As he took the vial from her, Gino felt he was no better than the quack doctors who hawked their magic remedies at the mercato. Ever since he had worked with Signor Morelli in the apothecary in Poppi, he had viewed speziale as an honorable profession. Now he questioned whether his selling false hope to this woman was a crime or at least a sin.

Noticing the woman was without her usual companions, Gino remarked, "You're alone today." Although fearful of hearing another gruesome story, he was eager to learn why her friends were not with her.

"Some of my friends were taken by this scourge; the others worked in a woolen mill," she responded in a labored voice. "Last week, the mill owner, like so many others, left the city with his wife and two sons. He had charge of buying raw wool and selling the finished fabric while one of his sons managed the spinning and his other son managed the looms. The owner decided the mill couldn't function without the three men, so he closed it. With the mill closed, all the women who operated the equipment, including my friends, have no work."

"What are they doing now?"

"Shops are closing everywhere for the same reason the mill closed, so the women can't find other work. All they can do is stay at home. Fortunately, those women have husbands who are still working, but others are less fortunate. Men and women worked at the mill, so in some families, both the husbands and wives have no work. I don't know how long they can survive."

"You don't work at the mill?" Gino asked.

"I work for a tailor, but his business is also suffering. He makes custom shirts and cloaks for the men in Florence's most prominent families. With more of the aristocrats leaving the city every day, the tailor gets few new orders." Her lips turned down. "His kindness keeps me working, but unless he gets additional orders soon, he won't be able to keep me much longer."

As Gino forced himself to refill the vial, he said to himself, this woman has lost her friends and fears she may soon lose her job. Isn't it kinder not to crush her remaining fragile hope by telling her perfume won't save her?

The woman uncorked the vial and dabbed drops of gardenia-scented oil under her chin. After she left, Gino checked the supply of gardenia perfume. A month ago, he would have been mixing another batch by midday, but now the urn was still half filled. Many of those who had anointed themselves with the scent now filled the graveyards. He stared into the murky liquid. How can I continue with the fiction of a scent protecting people from disease? Are there speziali in Pisa dispensing gardenia perfumes? My mother never wore perfume. She would have thought it foolish had anyone suggested she could be protected from sickness by a perfume. What would she think of her son selling false beliefs?

***

For reasons Gino couldn't understand, men who came for elixirs also frequented the shop less often than they had months ago. In mid-afternoon, a man who had previously come for Virile elixir each week bounded into the shop. This was his first visit in a month. Smiling, he danced up to the counter and tapped his fingers to the rhythm of the song he was singing.

The woman's story of people having no work and the lingering pain of his mother's death made Gino want to thrash the man for being happy, but he held his rage and said with a hint of sarcasm, "You must be one of the few who still has work and has not lost a dear one to the plague."

Seeing Gino's scowl, the man stopped tapping and suppressed his smile. "You're right on both counts. I feel sorry for the poor bastards who have lost their jobs. Some of my closest friends are struggling to make it from day to day with no money coming to them, but the goddess Fortuna has blessed me. My job will last for all eternity. I work for the city repairing roads and if you go walking in any of our neighborhoods, you'll surely come upon roads needing repair, many of them. There will always be roads needing repair."

He held out both hands, palms up. "And of course, I shed a tear when I hear of another death, and every day brings more deaths than the day before. Only a devil could be so uncaring not to share the pain of those dying everywhere around us." He raised a finger in the air and his smile returned. "But we each choose how we deal with the peril. We can't tell which of us this fickle sickness will strike next. So rather than be despondent, I gather after work every day at a tavern with my cohorts singing and drinking until the barkeep sends us staggering out while we're still able to make it home. And we're not the only ones who think this plague may presage Armageddon. Taverns everywhere are filled with men enjoying the end of days.

"But today I was headed to the tavern when two young women crossed the street in front of me, close enough for me to smell their perfume and see the fullness of their breasts. The sight got me stirring and made me remember how long it's been since I chased my wife around the bedroom, so today, instead of going to the tavern, I came here for a mug of Virile."

Gino bit his lip to keep himself silent, filled a mug with the elixir, and set it down hard on the counter. Oblivious to Gino's ire, the man grabbed the mug, swallowed its contents in one gulp, and said, "Enjoy the day, my friend, there may not be many more," as he rushed from the shop. While Gino's eyes followed the departing man, he thought, the fool proclaims sympathy for those who have lost their jobs and he claims to share the pain of the bereaved, but his actions say otherwise. Drunkenness and lust don't fit together with compassion. He's oblivious to the pain of others.

At day's end, Gino walked along the river and stopped to gaze at the mill where he had spent his first night in Florence. The miller had just returned from a granary with a wagonload of grain to be ground into flour. He labors so people have something they need to sustain life, Gino said to himself. On the farm, I did the same. It was hard work, but satisfying and worthwhile. Now people are dying, and I can do nothing to help them. All I do is sell them perfume and elixirs. Gino sat staring at the river until night darkened the sky.

37

Monday April 14, 1348

Visiting his sister at Casa Pagholi gave Gino the opportunity to explore new areas of the city by choosing different routes for his walks from the apothecary to the casa. In the Sant Ambrogio district, he came upon narrow streets with rows of small houses for the working poor. Unlike some of the other neighborhoods touched by poverty, this one had no garbage or sleeping drunks in its alleys. Its air carried a strange odor, but not the most offensive Gino had encountered in his travels.

Ahead, he saw a young girl standing in the middle of the street. She looked in Gino's direction for a time, then turned and looked in the opposite direction, as though she were unsure which way to go.

"Are you lost?" Gino asked when he reached her.

"No, I live there," she said, pointing to a nearby house.

"Does your mother know you're out of the house, standing in the street?"

"My mother died."

Shocked by the girl's dispassionate statement, Gino asked, "Did you call a doctor?"

"My mother had the black disease. No one could do anything for her."

Gino stared at the girl, momentarily stunned by her perception. "Wait here," he said and went to the house. From the doorway, he caught the stench of death. He entered, passed through the tiny front room, the kitchen and sitting space, and stopped at the entrance to the bedroom. To his right was an empty cot, the girl's bed, and to his left a woman covered by a thin sheet lay on a bed. From the doorway, he strained to see if her chest rose and fell with her breaths. There was no movement. She was deathly still. He saw only telltale black swellings on her neck.

Outside, the girl had remained where Gino had left her. He was certain she would be horrified by his next words, but he saw no other course. "Come with me. We need to find a carter so your mother can be buried." Gino knew carters avoided poor neighborhoods because people who lived there couldn't pay their fees.

The girl took Gino's extended hand and walked with him. They went south toward the river, and when they approached Piazza Santa Croce, they saw a carter crossing the piazza and coming toward them. Gino approached the wagon and told the driver about the dead woman. "Who's going to pay?" the driver asked in an acidic voice.

"I will," Gino snapped.

"I get no other business in that neighborhood, so the cost is double," the driver snarled.

Gino agreed to the fee and led the carter to the girl's house. "Take the bed linens," he directed.

"If we wrap the body in a bedsheet, then no shroud," the carter growled.

The girl watched her mother's body being loaded into the wagon and driven away. Puzzled by her lack of tears and apparent composure, Gino asked, "Aren't you sad?"

"I was sad when my mother was sick, but now she's with God, so I'm happy for her." The reaction astounded Gino. Never had he witnessed someone set aside their own loss and view death from the perspective of the deceased. And this from a child.

When the wagon passed out of sight, Gino said, "I'm Gino. What's your name?"

"Mea."

"Where is your father, Mea?"

"I don't know. I've never seen him."

"Do you have any other relatives? Grandparents or an aunt or uncle?"

"No."

The small house and the girl's frayed dress showed the family was poor, but they weren't living in the streets, so they had income from somewhere. "Did your mother have a job?"

"She worked at a tannery."

"What did you do while your mother was working?"

"I worked there too." The girl looked to be no older than seven. Just as Gino wondered what such a young girl could do at a tannery, Mea provided an answer. "I sweep the floors and when wagons come, I give water to the horses."

Spending her days at a tannery explained her strange smell, Gino reasoned. Chemicals boiling in vats eventually stain every worker's clothes, hair, and skin. He went to the nearest house, knocked on the door, and told the woman who answered that the girl's mother had died. "Is there a family here who might take her in?" he asked.

The woman looked with pity at Mea. "Everyone in this neighborhood struggles to get food for their families," she explained. "If the girl were older, old enough to earn her keep ... But at her age, no one wants another mouth to feed."

He returned to where the girl was standing and said, "You can't stay here by yourself. Let's gather your clothes." While Gino looked around the kitchen, Mea went to the bedroom and returned with one dress as threadbare as the one she was wearing. Even without getting close, Gino could smell the harsh acrid odor of tannery chemicals. He shook his head. "Leave it. I'll take you to get a new one."

On their way to the Santa Maria Novella district, Mea stared in wonder at the churches, tower houses, and palazzos they passed as if she had never seen the sights of her city. Watching the girl's reactions, Gino understood she had already made peace with her loss while he continued to mourn his mother's death. His mother was a wonderful woman. Certainly she was with God and His angels. His sister had been right in saying he should look forward, not backward, but it had taken this girl to show him that his continued grief had distanced him from his friends, let his work suffer, and made him question his faith.

"Is this your young sister?" Ercole questioned when Gino and Mea walked into his used clothing shop. His nose twitched as it detected her unusual odor.

Before Gino could respond, the girl said, "I'm Mea. I'm not his sister."

Gino smiled at her assertiveness and said to Ercole, "Her clothes have spent too much time in a tannery. She needs replacements."

"Ah," Ercole acknowledged. From a shelf, he pulled a selection of dresses suitable for a young girl and spread them across the counter. "Do any of these appeal to you, young lady?"

Mea pointed tentatively to one dress.

"A fine choice," Ercole said and held the dress up in front of her. "And it's the perfect size for you."

"Choose two more," Gino said. She looked up at him questioningly, unsure whether she had heard him correctly. He nodded, and she chose two others.

After they left Ercole's shop, she asked, "I've never had three dresses. I don't understand why you bought them for me."

"You told Ercole you're not my sister, but you have no one else and my family is away, so maybe you can be my sister, at least for a while. And I like to do things for my sisters." She seemed comfortable with his explanation. "But before you wear the dresses, we need to get you clean so the new dresses won't smell like a tannery."

"My mother and I bathe in the river behind the tannery. I could go there to get clean."

"I know someplace closer," Gino said.

***

In the room above his own, the one where the healer Masina had lived until she was driven from the city, Gino heated two buckets of water at the fireplace. He poured one bucket into Masina's large wooden tub. After Mea climbed into the tub, he poured the second bucket onto her head and handed her a piece of washing paste. When she was clean and wearing one of her new dresses, he led her down to his room, where she helped him prepare a meal.

***

The following morning, Mea went with Gino to the perfumery. She astonished Signor Roselli by telling him, "I'm Mea, Gino's new sister." She sniffed every perfume urn and dabbed a few fragrances on her arms, cheeks, and neck. Mea keenly observed the women customers and told Gino they weren't like the women who worked at the tannery, but she didn't explain how they were different. In mid-morning, Signor Roselli took the girl to meet his wife. "She'll have a treat for you," he said. Gino didn't see Mea again until closing time.

Throughout the afternoon, Gino considered the girl's fate. She doesn't need a new brother; he reasoned. She needs a new mother who can teach her all the things women teach their daughters. She had no relatives, and her neighbors weren't prepared to take her.

At closing time, Gabriela brought an excited Mea to the perfumery. "She taught me a song," the girl cried out. "She played it on the lute, and we sang it together."

Looking at Mea while clasping Gabriela's hand, Gino said, "Maybe someday she'll teach it to me." He held Gabriela's hand as the three walked outside and released it only reluctantly when he and Mea walked away toward Casa Pagholi.

Passing a tower house, Mea asked, "Who lives in that high house?"

The question made Gino recall a person he knew who lived in a tower house, Tomasia, the woman who had come to Florence as a refugee from Poppi Village during the famine. He answered, "I'll take you to meet someone who lives in a tower house."

He had helped Tomasia get a room in one of the tower houses and find work at Piero Roselli's funeral services business. Initially, her job was washing bodies to prepare them for burial. Now, with the uncountable deaths caused by the plague, the washing of bodies had been abandoned despite objections from the bishops. Roselli's business had expanded. He had teams of carters collecting bodies throughout the city, and he tasked Tomasia with assigning locations to his crews.

Gino remembered Tomasia grieving over the death of her young daughter. She hadn't mentioned the girl's age when she had died of an incurable illness, but Gino wondered whether Mea might fill the sorrowful hole in Tomasia's heart. His intuition was validated by Tomasia's beaming smile the instant she saw Mea. "Her face. Her eyes. They're just like my sweet Tessa."

"I've never seen so many women living in one house," Mea said in a soft voice as Tomasia led her through the tower. On the top floor, Mea looked out wide-eyed through a window at the city below.

***

The following afternoon, Gino and Mea brought Tomasia to the house where Mea had lived with her mother. The three ate a filling supper cooked by Tomasia. Gino left the pair when Mea took Tomasia for a walk to show her the neighborhood. Holding Tomasia's hand, Mea said hopefully, "You could live here with me instead of in the crowded high house." Later, Tomasia tucked Mea into bed for the first time.

38

Monday May 6, 1348

Earlier in the year, news had reached Florence of a mysterious sickness ravaging the trading partners that the city depended upon: Sicily, Genoa, and Pisa. But few Florentines had known the deadly disease had already invaded their own city. The Signoria had been congratulating itself for ending the famine. Even though thousands had died from malnutrition, the members praised themselves for having prevented even more deaths. They couldn't foresee the looming plague.

Just two months later, the pestilence had also overrun Florence. Thousands of Florentines had died, with hundreds more deaths occurring every day. The Signoria and their advisors struggled to deal with the consequences. Shuttered businesses caused the soaring prices of scarce goods and services. Growing numbers of out-of-work people overwhelmed the public's charity. Desperate people resorted to crime and looting. A prominent banker, shortly before he fled the city, had proclaimed, "Corpses rotting in the streets have turned our once lovely city into a stinking sewer."

Messer Pagholi spent long hours at the Palazzo della Signoria with other government advisors trying to craft solutions to the burgeoning problems, so it surprised Rina, his wife, when he came home in mid-afternoon. Color drained from her face upon seeing him. "What's wrong, Avito? Are you not well?"

Avito embraced his wife and said softly, "I'm well, but we just received word of another member of the Signoria who's been stricken. And he's only the latest. Earlier in the week, the disease afflicted two other men who had been consulting with us."

Lucia stood across the room, watching. She couldn't hear Pagholi's words, but she saw the tension in his movements and sensed his fear.

He took a step back, rested his hands on his wife's shoulders and said, loud enough for Lucia to hear, "The city is not safe. The disease is everywhere."

His pronouncement did not surprise Rina. Her weekly card games with her friends had been suspended because two of the women had left the city with their families. The constant reminders of death everywhere kept Rina from venturing outside.

Avito announced, "It's time for you to leave." He turned enough to see Lucia was also listening. "You and Lucia will stay with my brother at his vineyard."

His tone and words told Rina he wanted to send her away, but he didn't intend to accompany her. "No! No!" she protested. "You must come with us."

He spread his hands in resignation. "I cannot. The city is in a crisis. There is work to be done, so I must stay."

Rina stepped away and faced her husband defiantly with her hands on her hips. "Lucia and I are protected in this house. There is no foul air here. You are the one at risk, in a place where men are losing their lives. If there is bad air, it is at the Palazzo della Signoria."

He went to her and wrapped his arms around her. "We're dealing with crucial matters at the palazzo. When they're settled, I will join you."

"Promise me it will be soon."

"Soon, *cara mia*. I promise."

Rina felt his determination and realized further protest would be futile. She lowered her head onto his shoulder and wept. Lucia tucked a handkerchief into Rina's hand.

Avito held his wife until she stopped crying, then said, "A carriage is coming to bring you to Domenico's vineyard. The carriage and a wagon to hold your belongings will be here within the hour, so you should start packing."

"Does Domenico know we're coming?"

Avito shook his head. "I've not spoken with him, but I'm sure he knows what's happening in Florence. He's probably wondering why you haven't left the city already. While you pack, I'm going to the butcher to get a hog hind for Domenico."

"I thought he raised hogs."

"No, he has only sheep at the vineyard, so pork will be a welcome treat for him. I'll return later to bid you off." He kissed his wife lightly on the forehead, then tenderly on the lips and left.

Signora Pagholi took Lucia by the hand and headed toward the stairs. "We haven't much time. Bring the trunk from the storeroom to my bedroom."

Rina was poring through two chests of clothes when Lucia dragged the trunk into the bedroom. "It's heavy. I couldn't lift it."

"I wasn't thinking, or I would have helped you. The trunk is heavy because it isn't empty." Rina released the two clasps and opened the trunk, which was half full of simple dresses and blouses, unlike the fashionable clothes she usually wore. "These are my country clothes. In the good times before the plague and the famine, Avito and I spent our holidays in the mountains. That's where I wore these clothes."

"Are these what you'll take to the vineyard?" Lucia asked.

"Yes, those and some of these." She pointed to the chests holding the clothes she normally wore in Florence. "Life is usually rustic at the vineyard, but occasionally Domenico hosts gatherings of his neighbors where stylish dress is appropriate." After thinking for a moment, she said, "Although if the plague has reached the countryside, he may have dispensed with his celebrations."

After winnowing her selections to fill the trunk and a single satchel, she dismissed Lucia. "You'd better pack your things. The carriage will be here soon."

Lucia had only the farm clothes she wore when she came to Florence, two dresses Gino had bought for her, and a dress she had bought for herself. They hardly filled her satchel.

Avito returned to the house in a wagon following the carriage. The wagon bed behind him held a hog hind wrapped in heavy cloth. He led both drivers into the house and directed them to fetch the trunk and the satchels.

Rina said, "Remember, you promised to join us as soon as you can. The Signoria would keep you with them forever if they could. Don't let them."

"I won't." Avito responded and kissed her hand as he helped her climb into the carriage. Then, helping Lucia, he said, "I think the vineyard will feel familiar to you. It's like a farm, except it grows grapes rather than vegetables."

Lucia didn't respond to his comment, which made him question whether she would find the vineyard comfortably familiar or whether memories of the farm would make her homesick for her village and her family. He closed the carriage door and watched as it moved away and turned out of sight, heading south toward the San Trinita bridge.

As the carriage approached the river, Rina looked across at her young house servant and said, "I'm going to miss him. Avito and I have been married nearly ten years and we've rarely spent time apart."

With tears filling her eyes, she shifted her gaze to the window and continued speaking as much to herself as to Lucia. "He was a handsome new lawyer when we first met. My father had hired him, and he came to our house to prepare a contract for something to do with father's business. He had intelligent eyes and spoke with a confidence rare in someone so young. Everything about him said someday he would become successful and important. But what heightened my affection was his gentleness and the respect he paid to my mother." She laughed. "I don't think he even noticed me until his third visit." Suddenly embarrassed, she pointed out the window and exclaimed, "Look! That boy just caught a fish!"

The carriage stopped briefly at Porta San Pier Gattolino to wait for a family to pass through the narrow gate. After clearing the gate, the family moved aside. One of them, a young boy, looked up wide-eyed at the carriage moving past him. Lucia noticed he didn't have shoes. His feet were wrapped in cloth. His parents and older siblings carried bags and satchels. A woman, probably the boy's mother, struggled with an infant, squirming to free itself from her arms.

"Where can they be going?" Lucia wondered aloud.

"In this direction, there are only vineyards. They're probably hoping to find work," Rina responded.

"How far is it to the vineyards?" Lucia asked.

"A hiker could reach the nearest vineyard in about two hours," Rina replied. "For them, it will take twice as long, or more."

In safer times, Rina would have invited the woman and her child to ride in the carriage, but she couldn't be sure the woman wasn't infected. Some people claimed infected people spread the disease by contaminating the air. Constantly, there were new claims and beliefs. Some sounded plausible, others seemed outrageous; there was no measure to tell which were true. The only satisfactory course was to avoid all risks.

Lucia was seated facing the rear of the carriage, giving her a view of the receding city. As they climbed into the hills, she could see the steeple of Santa Maria Novella in the distance. Later, when Gino walks past the church on his way home from the apothecary, she thought, he won't know I've left the city. Eventually, he'll go to Casa Pagholi and probably find the house empty. Until he chances upon Messer Pagholi, he won't know what had happened to me. Once again, our family is scattering.

They were traveling on the road connecting Florence to Siena. In normal times, the road was busy with wagons of merchants transporting goods between the two cities. Now, with so many shops closed in Florence, and perhaps also in Siena, the road saw only a few farm wagons.

The carriage driver turned off the main road at the village of Calzaiolo. Either he had been to the vineyard before, or Messer Pagholi had given him detailed directions. For several miles, they wound among hills covered with precisely spaced rows of grapevines. At a stone marker, the carriage turned onto a narrow road headed toward a distant villa. They were halfway along the road when a man on horseback raced out to meet them.

He stopped directly in front of the carriage and shouted to the driver. "You can't be here! Turn around!"

Rina recognized the voice as that of the vineyard manager. She leaned out the carriage window and called, "Antonio, it's Rina."

He walked his horse around to the side of the carriage. "Rina, Domenico didn't tell me you were coming."

"He didn't know I was coming. It was a sudden decision. Avito believes it is no longer safe in Florence, so he sent me here."

Antonio's face showed a pained expression. "Domenico isn't here. He won't be back until night. He ordered me to let no one go to the villa."

"Antonio, you know me," Rina said anxiously.

"Domenico is afraid for his family. Even I don't go into the villa. He heard half the people in Florence have died … and you have come from there."

"The plague is bad in Florence, but it hasn't taken half the people." Or has it, she wondered.

"I don't know," Antonio said, befuddled. "Domenico said let no one into the villa … but you're family." He bit his lip, unsure what Domenico would expect of him; then his expression brightened. "You could stay at an outbuilding until Domenico returns."

"The outbuilding will be fine," Rina agreed.

As Antonio led the carriage forward, Lucia asked, "What are the outbuildings?" She was familiar only with the crude sheds on her family's farm used to store tools and animal feed. She couldn't imagine Antonio expecting Rina to stay in a smelly, dirty storage shed.

Rina replied, "They're simple housing quarters. At harvest time, pickers move from one vineyard to another. When they're here at Domenico's vineyard, they stay in the outbuildings. The outbuildings are rustic, but they're clean and more comfortable than this carriage."

Lucia laughed. "I'm sure they'll be fine for me. Until I went to live at your house, all I knew was rustic."

The drivers unloaded the luggage. Antonio slung the hog hind onto the back of his horse. "I'll take this to the villa, and I'll let Domenico know you've arrived when he returns."

The brightest stars were already lighting the night sky when Rina answered a knock on the door. Domenico greeted her with an apology when she opened the door, "Rina, Antonio was only following my instructions when he brought you here," but he made no move to enter the building. His angst was apparent. In the past, he had always welcomed her with a warm embrace; now he remained a distance away.

"We've settled ourselves and are quite content here," Rina said.

"Let me explain," Domenico said, still keeping his distance from her. "My neighbor, a man I've known since childhood, had his wife and two children taken by the plague. They went to Florence to visit a friend and never returned. They died horrible deaths. Thinking of his tragedy keeps me awake at night. I couldn't bear losing my wife."

Not wanting to increase his anxiety, Rina said, "I understand. We can stay here until Avito joins us. He'll be coming as soon as his business in the city is finished."

Torn between concern for his wife's safety and duty to his brother's family, Domenico merely nodded and turned away. The next morning, Nedda Pagholi, Domenico's wife, burst into the outbuilding, embraced Rina, and said, "Come, breakfast is ready at the villa. Both of you, come."

Rina raised an eyebrow. "Will your husband be comfortable with us coming to the villa?"

"Domenico takes great measures to protect me, and I love him for it, but I'm sure you didn't bring a carriage full of bad air with you from Florence. There's no reason for you to be sequestered."

***

Two days later, near closing time at the apothecary, a young man wearing a leather cape and leather boots entered the shop. "Are you Gino Liani?" he asked.

"I am," Gino replied.

"I'm a courier for the Signoria. This letter is from Pisa. It's addressed to you."

He took the letter and stared at it, but didn't open it. Thinking Gino might not know how to read, the man said, "Would you like me to read it to you?"

"Thank you, but I can read."

"If you read it now, I can have your reply sent to Pisa."

Gino cradled the letter in his hands as though it were a valuable jewel. "I need to share it with someone."

The man nodded. "If you wish to send a response, go to the Palazzo della Signoria and tell a clerk to deliver your letter to me, Manzo."

***

Crossing the city to Casa Pagholi, anxiety made Gino pat the pouch fastened at his belt that contained the letter from his brother. If it held good news, he would delight in learning it simultaneously with Lucia. Bad news would be less overpowering if they were together to comfort each other, although he questioned whether he could endure any more dreadful news.

Gino stepped to the side to give a wide berth to a woman and two young girls who were walking toward him. As they passed, one girl looked up at him and smiled. He judged her to be about eight or nine, the same ages as his younger sisters when he had left the farm. In his mind's image, his sisters hadn't aged. He could see them in a field picking beans on a warm summer day. And he could see them waving goodbye to him as he left the farm in Taddeo's wagon, heading for Florence. His memories had not aged in three years, but his sisters surely had. Now the girls would be eleven and twelve … if they had escaped the plague. How could a loving God not protect those innocent girls?

When he reached Casa Pagholi, he found the house empty. He couldn't imagine where the two women might have gone with the plague raging in Florence. Signora Pagholi had suspended all her social engagements and merchants came to the casa, so there was no need for them to go shopping. Gino sat on a bench in the small garden at the rear of the building to wait for the women to return. Before long, he began fidgeting, stood, paced through the garden, then returned to the bench. He tore open the envelope and began reading.

My dear brother Gino,

Shortly after we met in Florence, I was assigned to a canal barge, so I'm sorry to tell you I won't be coming there again. Now my job is ferrying goods between ships at the seaport and the warehouses in Pisa. Men on the other canal barges complain about the long hours, but they never worked on a farm. I have no complaints. The work is steady, and the pay is good.

Our young brother Laro has taken a job as a cabin boy on a ship carrying goods between Sicily, Calabria, and Pisa. On his first voyage he was seasick, but he's become accustomed to the rocking motion of the ship. He claims it helps him sleep at night. What a change he's made from a farm boy to a sailor. His voyages take him away for a week or two at a time, so I only get to see him for a couple of days when his ship is in port.

Father is kept busy at the carpentry shop, but he finds it depressing to spend his days building coffins. He enjoyed the work more when he was making furniture.

The plague is still strong in Pisa but not outside the city, so father arranged for Ciosa and Fiora to stay with the family of a man who owns a lumber mill and delivers wood to the carpentry shop where father works. At first the girls protested, saying they were old enough to take care of themselves, but father didn't want them exposed to the plague, so he insisted. They stopped complaining when they learned the family has a daughter the same age as Ciosa. I miss the girls, though. Without their laughter, the house feels empty.

Father and I miss you and Lucia. We're told the plague is also strong in Florence, maybe even worse than here in Pisa. We pray you both stay well.

Your loving brother, Fanto

Thank God no others in our family have gotten sick, but we keep wandering farther apart with Ciosa and Fiora at a lumbermill and Laro on a ship. "Will we ever be together again?" Gino wondered.

As daylight began to fade, Gino headed back to his room, disappointed that he couldn't share the news with Lucia. Still puzzling over where his sister had gone, he took solace in believing Messer and Signora Pagholi would keep her safe.

***

The following day, Messer Pagholi greeted him when he arrived at the house. Pagholi explained, "I sent Rina to my brother's vineyard three days ago, and Lucia went with her. It was a sudden decision I made after hearing of another death among my close associates. I should have gone to the apothecary to tell you, but I've been busy. I miss Rina and I'm sure you miss Lucia. Maybe we can visit them soon."

Messer Pagholi's explanation left Gino torn. He felt comforted knowing his sister was in a safer place, but now he was more alone than ever.

39

Tuesday May 13, 1348

Decades of mistrust and fear of corruption had shaped the Florentine government. Its principal ruling body, the Signoria, consisted of nine men chosen to serve for the exceedingly short term of two months. With such brief tenures, it became common practice for the men in power to defer the burden of addressing difficult and unpopular matters to their successors. Neglect caused manageable problems to fester until they grew into crises, when public outcry finally demanded they be resolved.

The Signoria had two councils with comparably short terms to advise them on policy. Members of one council, known as the Council of Twelve, served for three months. Members of the Council of Sixteen were appointed for four months. Messer Pagholi was nearing the end of his tenure on the Council of Twelve. During the famine crisis, he had served, along with a few other esteemed men, as unofficial advisors to bring continuity to the fragmented government. Pagholi had decided, although not yet let it be known, that he would also stop serving as an unofficial advisor and return to his post as a senior magistrate when his term on The Twelve ended.

Panic gripping the city forced the Signoria to take action to combat the plague. They responded by convening a meeting in the large Hall of the Two Hundred. Besides their official and unofficial advisors, the Signoria invited representatives of the major guilds, the bishop of San Reparata cathedral, the Captain of the People, and managers of the funeral services companies. The people of Florence had been avoiding contact with others as much as possible, so the Signoria hadn't expected people would flock to the meeting. They had made no provisions to limit attendance by the public and were surprised by how quickly the hall filled. The derisive comments of those crowding into the room made clear they had been embittered by the Signoria's inaction. One angry man, as he pushed his way toward the front of the room, grunted, "Bodies in the streets didn't move them. They did nothing until the plague claimed one of their own."

Only six members of the Signoria sat on the chairs lined up at the front of the room. Besides the member who had succumbed to the plague, two others had been stricken and were likely on their deathbeds. Signor Sfortunato, the Signoria's most senior member, stepped to the lectern, ready to start the meeting. He was a small man with thinning hair and a weak chin, but despite his meek appearance, he held Florence's most prestigious elected office with the title Standard Bearer of Justice. Earlier, he had approached the Captain of the People and suggested, "Some of the uninvited people might cause trouble. If they become unruly, they will need to be removed. Can you summon your *berrovarii* to enforce order should it become necessary?"

"Yes," the Captain agreed and dispatched his assistant to fetch some of his men who served as the city's law enforcement officers.

Sfortunato pounded his fist on the lectern and called for quiet. "We are here to consider actions to combat the plague. Some of you have proposals to discuss, but first, we'll begin by describing the actions we have already taken."

He gestured to the captain, who rose and scanned the crowd. He gave a quick nod to three of his men who had just arrived and taken positions at the rear of the room. His narrow frame and prominent brow gave him the appearance of an academic, but everyone in the audience knew him as Florence's top law enforcement officer and criminal magistrate.

His powerful voice, carrying to the furthest corners of the room, proclaimed, "We issued an edict last month forbidding anyone who had traveled to Pisa or Genoa from entering our city. Goods being brought to Florence by Pisans must be delivered to a location outside the city and brought into the city by Florentines. The crews of river barges coming from Pisa must remain onboard while their barges are unloaded. My berrovarii are stationed at the city gates and the docks to ensure the ruling is enforced. I'm carefully monitoring the situation in other cities and I will extend the prohibition to include Siena if the plague there continues to worsen." He remained standing for a few moments to see if anyone was foolish enough to question his ruling.

Next, Sfortunato called upon the representative of the Doctors' and Apothecaries' Guild, who was seated in the front row and wore the traditional red robe of his profession. He had served twice as a guild consul and twice also as its secretary. Although he was not currently an officer, he had been chosen to present the guild's position. Rumors claimed both current consuls had fled the city, but the guild would only admit the men were unavailable. The doctor remained seated as he began addressing the members of the Signoria. "Those who have unbalanced humors are most susceptible ..." He got no further before shouts from the audience interrupted him.

"Is he speaking yet?" one voice shouted.

"We can't hear him," another complained.

Two berrovarii moved toward the disrupters, ready to eject them from the meeting until the captain raised his hand, signaling his men to withdraw.

With the help of an associate, the doctor pushed himself up and turned to face the crowd. He spoke louder, although those in the rear still had difficulty hearing him. "We have long known humid vegetables and fruits can unbalance the humors and increase the severity of all sicknesses, including this plague. Therefore, we must ban the sale of humid foods."

"What are humid foods?" a man blared. He was recognized as an official of the merchant's guild, so no effort was made to silence him.

The question startled the doctor, but he quickly recovered. "Figs, plums, beans, and melons are some of the humid foods ... and there are others." He thought for another moment, then added, "Mushrooms, too. Even milk can cause imbalances."

"We can't ban all foods," the merchant retorted. "What will people eat?"

With memories of the famine still fresh in people's minds, the crowd voiced support for the merchant's objection. Sfortunato again pounded his fist on the lectern and declared, "Our intent is to listen to all proposals today and to issue our rulings tomorrow. We will consider the information provided by both the doctor and the merchants." He glanced at the other Signoria members to confirm they agreed with his statement.

Florence had several bishops, but only one, the bishop of San Reparata, had been invited to the meeting. He received special treatment because San Reparata was the city's cathedral. Hoping for an even higher status, he fervently prayed for a promotion to archbishop.

Sfortunato admonished the crowd. "Listen respectfully to the words of Bishop d'Santo."

The bishop rose, turned to face the crowd, and in a powerful voice trained through years of delivering homilies, he began, "My children. As the good doctor told you, unbalanced humors can intensify the effects of disease. In the past, we have all suffered ailments caused by unbalanced humors, but this plague is different. Yesterday, a friar from my church was summoned to the home of a family stricken with the plague, a mother, father, and three children. While the friar prayed at their bedsides, the mother, father, and one child were taken by the Lord. The other two children, who lived in the same house, ate the same foods, and breathed the same air, suffered no illness whatsoever. There can be only one explanation for this: the hand of God tapped three members of the family, and for reasons known only to the Almighty, did not touch the other two children."

Raising his voice, he continued, "We should not be surprised by this because the Bible gives us warning. In Deuteronomy 28, it says if you do not follow God's laws, the Lord will bring upon you great plagues and all the diseases of Egypt will cling to you." Enumerating with his fingers for emphasis, he stressed, "The Holy Book tells us the only way to end this plague is to rid ourselves of fallen women, of drunkards, and of gluttons."

He turned to target the members of the Signoria, but kept his voice loud enough for everyone to hear. "You must expel prostitutes from the city, and you must limit the consumption of beer and wine." He didn't mention gluttony because, with the high prices of food, few could indulge in that sin. Everyone looked at those standing nearby, expecting someone to speak in favor of beer and wine, if not the prostitutes, but no one did.

Sfortunato held a hand in front of his face to hide his smirk as he wondered how his colleagues would respond to the bishop's repressive proposals. He thanked the bishop for his suggestions, then called upon another member of the Signoria who came to the lectern. "Bad air is everywhere in our city," he began.

A heckler shouted, "You can call the air bad in your district, but where I live, it stinks like shit." Two berrovarii moved forward quickly and grabbed the disrupter by the shoulders. He continued his protest as they dragged him from the room. "We can hardly walk through the streets without retching," he bellowed.

When the man was removed and the excitement subsided, the Signoria member resumed speaking. "The causes of the bad air are many. Carters collect the bodies of those whose relatives can pay." He glared at one group of funeral services owners as he added, "Even though some charge obscene fees for their service. But we have too many shameful cases of families abandoning their dead relations, leaving them in houses to die alone. And with no one to pay the carters, those bodies remain festering, sometimes for days, before neighbors are overwhelmed by the stench. Corpses of paupers lie fallen in alleyways. In some neighborhoods, garbage is left to pile in the streets. Sewer systems are clogged. Butchers have putrid meats and markets have rotten produce."

A butcher in the audience yelled, "My shop doesn't sell putrid meat."

The speaker shot him an icy stare; then he addressed the comment. "I'm sure you don't sell putrid meat and when your beef gets too old to sell, you probably give it to dogs. I'm talking about beef so tainted even dogs won't eat it. What becomes of it then?" The butcher slunk down and hid himself in the crowd. "Markets are littered with vegetables and fruit so rancid they are rejected even by rats." He spread his arms wide. "All these sources contribute to our bad air, and all must be eradicated. I propose a special commission be appointed with the power to correct all unsanitary conditions." He returned to his seat, pleased to see heads in the audience nodding approval of his recommendation.

The Signoria was the only government body empowered to propose ordinances, but their proposals needed approval before being enacted into law. Not only did they require the consent of the Council of Twelve and the Council of Sixteen, but they also needed a two-thirds majority in the three-hundred-member Council of the Popolo and the two hundred member Council of the Commune. Experience had taught the members of the Signoria their proposals could be turned into law only through compromise.

Later, in the confines of their meeting chamber, the members discussed each proposal. They had before them a list of a dozen fruits and vegetables the doctors' guild representative deemed as humid. "We can't ban all these," one member declared. "Some are grown on farms right here in Tuscany. Surely we won't ban those," another member observed. Sfortunato said, "My doctor claims raw fruits are most harmful. We should begin by banning fruit brought from the south."

As they struggled to reach consensus, laughter from the member at the far end of the table interrupted the discussion. "At least no one will object to Bishop d'Santo's proposal to expel the prostitutes. I suspect half the members of the Council of the Popolo frequent prostitutes, but none will admit publicly."

"We can't just send them away." Sfortunato said. "Where would they go?"

The laughing member suggested, "We should instruct the bishop to provide space for them at a convent in the countryside." Even Sfortunato chuckled at that suggestion.

Two days later—May 15, 1348

Throughout the city, town criers announced the measures proposed by the Signoria and approved by the councils to combat the plague.

Until such time that the plague ends:

*Figs, unripe plums, fresh beans, and unripe almonds are banned from entering the city.

*Prostitutes are exiled from the city.

*Fines will be imposed on butchers, taverns, and other shops having materials that emit a stench.

*A commission of eight honorable men will be appointed to enforce sanitary regulations. They shall have the authority to remove putrid matter and infected people who might corrupt the air.

40

Thursday May 15, 1348

In mid-afternoon, Messer Pagholi entered the perfumery carrying a bottle of wine. Surprised by his presence, Gino said, "It's rare to see you here at this hour. I heard about the new ordinances. Did the Signoria release you early today or is your work with them finished?"

"I released myself," Pagholi replied. "There's little reason to expect the new ordinances will eradicate this plague, but whatever more is needed will be the responsibility of others. It was my pleasure to serve the Signoria, but doing so has kept me from my wife far too long. When we were together in Florence, the city's business kept me from giving her the attention she deserved. And now, I haven't seen her at all in too many days."

"I imagine the separation has been difficult," Gino said, recalling the last time he saw Gabriela's smile and felt the warmth of her touch.

"Tonight, I'll sleep in my bed alone for the last time. Tomorrow I'm going to my brother's vineyard to be with Rina." Smiling, Pagholi opened the wine bottle. "Join me in a drink to mark my freedom from the problems of our beleaguered city."

Gino set two mugs on the counter. "We have only mugs; no wine glasses," he said apologetically.

"They'll do," Pagholi said as he poured and raised his mug. "May the future of our city rest on the shoulders of wise men."

As the men touched mugs, Gino said, "May those men have wisdom matching your own, and may you now be free to enjoy your wife's company." After taking a long drink, Gino asked, "Why wait until morning? Why not leave for the vineyard now?"

"There's a vegetable garden at the vineyard, but it lacks the variety of goods available here in Florence. My dear wife enjoys tropical delicacies, so in the morning I'll go to the central market in search of her favorites, figs, plums, and apricots. Nuts too, if there are any to be found."

"Aren't tropical items banned by the new ordinances?" Gino asked.

"Yes, they are, so tomorrow may be my last chance to get them until the plague ends. The captain is a practical man. He'll have the berrovarii wait a day or two before enforcing the new laws, so merchants have time to sell their remaining stock." Pagholi grinned. "And to give members of the Signoria time to make their purchases."

Pagholi took another drink, set his mug down, and said, "You must miss your sister, Gino. Come with me to the vineyard to visit her. We can travel together. I've a wagon reserved for tomorrow morning."

Signor Roselli, who had overheard the conversation, poked his head into the perfumery and said, "You should go, Gino. I can't count how many times in the past weeks I've heard you mention your sister. I know you'd like to see her."

***

The next morning, Gino met Pagholi at the central market. As the magistrate had predicted, vendors' carts still displayed the banned items, yet two berrovarii strolling through the market didn't arrest the sellers. One even stopped for a friendly chat with a merchant and didn't mention the contraband in the seller's cart.

When Pagholi spotted Gino, he held up two bulging sacks. "Figs and apricots," he said happily. "Rina will be delighted. But I'm still hoping to find a vendor selling almonds."

"The sacks look heavy," Gino observed. "Did you buy the vendor's entire stock?"

Pagholi laughed. "I had to wait in lines to get these. I wasn't the only person eager to buy tropical fruit before the embargo is enforced."

Gino scanned the carts in the marketplace as Pagholi drifted away in search of an almond merchant. Pagholi had already merged into the crowd when Gino said, "I'd like to get something for Lucia." He spotted Ercole's cart in the used clothing vendor's favorite spot near the portico.

"The air must not be bad in this marketplace," Ercole joked. "I come here several times each week and I've survived."

"Maybe your good Christian soul is protecting you," Gino quipped.

"It can't be purity, my friend, for my soul is no less clouded than those of my colleagues who've been struck down by this horrible plague."

"Is the plague affecting your business?"

"It's taken half of my customers, so sales are sluggish while my shop is bursting with a stockpile of goods ready to sell. Once people get past grieving, they're eager to dispose of their dead relatives' clothes and they remember Ercole's shop. Every day people come in with armloads of clothes for me to sell."

"Then perhaps you can help me. Lucia has been staying outside the city. I haven't seen her in two weeks, so I'd like to bring her a gift, nothing extravagant, just a token."

Ercole raised a hand. "I have the perfect gift." He searched through an assortment of items on his cart and pulled out a selection of silk bandings.

"What are they?" Gino asked.

"*Cordoni*, narrow belts. They're the newest fashion replacing the wide *cinture* women have been wearing. Cordoni are the most sought fashion accessory by wealthy Florentine women. And these are not used, they're new. I got them from the owner of a silk mill who wanted to sell his finished goods before he fled the city. He claimed Signora Peruzzi, the banker's wife, has a different color cordino for each day of the week."

"Lucia is a simple farm girl. I'm not sure she's ready for fashion."

Ercole laughed. "Your sister is no longer the little farm girl stuck in your memory, Gino." He held out a dark brown cordino. "This one matches her eyes and will contrast well with the wheat-colored dress she bought."

Gino's jaw dropped. "You remember her eyes and the color of the dress she bought?"

"Attention to details is necessary for success in my business. Is she still a house servant at Casa Pagholi?"

"Yes. Although now she and Signora Pagholi are staying at Messer Pagholi's brother's vineyard."

He handed Gino a dark blue cordino. "Have Messer Pagholi give this one to his wife. He can pay me for it when he returns to the city. It would be unbecoming of Signora Pagholi to be less stylish than her house servant."

From the market, Gino and Pagholi walked to the stable. The magistrate was pleased to have fruit and a new fashionable accessory for his wife, plus a sack of oranges for his brother. Despite Ercole's endorsement, Gino remained unsure how Lucia would react to the cordino.

As they climbed aboard the wagon, Pagholi said, "Vandals have been breaking into houses abandoned by families who've left the city. My house is in a safe neighborhood frequently patrolled by the berrovarii; still, I'm concerned. If this is not too great an imposition, would it be possible for you to stay at my house one or two nights each week so any thugs will see lights inside and window coverings moved?"

"You've treated my sister as a member of your family. It would be my pleasure to do that for you," Gino said, touched that this important man put such trust in him.

***

Messer Pagholi turned the wagon off the main road at the stone marker and headed into the vineyard. No one rode out to intercept them as they continued along the dirt track and approached the villa. In the distance, to his right, Gino noticed two figures walking along a row of grapevines. He lost sight of them momentarily when they bent down to tend the vines. They were laughing when they straightened up and continued walking.

Gino squinted, held his hand above his eyes to block the bright sunlight, then burst out, "That's Lucia! I'm sure it's her!"

Pagholi glanced in the direction Gino was pointing and said, "They're walking toward the house. You can meet her there." He kept the wagon moving forward and when it reached the house, he jumped out and called to his wife, who rushed outside and embraced him.

Gino kept watching Lucia and the man with her as they stopped several more times to tend vines. "What a surprise!" Lucia shouted when she saw her brother. She raced to him and hugged him.

Gino wrapped his arms around his sister, but his eyes were on the man following behind her. It was only the middle of May; yet the man had the healthy color of one who had been toiling under a summer sun. His short-sleeved smock exposed his muscular arms. Gino judged him to be about four years older than Lucia. When he got close, Lucia said, "This is Berto. I was helping him tie vines to the trellises."

After she introduced Gino, Berto said, "Your sister is a great help. She learns everything quickly." Moving away, he added, "I need to inspect some other vines. Perhaps I'll see you again later."

Gino waited until Berto left, then said, "You seem to be enjoying yourself here at the vineyard."

"I am," Lucia responded, her eyes still on Berto. "The vineyard is a cheerful place, very different from Florence. I went to Florence during the famine. It was a depressing time, with half-starved people teeming into the city from the countryside. Our own family was forced to leave their farm. Now it's even worse. Florence is engulfed by the plague. I was fortunate to be sheltered from the horror at Casa Pagholi, but outside, there was death everywhere in the city. Just knowing of the horror haunted me. Here it's different. The plague hasn't taken a toll in the vineyards or the nearby village. I'm happy … the way I was when we were children on the farm. I've put the misery aside."

A long silence passed before Gino asked, "Will you be going back to Casa Pagholi when the city is safer?"

"I don't know."

Although fearful of hearing her response, Gino asked, "Is Berto part of your uncertainty?"

"I don't know. I've only known him for a week." But the smile Lucia tried to conceal told Gino a week's acquaintance had been enough to change his little sister into a young woman who could fall in love.

41

June 1348

Even though Gino lived a distance away from the apothecary, he often arrived earlier than Signor Roselli, who lived directly above the shop. But never Roselli been so late that Gino had time to help several customers before Roselli arrived. When the shop door opened again, it was Gabriela Roselli, Carlo's daughter, who shuffled in, her face streaked with tears. Gino rushed to her and wrapped his arms around her. "Gabriela, what happened?"

Her crying grew louder as she lowered her head onto his shoulder. Eventually she managed to say, in a quivering voice, "My father is sick. My mother sent me away."

"This isn't the first time he's been sick. He'll recover," Gino said, hoping to reassure her.

In a barely audible voice, Gabriela said, "He won't recover. Not from this. No one does."

They stood motionless for several minutes. When her crying slowed, Gino led her to a chair. "Stay here. I'm going to speak with your mother."

Gino locked the shop, climbed the stairs to the second level, and knocked on the Rosellis' door. "It's Gino," he called.

"You can do nothing here, Gino. See that Gabriela is cared for," Signora Roselli asserted from inside.

"I'll fetch Doctor Guarino."

Gino couldn't understand Joanna Roselli's muttered response. Descending the stairs, he recalled Guarino saying he visited the houses of plague victims, not to care for the sick but to care for others in the house, to strengthen their immunities. "Come with me," he said to Gabriela. "We're going to fetch Doctor Guarino." He took her by the hand and led her. She moved like someone in a trance.

Guarino pounded a fist on his desk when Gino described the reason he and Gabriela had come to his office. "Damn this disease. It's impossible to tell who'll be next," he snapped, then to Gabriela, he said, "Your father is a good person. I'll do everything I can for him."

He accompanied Gino and Gabriela to the apothecary, where he requested of Gino, "A vial of belladonna." To Gabriela, he said, "Belladonna will relieve his pain."

"A full vial?" Gino asked.

"Yes, a full vial." His sharp reply told Gino he intended to administer a small dose and then entrust the rest of the lethal drug to Roselli's wife. She would find the courage to end Roselli's suffering when his pain became unbearable.

As soon as the medication was ready, Guarino took the vial and left the shop. Gabriela sat alone in the preparation room and Gino served customers while they waited for the doctor to return. When Guarino came back to the apothecary, he merely nodded his head, acknowledging to Gino that Roselli had the incurable sickness. He continued into the preparation room, where Gabriela sat stiffly, her hands gripping the sides of her chair. Guarino announced, "I examined your mother, and she shows no signs of the disease. Her humors are balanced, so I don't expect her to be stricken."

Gabriela's hands relaxed, and she folded them on her lap. "Thank God," she said, her voice faltering.

"I want to test you as well," Guarino said.

After analyzing Gabriela's urine, Guarino reported, "Your humors are also balanced, but your mother insists you stay away from the house as a precaution, and I share her vigilance. This pestilence is unpredictable, so it's best to take whatever measures you can to keep yourself safe." He placed a sympathetic hand on Gino's shoulder as he left the shop.

***

Gino closed the shop early and took Gabriela to Casa Pagholi. She merely picked at the supper he had prepared, then pushed the plate away and said, "When I was younger, we took our holidays at a lake in the hills near Arezzo. With two years of famine and now the pestilence, we haven't taken a holiday in recent years, not even once since you started working at the shop. Father promised when life returned to normal, we would go back to that lake." Tears came again as she realized her family's life would never return to normal and her father's promise would never be fulfilled.

Gabriela slept fitfully. From the room across the hall, Gino heard her tossing. Twice her outcries woke him. The second time, he went to her room and lay down next to her. His arm around her calmed her and let her sleep until morning.

She opened her eyes, looked around the room, confused, and asked, "Where are we?"

"Casa Pagholi."

"Casa Pagholi? How did we get …" Then the memory came like a stabbing pain. She declared, "I want to see my father."

"Yes, but first you need to eat something. You ate nothing last night.

They compromised by Gabriela eating a sweet roll as they walked from Casa Pagholi to her home above the apothecary. She banged on the locked door. "Let me in, mother. I want to see father."

"No," her mother declared adamantly. "He's sleeping."

"How is he?" Gabriela asked in a softer, fear-filled voice.

Joanna didn't believe in lying to her daughter even when she had to deliver tragic news. "He's doing poorly. He worsened steadily through the night, but I gave him a dose of the medication from Doctor Guarino, so he's not suffering."

"Please, may I see him?"

"It's better you not see him while he's so ill," Joanna said, her voice cracking with emotion. "Remember him as you've known him your entire life, his strong shoulders carrying the weight of the world, always there to protect you."

Gabriela knew from experience that protesting would be fruitless. Her mother was unyielding once she had set her mind. "And you, mother? Are you well?"

"Don't fret about me. I'm fine. I have no symptoms."

Gino said, "We should tell his brother." Neither woman responded to his suggestion, but Gabriela followed him as he went down the stairs.

They started walking toward the Ponte Nuovo, the bridge connecting to the Oltrarno district, when Gino stopped abruptly. He clasped Gabriela's hand tightly and said, "Your father should have a priest."

Gabriela whimpered, "Father Foscari."

They walked east to the Rosellis' parish church where Gabriela waited in a side chapel while Gino spoke with the priest. Minutes later, Gino rejoined Gabriela and told her, "Father Forscari will go to your house now."

***

At Piero Roselli's funeral services building, Gino entered the office and moved close so Roselli could recognize him. Roselli noticed another figure behind Gino, but his poor eyesight kept him from identifying the other person as his niece. "Ah, Gino, have you brought me someone else looking for work? Is she as good as Tomasia? Never have I seen a woman more skilled and dependable. She handles any task I give her." Gabriela stepped around Gino and moved close enough for her uncle to identify her. "Ah, my lovely niece. It's always a joy to see you, and a shame you rarely visit me."

He studied her expression and suddenly his tone changed from jovial to somber. He stood and took her hands in his. "What's wrong?"

Gabriela uttered, "My father has the sickness."

Piero pulled his niece close, his arms around her. "Oh, my dear child." He looked at Gino and mouthed the words without speaking, "How many days?"

Gino said softly, "This is day three. The priest is with him."

Piero knew the plague usually claimed its victims in four days. "What good are prayers if they go unanswered?" he scoffed. He shook his head, then called out, "Luigi!" When the thin man with the bent nose poked his head into the office, Piero said, "I need a wagon, now."

***

Piero rapped on his brother's door. "Let me in, Joanna. It's Piero."

The latch clicked. Piero pushed the door open and rushed in, followed by Gabriela and Gino. Piero went to his brother's bedside while Gino and Joanna held Gabriela at the bedroom doorway.

Joanna had arranged a sheet to hide the swellings at Carlo's neck, so just his head was visible. He could move only his eyes. He swept them from his brother to his daughter. His lips trembled, but he lacked the strength to produce sound. Piero bent low and said his last words to his brother. Gino took Gabriela, again in tears, to the other room. "The doctor gave me this," Joanna said, and showed Piero the vial of belladonna. "But I can't do it."

"Has he received last rites?" Piero asked. Joanna nodded. "Give the vial to me," Piero said. "And go be with your daughter."

42

September 1348

Many believed the plague would continue only until winter. "Icy winds from the Northern mountains will drive away the bad air," they predicted.

Others maintained the pestilence would persist until not a soul remained in Florence. "We have offended God. This will end only when His vengeance is complete."

Both were proven wrong. In the nightmarish days of mid-summer, hundreds perished every day. By mid-September, after claiming more than half the city's population, the hellish disease abated for reasons no one could explain, with plague deaths numbering little more than a dozen each day.

Gino worked by himself, serving customers in both the apothecary and the perfumery. Since women no longer came to the shop seeking gardenia perfume, and the population of the neighborhood had fallen to half, the pace of work had slowed. Gino picked up a container to prepare a curative for a customer who was having difficulty sleeping and noted the label, *Ballota*, had been written by Signor Roselli. The handwriting triggered reminders of his mentor. Signor Roselli had taken a chance by giving a job to a young immigrant from a farming village. Roselli had helped Gino meet the guild's qualifications to become a speziale, and he had even loaned Gino the money to pay the guild application fee. While he waited for guild approval, Roselli had found him a temporary job with

Piero Roselli's funeral services business. He treated Gino like a member of his family.

His reverie was interrupted by Signora Roselli, who strode into the apothecary, carrying a dish with a tasty-looking pastry. "It's a blueberry torta … freshly baked," she announced and with motherly caution, added, "Blueberries can stain, so take care to keep them from dripping onto your tunic."

Gino thought, I should be supporting her; instead, she's caring for me.

"Gabriela and I are going to the market. Is there something you need?" Joanna asked.

Seemingly at the mention of her name, Gabriela stepped into the shop. It had taken her a month to recover from the shock of her father's death, and during that time, she had rarely gone anywhere and never came into the apothecary. In that month, Gino saw her only twice when her mother had invited Gino to supper. Signora Roselli had hoped Gino's presence would help ease her daughter's mourning. Gino shared the same hope, but those occasions only made for awkward meals. The young orphan girl Mea had shown Gino how to view death as the ascension of the departed into the kingdom of God, not as the loss felt by those left behind. Her youthful insight had removed Gino's pall. He had tried to do the same for Gabriela. Despite the comforting words, "Your father is with God," she couldn't shake the deep sorrow of losing him.

Now, three months later, Gabriela had finally cast off her gloom. She flashed a wide smile upon entering the shop; she had resumed playing her lute, and she had accompanied Gino on a visit to Tomasia and Mea.

"We're getting into chestnut season," Gino replied in response to Joanna's offer. "If there are chestnuts, I can make soup using my mother's recipe."

"I wonder if her recipe is the same as mine?" Joanna asked.

Before they could compare recipes, a man entered the perfumery. Gino went to serve him while the two women headed to the market.

"Professor," Gino greeted Professor Vianello warmly and began preparing his special elixir. "I'm delighted to see that you are safe. I can't even remember the last time you were here."

"My students were among the first to leave the city when the plague struck. Their family went to a villa near Fiesole." Laughing, Vianello said, "It wasn't long before their father sent for me. He said without daily tutoring, his children were falling into ignorance."

"How many students did you have?"

"That family has two boys and a girl. I had also been teaching two girls of another family. They left the city too, but I don't know what happened to them."

"Did you stay at the villa?"

Vianello nodded and took a swig of his elixir. "Ah, I missed this. I can already feel the fog leaving my head." He took another swig. "Yes, I stayed in the villa. I had two rooms, one for my personal use and the other for lessons with the children."

"What was it like being with the children constantly?"

The professor held up his hands, spread apart, and shook his head. "They're wonderful children, well-behaved and excellent students, but they talked constantly. Thankfully, they went horseback riding for several hours every day." He tapped his empty mug, cuing Gino to refill it. "I would have liked more time to myself, but I consider myself fortunate. The pay was ample ... more than ample, and the food was excellent. Old professors rarely find such lucrative opportunities."

With trepidation in his voice, Gino asked, "Have you seen any new omens in the sky?"

"Nothing to match the triple conjunction." Vianello's tempo increased and a touch of excitement entered his voice as he said, "Our future came to pass exactly as the omen prophesied: Jupiter and Saturn, the water planets, gave us two years of rain, then Mars, the god of war, gave us the deadly plague."

"How can the planets know the future?" Gino wondered.

"To that question, I have no answer. I merely interpret the heavenly signs based on my study of past events. However, some of my colleagues believe God uses the planets to send us messages."

"Why would God tell us he intends to unleash a plague?"

Vianello chuckled, "Ah, another tough question, and maybe one best answered by a man of the cloth. Fortunately, triple conjunctions occur at most once per century, so there will be no recurrence in our lifetimes."

"Has the family decided the city is now safe enough for them to return?"

"Safe enough, I suppose. The head of the family is a lawyer, and he's eager to restart his business. Hundreds of houses were left empty in the city when entire families died. He expects legal cases contesting the inheritances of those houses will give him more business than ever." Vianello ran a finger slowly along the rim of his mug. "Some find profit even in the worst of tragedies."

The professor swayed slightly as he turned to leave. "I've been away from my elixir far too long," he quipped.

After Vianello left, three other men, whom Gino had not seen in many months, came for mugs of Virile elixir, another sign of life in Florence gradually returning to normal. Gino swept the floor, ready to close the shop, when Gabriela pranced in carrying a sack. She held it out to Gino, "The chestnuts you wanted. My mother bought some as well. She'd like to compare her version of chestnut soup with yours."

Gino took Gabriela's extended hand, then her other hand, pulled her close, and kissed her. "I'll soak these chestnuts tonight and gather the other ingredients so I can make the soup at your house tomorrow."

They left the shop together. He kissed her again and watched her climb the stairs to her house.

***

Although vandalism had declined as the plague receded, Gino kept his promise of spending two nights each week at Casa Pagholi. Seeing two shabbily dressed men sauntering along the street, Gino took a position at the casa's front entrance, his arms folded across his chest and a scowl on his face. Vandals or merely beggars looking for handouts? Only when they had passed Casa Pagholi, reached the corner, and turned out of sight did he relax. Gino had become accustomed to using the servant's entrance when he visited his sister, so he went around to the rear of the building. Upon entering the rear hallway, he heard sounds coming from the second level, someone walking, not voices. "Who's there?" he shouted as he started up the stairs.

A shadow flashed across the wall of the second level landing. Climbing cautiously, Gino poked his head above the top step. To his left, a silhouetted figure stood in the doorway of Pagholi's study.

"I didn't mean to surprise you," said Pagholi's familiar voice. "I just returned to the city this afternoon. Thank you for caring for the house in my absence."

Gino released his tension with a long exhale. "It was my pleasure. There were no incidents."

Gino cast a quick glance to each side. Noting it, Pagholi said, "They're still at the vineyard. I got a ride with a merchant who was coming to the city. I'll arrange a carriage for Rina and Lucia tomorrow."

He motioned for Gino to join him. "My first act upon returning to the house was to open a bottle of wine. Come help me finish it." Pagholi poured a glass for Gino, displayed a devilish grin, and quipped, "Rina is eager to return home, but Lucia would be happy to remain at the vineyard. She and my nephew really enjoy each other's company."

"Your nephew?" Gino said, confused.

"Yes, Berto. You met him when you visited the vineyard."

"I thought Berto was one of the workers."

"He gives the impression of being a worker because he's an ambitious young man. Every year, my brother does less and relies more on his son to manage the vineyard."

"How close ..." Gino began, unsure he wanted to finish the thought.

Struck by Gino's concern, Pagholi turned serious. He thought for a moment of offering his own opinion, but decided Gino should discuss the relationship with his sister. "You can ask Lucia tomorrow. She'll be coming to the city with Rina."

43

Twenty months later - Thursday May 5, 1351

Even in the Tuscan hills, spring was giving way to summer. Vivid green painted over the pale chartreuse of leaves on the shortest bushes and the tallest trees. Moisture lingering from a shower the previous day made the air heavy, while dampness clinging to moss on the forest floor gave it a strong, earthy scent. A hawk circling above dove to the ground and, an instant later, winged skyward with a small rodent in its beak.

Gino stopped his horse next to his father's at the crest of a hill, where the Casentino Valley spread out below. "Taddeo said whenever he looked into the valley during the famine, he became sad. He said small green patches marked the few farms struggling against the endless rain, while nearly everywhere else were the brown dirt fields of abandoned farms."

"Ours among them," his father said. "But look; life has returned. Only a few farms appear neglected. Most look prosperous."

"Will you ever go back to the farm?" Gino asked.

"I had considered going back, but now I have a good job in Pisa and my children have made lives for themselves away from the farm." He looked at Gino. "You were the first to leave, then Lucia. Fanto, Laro, Ciosa, and Fiora still live in my house, but soon they too will be off on their own. When the rains stopped and farming could resume, I contacted the abbot at San Fedele asking if there was someone who could look after the farm. The abbot said many men driven from the cities by the plague needed work, and he helped arrange for a man to work the farm. The man, his wife, and four children live on the farm and pay a modest rent. I've never met the man, but the abbot says the farm is producing well."

Riding through the valley, they passed the farms of people they had known, and everywhere the men they saw working in the fields were strangers. None of the old families had returned. When they reached their farm, they rode toward the farmhouse, past young boys working in the fields, boys they had never met.

At the house they dismounted, knocked, and introduced themselves to the woman who answered. She called to her husband, who was harvesting artichokes in a nearby field. When the man joined them, Gino's father said, "I'm Alberto Liani, the owner of this farm. I see you and your sons have taken to the land. The crops look healthy."

"The farm has been a blessing. When my family fled from the plague, we had no place to live. We slept in the forest until the abbot told us you wanted someone to farm your land. No man can be proud when he makes his family sleep on the ground."

Suddenly, the man stiffened. With alarm in his voice, he asked, "Are you coming back to the farm?"

Alberto smiled reassuringly. "No, I'm not returning to the farm. When the rain became intolerable and nothing would grow, my family and I left this farm and went to Pisa. We're settled there now. The reason I came to Poppi is to have a notary in the village separate a section of the farm to be my daughter's dowry. However, the change will not affect you. I've spoken with my future son-in-law, and he's content to have you continue farming his section. His father owns a vineyard south of Florence and the grape vines keep them busy enough. They don't need the added work of a farm."

***

Saturday May 7, 1351

The sky was a lustrous blue, the air warm with just a slight breeze, birds chirped in flowering bushes; a perfect day for a wedding.

Neighbors of the Pagholi vineyard milled around the outside of the Church of Santa Margherita in the Chianti Hills south of Florence when the carriage carrying Gino, Gabriela, their two-year-old son Carlo, and Joanna Roselli arrived. Joanna took Carlo to explore a nearby field while Gino and Gabriela chatted with Avito and Rina Pagholi.

Berto, the groom, arrived with his brother and his parents. Smiling, handsome Berto stepped from the carriage, then held his mother's hand as she climbed down. Berto wore a magenta tunic with silver buttons; in keeping with tradition, his best man had a long sword at his waist, although no one expected the wedding party to be attacked by brigands in the peaceful Tuscan village. The parents mingled with their relatives and friends while Berto and his brother walked to the church door where their parish priest was already waiting. If the most important day in Berto's life caused him stress, he showed no signs of it.

The last, and largest, carriage to arrive held the bride, her father, and her three bridesmaids, Ciosa, Fiora, and Berto's sister. The bridesmaids wore their best dresses and flowers in their hair. Lucia wore a form-fitting blue silk gown with full-length white sleeves. The crowd hushed as Alberto escorted his daughter to the front of the church. He kissed her on the cheek, then moved away, leaving her standing beside Berto.

The priest welcomed the assembled guests as witnesses to the sacrament of Holy Matrimony and cued Berto to recite his vow. In a firm voice, loud enough for everyone to hear, Berto said, "I promise to love and honor you, Lucia, to keep you and protect you in sickness and health as long as our lives shall last." Following a brief homily on the sanctity of marriage, the priest blessed the ring and gave it to Berto, who placed it on Lucia's finger.

The priest opened the door and entered the church, followed by Berto and Lucia, their attendants, family, and guests. Berto and Lucia walked to the altar and kneeled facing the priest. The bridesmaids and best man held a canopy over the bride and groom while the priest said mass. Alberto Liani beamed, delighted his daughter had passed through the tribulations of a troubled world and found happiness. Gino squeezed Gabriela's hand, hoping his sister would discover the same joy he always felt with Gabriela.

The attendants removed the canopy when the mass ended. Berto took Lucia's hand and led her toward the church door. Midway through the cheering crowd, he stopped and announced in a commanding voice, "My wife and I invite you to join us for a celebratory meal at the Pagholi Vineyard."

About the Author

Ken Tentarelli is a frequent visitor to Italy. In travels from the Alps to the southern coast of Sicily, he developed a love for its history and its people. He has studied Italian culture and language in Rome and Perugia, background he used in his award-winning series of historical thrillers set in the Italian Renaissance. He has taught courses in Italian history spanning time from the Etruscans to the Renaissance, and he's a strong advocate of libraries and has served as a trustee of his local library and officer of the library foundation. When not traveling, Ken and his wife live in beautiful New Hampshire.

Note from Ken Tentarelli

Word-of-mouth is crucial for any author to succeed. If you enjoyed *The Blackest Time*, please leave a review online—anywhere you are able. Even if it's just a sentence or two. It would make all the difference and would be very much appreciated.

Thanks!
Ken Tentarelli

Also from the Author

The Laureate: Mystery in Renaissance Italy

The Advisor: Intrigue in Tuscany

Assignment Milan

Conspiracy in Bologna

Rebels in Pisa

Deadly Rivalries

www.ingramcontent.com/pod-product-compliance
Lightning Source LLC
Chambersburg PA
CBHW060535190726
48283CB00003B/733
9781685136536